La Familia 2

La Familia 2

Paradise Gomez

www.urbanbooks.net

Urban Books, LLC
97 N18th Street
Wyandanch, NY 11798

ISBN 13: 978-1-60162-586-1
ISBN 10: 1-60162-586-3

First Trade Paperback Printing April 2015
Printed in the United States of America

10 9 8 7 6 5 4 3 2 1

This is a work of fiction. Any references or similarities to actual events, real people, living or dead, or to real locales are intended to give the novel a sense of reality. Any similarity in other names, characters, places, and incidents is entirely coincidental.

Distributed by Kensington Publishing Corp.
Submit orders to:
Customer Service
400 Hahn Road
Westminster, MD 21157-4627
Phone: 1-800-733-3000
Fax: 1-800-659-2436

Prologue

Click!

The loaded clip to the 9 mm easily slid into the chamber like dick into pussy and the tool was ready for death. The hammer was cocked back and the safety switched off. The gun, in the hands of a killer, was ready to create a homicide on a cold Friday night. The young boy with the gun in his hand was only sixteen years old, and already was a hardcore gangster to the bone: wired for murder, being numb to violence and taking a human life by the gun. He had already seen things that scarred his mind for life: murder, rape, violence, and jail. His eyes and heart were cold as frost forming on a car windshield on an early winter morning.

The burning weed was being passed between the four hoodlums riding in a stolen Chevy Impala with tinted windows. The four young hardcore hoodlums with rap sheets as long as their arms were part of a notorious gang who called themselves the Bronx Mafia Boys, one of New York's most infamous and violent gangs with over 2,000 committed members. They intentionally drove into enemy territory seeking out their rival to kill, the Young Gangster Crew.

Rap music blared inside the car. It was a dark and wintry night; the Chevy slowly turned corner to corner, seeking to destroy. Young DJ took a pull from the weed between his lips and inhaled the potent drug to soothe his mood. He took several more pulls and then passed the joint to one of his cohorts next to him and leaned into the back seat of the car. He gripped the gun and was ready to see some action. The Bronx was his home; the gang was his loyalty and nothing else in his life mattered but his street family and his violent reputation.

For months now, both of these violent drug crews, The Bronx Mafia boys and Young Gangster Crew had been warring over northern territory in the Bronx and residents and the neighborhood found themselves in the middle of World War III. Since the life sentence Rico received in his RICO trial, the streets and the drug market was left wide open for fledging gangsters and drug crews making their way up the ladder and solidifying a position on the streets. Bloodshed started to become a regular in the Bronx streets. People were scared to leave their homes. Edenwald was starting to look like Baghdad; gunshots and bloodshed was becoming a common thing like children playing and traffic going by.

Muppet, the alpha male in the car, took a pull from the blunt and exhaled. His attire screamed hardcore gang banger: red bandanna tied around his head, the dark teardrop underneath his eye, jeans sagging, Timberlands on his feet, and an automatic resting on his lap. As the car moved about, he kept a keen eye out on the streets. The members were going head hunting, meaning first rival they saw on sight, it was a shot to their dome.

"Yo, damn it's a slow fuckin' night, ain't nobody out this bitch," the driver said.

"It's cold as fuck out here, that's why," Muppet replied.

"Been drivin' around this bitch for an hour and ain't no action happening," Young DJ chimed.

"We gon' find sumthin'."

"Shit, we better. I'm gettin' tight just drivin' around this bitch," the driver said. "Gas ain't fuckin' cheap."

"Doe shut the fuck up! This ain't even ya fuckin' car," Muppet hollered.

"I'm sayin', Muppet, we almost riding on E out this bitch."

"And? We gonna keep ridin' out this bitch until we prove our point, and I don't give a fuck if we gotta ride around on fumes, fuck that shit, I'm tryin' to make this money out here and ain't no fuckin' body stepping on my ends! Ya niggas fuckin' hear me?" Muppet exclaimed.

"Yeah, we hear you," everyone answered simultaneously.

"So shut the fuck up, stop acting like some whining-ass bitches, and let's do this shit."

The driver and Young DJ nodded.

Everyone knew not to argue with Muppet. He was crazy, a fuckin' lunatic, and his violent and deadly reputation preceded him. The entire Bronx borough heard of Muppet's name; from Sound View to Yonkers, he was a stone-cold killer. And the reason why he wasn't locked up yet for his transgressions was because he had the streets on lock with fear and there weren't too many folks lined up at the district attorney's office ready to snitch on him. He beat two murder cases, one drug case, and seemed to be the urban Teflon Don.

Now Muppet had his sights set on Rico's old hood. It was highly profitable; the traffic in the area was rich, from 233rd Street stretching to Laconia Avenue, down to 225th Street, and it was a fuckin' goldmine. And every crew looking to expand into Edenwald wanted control of it.

Muppet took a strong pull from the blunt and sat back. His eyes were glued out the window. The cold didn't seem to affect him. He wore a T-shirt along with his gang attire. He made his affiliation strongly known wherever he went, making him not just a mark for other rival gangs, but to the police also. But Muppet had this agenda: come up by any means necessary.

The Chevy slowly rounded the corner on Baychester Avenue and headed south. Weed smoke engulfed the car, and another joint was lit. As they approached Boston Avenue, the group spotted three young hoods exiting the KFC on the corner. It was dark and frigid and everyone was bundled snuggly in their winter coats and wool ski hats. One of the men leaving the fast food KFC lit a cigarette and laughed with his cronies. They were members of the YGC (Young Gangster Crew), and it was written all over their street garb like walking advertisements.

The three men paid no attention to the dark Chevy slowly approaching their way. The traffic on the street was sparse because of the winter month and the cold. KFC was closing up; the trio was walking toward a parked Dodge on the street.

Muppet lit up like a Christmas tree when he noticed his foes out in the open cold like the wind blowing. He gripped his automatic with a steely glare and sang out, "It's time for some action. Time, time, time for some action. Get up real close on these clown-ass niggas, yo," he told the driver.

The car came close; the window slowly came down with the cold rushing into the car like hurricane wind. Muppet flicked the dying joint out the window and focused his attention on his targets. The men walked and talked unknowing of the danger. Muppet leaned out the window with his arm outstretched with the pistol at the end of it. He set his sights on his kill. The cold and the late night made the streets empty. Muppet aimed as the car he was riding in approached closer, his foes had their backs turned to him. He smirked, shouted out, "Punk-ass bitches!" catching the men's attention and when they turned around to see where the insult was coming from, Muppet didn't hesitate to fire.

Bak! Bak! Bak! Bak! Bak!

The five gunshots echoed through the cold night and all three men dropped to the cold pavement like timber wood being cut down. Muppet hit all three like the deadly marksman he was. But it was evident that they all weren't dead. Only two lay lifeless against the cold concrete; the third was still alive, crawling to some unseen safety on his hands and knees. He was bleeding badly being shot twice in his side.

Muppet told them to stop the car. He wanted to finish the job. He didn't want to see any survivors. He had a deep-rooted hatred for the YGC and wanted to send them all to hell. He climbed out the car with the smoking gun in his hand and hurried toward his helpless foe. Muppet was about to enhance his murderous street reputation by tenfold. He stood over the powerless soldier smirking, then aimed his gun at the back of the man's head and fired multiple rounds. And when he saw the back of his head explode in bloodshed it gave him a pleased feeling of accomplishment; three less YGC niggas to worry about in the Bronx.

Muppet climbed back into the car and jubilantly shouted, "Now that's how you kill a muthafucka!"

His peoples weren't shocked; it was their way of life since they knew how to walk. Their enemies shot at them, and they shot back.

The Chevy sped away, leaving the bloody crime scene behind for police to figure it out. But it was obvious to the hood that the shooting would be considered gang related. And the boys murdered in cold blood ranged from fifteen to seventeen years old.

Chapter One

Mouse

Despite having an incarcerated and asshole baby father, he gave me the best thing a woman could ever want in her life: my daughter Eliza. She was my world of joy, the best thing ever to come into my life. I had no regrets in giving birth to her. She was my shining star, my angel, the joy of my life, and she was the only person I cared for. Everyone else could kiss my ass and stay the fuck away from me. I'd been through so much shit in my life, and been down and out so many times that there was no other way but to go up for me, and with Eliza to care for, I didn't have a choice. I wanted better for me and for her.

Eliza was one year old, and it was hard to believe that a year already had passed since she was born. Time flies, but I wasn't having fun. She started walking around eleven months and she was becoming good at it. Regardless of her falling down and crashing into things, my baby girl didn't cry and she would continually pick herself up and try again. I was proud of her already, because she wasn't a quitter; she mastered what life was about. You fall, but you don't stay down. You continue to get up, dust yourself off, and try again. I emulated my daughter. I was down, but it wasn't over for me. I'd been bruised, but I wasn't broken. I'd been up and down like a rollercoaster ride. I'd been beaten and broke, but I was still standing and pushing forward, in spite of living in a

Harlem shelter for women with kids. This wasn't the end for me, but only the beginning.

My options were either living on the cold streets with my daughter or taking residence in a shelter that a friend told me about. Of course I chose to stay in a family shelter. If I was on my own, I could tolerate the streets of New York. I'd done it before when living with my crazy fuckin' father became too unbearable and Sammy wasn't able to take me in. But now that I was a mother, things were different; I had to think of my daughter's well-being too.

The women's Samaritan family shelter on 155th Street provided transitional housing for up to twenty-five women and their children. And comprehensive services included individualized treatment for those who suffered from substance abuse, domestic violence or HIV/AIDS, and more. And emergency services were also provided for up to five women each night.

The shelter I was temporarily staying in was comfortable to some extent, but it would never become my home. We had our own tiny apartment, a kitchenette, TV, no cable, twin beds, and a place to do our laundry. The women here had been through hell and back, some worse than others, and I shared some of their pain. The abusive boyfriend, or absent father, drug addiction, gangs, probation, STDs: we been through it all and were only trying to find our way in a world that had forgotten about us or considered us undesirables because of our circumstances or background. A few were living with the monster, and hearing their story reminded me of Sammy's mom who was living with that sickness. I was thankful that I never caught it. I was healthy and my baby was too.

The staff in the women's shelter was cool, working to prevent homelessness through programs that provided budget management counseling, housing referrals, rent and legal assistance to more than 300 families each year.

From where I was over a year ago, living the high life with Rico, experiencing the glamour and finer things in life, and for the first time in my life, living in a luxurious home, to becoming pregnant and ending up in a family shelter for battered and abused women, I would have never thought in a million years that it would come to this. At one time in my life, I was on my way to reaching stardom with my best friend Sammy. We were two talented bitches from out the hood with a growing reputation in the music world. We had great management via Search and great material that we were writing ourselves. But then it all fell apart by the seams, and Sammy and I became bitter rivals. How and why? Rico.

He was the master of destruction, fucking and deceiving us both, turning friends against each other, and us both having his babies. We were out here trying to survive while becoming new mothers. We were hungry, and trying to find our way back to the road paved with gold and wanting better for ourselves and our kids. But every day it seemed things got worse. Every day it felt like I was drifting further away from my dreams and losing touch with hope.

I hadn't heard from Sammy in months; the last I heard about her was that she was stripping in some seedy club in the Bronx trying to make ends meet. And she was frequently taking her son upstate to visit Rico. It was her life and her son. I refused to visit Rico and take Eliza anywhere near him or a prison. She didn't need to know her daddy. I was her mother and father. Rico was hell in my life. He was shit disguised as sugar, and he would never taste like sugar no matter how many flavors he tried to add, and I wanted to eradicate every thought of him, but his daughter was the only exception, and thank God she was looking more like her mother than her daddy. My genes were strong, like the woman I was, and my daughter was going to be stronger. I was going to raise Eliza to stay away from men like her father, muthafuckas who were only wolves in sheep's clothing.

But dwelling on the past wasn't going to get me anywhere. I had to focus on my future, and this shelter, the people in it, the condition I was in; it wasn't going to be my future at all. This was not going to be forever. I had hope and was ready to scratch and crawl my way out of the ghetto like I almost did when Sammy and I were Vixen Chaos.

I sat in the family room in the shelter viewing an episode of *Love & Hip Hop: New York*. I sat among many female residents staring at the mounted TV in the room. It was the only place in the shelter where they had cable playing and *Love & Hip Hop* was the show to watch inside the shelter. It seemed like every bitch in the place would stop everything they was doing for that one hour and be glued to the TV show like it was some religious program on how to catapult your way into their world. These catty bitches on *Love & Hip Hop* were idolized by the majority of women in the shelter. They lived a life that we all dreamed of, and yearned to date and fuck the men they found attractive, and longed to wear the stylish outfits, shoes, and jewelry manifested on the show. I briefly lived that life, and I can't lie, it was fun for a moment, especially when Rico took me on a shopping spree on Fifth Avenue, spent thousands of dollars on me, and had me dining in some of the finest restaurants. But I was never on the level that some of the women on the show were on. They had their own: their own money, owned homes, and ran successful businesses, and had some respect in the industry.

I lived that life briefly, but I never had my own. I wanted to have my own. It was a dream of mines, to become like Yandy or Chrissy. These bitches were beautiful, bad with attitudes and smart, and they had a man holding them down and vice versa. I thought I found that with Rico, but it was only a lie.

"Damn, Joe Budden look like he got a big dick," Theresa said loudly, being the loud and obnoxious bitch she always was. "I know he can fuck a bitch right. That bitch Tahiry don't know what do wit' that dick, because she can't even hold on to her man."

The girls around her laughed at her blunt comment. I wasn't amused.

"Yo, I can't stand Erica trifling-ass. First off, that bitch can't sing for shit, and she's a fuckin' slut," Whitney chimed.

"True dat," Melanie agreed, slapping Whitney a high five.

They talked reckless about the female characters on the show, but in true life, they envied them all because it wasn't them living the life of luxury, having great sex, and going on lavish shopping sprees. Some of these ladies in the shelter were so broke down and battered that even a miracle couldn't help them out.

I watched the show, but I was in my own world. Eliza was asleep in my arms. I had just fed and bathed her, and now it was time for a little "me" time. But me time was useless when a bitch was broke, homeless, and with a baby on her hip twenty-four/seven. So me time was watching cable quietly while everyone else talked loudly and ridiculed each and every bitch on the show they deemed not keeping it real or was a whore.

During a commercial break, one of the young girls in the shelter came into the TV room looking upset. I saw her wipe a few tears from her eyes as she went toward some friends seated in the room. My focus went from the television to them knowing something went down somewhere. I knew the girl with the tears streaming down her face. She was a teen mother with twin girls and she was from my part of town, Edenwald. She was known to run with some heavy hitters on the streets. Her parents had kicked her out for selling drugs in their apartment. She was fighting with her parents for custody of her twins.

I overheard her say, "They killed String; they killed my fuckin' cousin!"

She was clearly upset and distraught. I knew String. He was part of a violent gang who called themselves the Young Gangster Crew, YGC, and they were at war with the Bronx Mafia Boys. That bit of news became more important in the room than *Love & Hip Hop*. Majority of the girls in the Harlem shelter came from the Bronx and we all had boyfriends, brothers, cousins, uncles, fathers, or baby fathers associated with the streets, drugs, or a violent gang, and murder wasn't anything new to us.

They said the murders were on the news; three men were gunned down in cold blood while leaving a KFC late at night. But that was life in the Bronx and I felt immune to the news. My father was gunned down in the same fashion.

I didn't have time to console anyone or get more information on what happened. I simply didn't care. I figured my heart just grew colder in the past year. Not anyone gave a fuck about me or my daughter, so why should I give a fuck about another life being snatched from this cold, hard earth? It was life; you have a birthday and a death day. While a few girls shed tears for String and his friends, I removed myself from my chair with my daughter asleep in my arms and decided to head into my room for the night. I had enough troubles on my mind and I didn't need anyone else's problems coming my way.

However, as I was about to exit the TV room, I saw one of my headaches and continuing problems coming my way. Her name was Dietra; the bitch was walking hate.

She was somewhat heavyset, black like tar and ugly like hell with a bad weave in her head and a constant attitude aimed my way. She didn't like me and I didn't like her. The main reason for her animosity toward me was she was Denise's older cousin. I beat the bitch down in front of the whole projects last year, and then Sammy and my homegirls put that bitch in the hospital over a year ago. She wanted revenge for her cousin, and she wanted to take it out on me.

But there was one golden rule in the women's family Samaritan shelter in Harlem: no fighting at all. If caught fighting in the shelter, it was immediate eviction, and being evicted was the last thing I needed in my life when I had my daughter. But despite that rule, there was constant friction between Dietra and me, hard glances thrown at each other, arguments and bickering, but physically we never laid hands on each other. But the pot was boiling between us and I knew it was inevitable that a fight was brewing. She was just itching to find a reason and try to fuck me up, and I was going to find a reason to fight back and knock that bitch's teeth out.

As I passed Dietra in the hallway, she glared at me and uttered, "Fake-ass bitch."

I was tempted to snap back, but I had Eliza in my arms and I couldn't risk endangering my daughter for this stupid bitch. I had to be better than that. And the fact that she had the audacity to talk trash while I had my daughter in my arms goes to show the type of ignorance and stupidity she was about.

I frowned heavily, locked eyes with the bitch for a moment, and kept it moving. She didn't want any part of me. Yeah, my name was Mouse, and I was small, but I was fierce like a tiger and my hands needed to be registered because I was lethal with them and Dietra was about to find out the hard way not to fuck with me. Because the bitches who used to underestimate me back in the days give me nothing but respect now when they saw me, because, like Dietra, they came at me for a fight and I held my own, tearing out many weaves, blacking eyes, breaking noses, and sending bitches to the emergency room when they came trying me.

I kept myself humble. It wasn't the place or time for a fight. I had too much to lose. Dietra walked into the TV room and I simply stared in the face of my baby girl. Her beauty and innocence kept me calm.

The minute I walked into my room I put Eliza in her bed and then pulled out my pen and pad and started to write as I sat on my bed near the small window overlooking the block. I yearned to write. Expressing my love, pain, sorrows, grief, and much more through rhymes and poetry was always going to be my passion. When I had nothing else, I still had my writing, my soul to take, my heart to wake, and my mind to say. I didn't want to ever give up on my dream, no matter what. Yes, I had a setback, a few over the years, but I had faith that success was going to happen to me.

I started with: "I'm my worse behavior, crime of the time, love of war, endless grind feeling gone, angry at time feeling time ain't never on my side, father time absence like the biological in my life, it's always dark on this side of town, sun don't come around no more, eclipse was what I was born on, look up and stars seemed too distance from me, black is all I see, the black is on me. Who is I, me and mines, turning my black into some success in me."

Chapter Two

Sammy

Motherhood was becoming a challenge to me, from my son catching an ear infection, then having a high fever and rushing him to the emergency room, along with him teething and then trying to put him to bed every night was a challenge. And when he cried, he cried very loud, with the lungs on my little man feeling like a blow horn was in my room. He was becoming a handful at six months, but that didn't mean I didn't love my son Danny to death. He was my world and my heart, and the most precious thing I ever had on this earth, more precious than diamonds and gold. I adored the way my son's small eyes lit up when he smiled and laughed while he looked up at me. The way Danny laughed when I would tickle him made me light up, too. The way he fell asleep when I held him in my arms always made me feel so motherly. He was my baby boy, and he was going to grow up to become my big strong man, my protector, and I knew he would become the one man in my life who wouldn't break his mother's heart.

I sat by the window in the kitchen of my project apartment gazing out at the ghetto once again. I was back in Edenwald, the place I grew up in, and I didn't like it. I missed the place I had in Co-op City when I was selling drugs for Rico. It was bigger, more comfortable, and a lot more lavish, but staying there came with a cost. I was fortunate that the feds didn't come for me too like they did for Rico's entire crew. I managed to stay under the radar and stay free. It was a blessing.

But then I still felt cursed. I was alone and basically living on ends. My life had changed dramatically. Never in a million years would I think I would become a single mother struggling to survive and barely paying rent. The icing on the cake was being blackmailed by Rico. He had this murder lingering over my head, threatening my freedom if I didn't comply with any of his demands. I was sick of him, but I had to put up with him; he was my son's father, and regardless of him serving a twenty-five-year sentence upstate, he still managed to have control over my life.

I would frequently visit Rico, like I had a choice, taking Danny on the six-hour trip by bus to see his father in Attica prison, and you would think Rico would be appreciative of it, seeing his son, but he wasn't. He barely held his son in his arms or played with him as we sat in the crowded visiting room being heavily watched by a half dozen correction officers. He said he cherished the boy, loved him, but I couldn't tell.

I had to admit, Rico did look good clad in his prison-issued gray jumpsuit and bald head glistening like a diamond. He seemed to be taking really good care of himself and was bulking up by weightlifting. But looks could be deceiving. Prison didn't age or change him at all. He still had that powerful image. But he was still on that bullshit, wanting to be controlling and a perpetual asshole in my life.

He glared at me and had the audacity to ask, "Who you fuckin' out there?"

I scowled. "What?"

"Sammy, you fuckin' heard me. I don't repeat myself," he uttered.

I was only coming to visit him with his son because he had this murder over my head, and if it weren't for that, I would have been ghost a long time ago. Fuck Rico! I hated him so much that I wanted to kill him at that moment. He had the nerve to grill me about my life, who I was fuckin', and how I did me. No matter what, he was always going to be a jerk.

But he scared me, now more that he was locked up than when he was on the streets. He was a sneaky nigga. It was also brought to my attention that he still had a handful of killers on the streets. I know he did. He made it known that I was being watched like a hawk. Why though? The man had twenty-five years to serve, so was I not allowed to move on with my life? He had the best of both worlds, some of the sweetest pussy from Mouse and me, two of the project's baddest bitches, and we both gave him some beautiful babies.

"You gonna always be mine, Sammy, you know that right?" he said. "You ain't going anywhere. Fuck that."

He looked at me with his cold eyes, apathy in his heart, and didn't even blink. The statement of always being his had me about to throw up. I was never his in the first place. It was a fling, a damn mistake.

I had no reply to his chilling comment. I just sat there like a damn fool. Danny was in my arms chilling; he was quiet and being a good baby by not fussing or crying. It was Rico who seemed to be throwing the temper tantrum. I felt trapped by Rico's words. He reached across the table to take my hand into his. I hesitated. I didn't want him touching me. I wanted to leave, but I had an hour visit with him and there was no way he was going to let me cut it short. I was there with his son, but he cared not to hold him for too long. His only concern was my business.

"What do you want from me, Rico?" I asked with such disdain in my tone and pulled away from his reach.

"I want you to marry me," he had the nerve to say.

"What?" I knew I didn't hear him correctly.

"I want you to become my wife."

It was like he had spit in my face. The muthafucka had to be delusional. Prison had made him go insane. There was no way in hell I was going to marry Rico. I didn't care if he threatened me by exposing me or murdering me. It was my word against his, and he was a felon.

"I'm not marrying you, Rico," I flat-out told him.

"And why not?" he responded through clenched teeth. "You think you have a choice in this?"

"What is wrong with you?"

"I always been in love wit' you, Sammy," he stated.

Love? Rico didn't even know what the word meant.

He always had been a self-centered and narcissistic bastard. He left behind so much pain from my life to the streets, that people was dying out there, fighting and killing over something he left behind. The Bronx was ugly. He was uglier. He was a twisted gangster with a hard on for drama.

"You got my son."

"Like you give two shits about him, Rico. You can't even hold and play with him while he's here to see you. And you think you can be a father to him in here?" I exclaimed.

"I still got my resources out there, Sammy, and I can take care of you. Remember who the fuck I am. You can't hide."

I didn't have any doubt he still had pull and clout on the streets, Rico would always be Rico, but while there was hell going on out there, muthafuckas dying, starving and homeless, Rico had three meals and a cot to sleep on. But his son and I, we were barely making it out there. He put this baby in me, didn't acknowledge my son like it was his when I brought him to the prison, and he left me out there to become a single mother with a baby daddy incarcerated; my worst nightmare.

I glared at Rico as he sat across from me. He might as well been the anti-Christ in my eyes. I had a right to be pissed the fuck off. I felt he took everything from me: my career; my best friends, Mouse and Search; my dreams; and, most of all, my damn dignity. I felt my dreams of breaking into the music business were becoming distant. I wasn't writing, singing, or rhyming like I used to, and I had no one to support me. I supported myself and my son by dancing in this strip club called Crazy Legs. It was a job, however; not the one I ever saw myself doing, but it paid the bills.

My first night I was so nervous that I threw up for a half hour in the bathroom. I had no idea what I was doing or what I was getting myself into. I knew girls who danced, and they always told me it was good money in it. It wasn't me though. Honestly, I felt I was always better than that, too good to take my clothes off for money. I left that scandalous occupation for the whores and birds who were stupid enough to get into it. I had bigger dreams.

But shit always comes back to haunt you.

My first night taking my clothes off in front of dozens of horny and howling strangers was nerve-racking and it was a total contradiction for me. Kawanda got me into it. She lived in the apartment down the hall from me. I would see her leave almost every night to go to work and hours later she would come back with at least three to five hundred dollars a night. She always paid her bills on time and had so much extra to spend on herself, especially since she didn't have any kids.

When your child is hungry, the lights are about to be cut off, and you need heat in your apartment, pride becomes a memory and you find yourself doing what you gotta do to take care of home and your child. I swallowed my pride and went to talk to Kawanda about dancing. She was more than happy to give me the details on it and to help me out.

"They would love you down there, Sammy," she had said. "You got a great body and you are a beautiful woman. You would kill it in the club."

I really needed the money. So the next night, I had a neighbor watch my son and I went with Kawanda to Crazy Legs. The club was in the south Bronx, and it was underground, really seedy with the atmosphere that anything goes. I mean, bitches got butt-ass naked and walked around like they were Eve in the Garden of Eden. The customers in the place were perverts, hoods, pimps, thugs, drug dealers, sex addicts, and more; they all went crazy over some pussy.

The minute I walked into the place, all eyes were on me. I guessed they smelled the new girl on me and couldn't wait to see what I was working with. It was a cold night, and I was bundled up in a snorkel jacket, hat, gloves, and some boots. I hid my figure, but it felt like every nigga in the place had X-ray vision and peeled away my clothes, and was picturing me naked.

I hurried behind Kawanda into the changing room. It was a joke, more like a ghetto walk-in closet cluttered with ratchetness. There weren't any lockers to place your stuff in, just a whirlwind of bags: trash bags of clothing and duffle bags, lying about the floor from the door to the back, and inadequate clothing everywhere. Every girl shared one long mirror and the paint on the walls was peeling, and had me worried about asbestos. The changing room looked disgusting. There was ass and coochie everywhere, bitches half dressed and talking shit, either to each other or about the men outside calling a few cheap or ugly, and it smelled. I mean it reeked of unwashed pussy, period blood, and just odor. Bitches were spraying their private parts with some scented coochie spray and wiping their asses with baby wipes.

It was crazy to see.

When I walked in, the seasoned dancers in the room smirked at me and knew I was fresh blood. I couldn't believe that I was about to do this. I wanted to back out of it, but when I saw one girl counting up money, mostly dollar bills, tens and fives, it became enticing.

Kawanda encouraged me to do my thing. She started undressing, getting ready to go on stage and make her money. I stood near her feeling lost. Kawanda was willing to share some of her clothing with me, because I had nothing to dance in. I was used to performing in front a crowd fully clothed while singing and rhyming; but this here, taking my clothes off in front of complete strangers and dancing seductively, was crazy.

Kawanda got dressed in a platinum bob wig, a red G-string, a faux fur light-up hood, and red six-inch stilettos. She oiled her body down with baby oil and sprinkled some glitter on her breasts and her transformation was absolutely amazing. She went from average to exotic in no more than twenty minutes. And I thought that I was a bad bitch. I sighed, knowing I had to do the same thing. I got dressed in one of her white short-sleeved tie tops, and a short plaid schoolgirl skirt. Underneath the skirt, I wore all-over sequined booty shorts, and sported a pair of black stilettos.

I took a deep breath and followed Kawanda to where it was show time. The DJ was blaring rap music, and thick weed smoke, along with cigarette smoke, lingered all through the club. The men were lively and loud, and the stage was in use by a dark-skinned, thick, big-booty stripper with pasties on her breasts, black knee-high boots, and nothing else. Her pussy was shaved and exposed, and she sported more tattoos than Dennis Rodman. She twirled around the pole looking like a professional and enticed the hordes of men surrounding the stage by booty clapping and pole dancing.

I noticed the eyes gazing at me. Men looked eager to see me naked. I was the new dancer, and being a new and beautiful dancer, especially with my curvy and jaw-dropping figure, was like being a virgin in the place. Everybody wanted you to become their first.

"I need a drink," I had said to Kawanda.

She had smiled and said, "We always do."

At the bar, I had ordered a Cîroc Peach and Sprite, and downed it like it would be my last. The scenery was overwhelming; something was going on everywhere in the club: lap dances, grinding and fondling, arguments, money raining down on the stage, flirting, drinking, and later on I found out that in the back of the club, bitches disappeared into one of the three rooms with men, and they sucked and fucked these niggas for a fee.

Yeah, everything went down in Crazy Legs for the right price. But I knew my pussy wasn't for sale. I just wanted to dance and make my money. Kawanda went on first to show me how it was done. She danced to the beat of Lucy Pearl's "Dance Tonight." I gazed at Kawanda and she was on point on stage, working that pole like it was a hard dick in her hand and she didn't hesitate to get buck-naked in front of these thirsty niggas. Gradually, the stage was being inundated with money. It was mostly the drug dealers and shot callers spending money on my friend. Kawanda had these niggas in awe for a half hour and when she was done, the bitch stepped off the stage with money in both fists. She had to have made at least $150 in that half hour alone.

When I stepped on the stage to dance, my heart was beating faster than rock drums in a heavy metal concert. But I was going through with it. I needed the money and had to feed my son. Right away, I had everyone's attention in the place; the new girl was about to perform. The DJ put on Rick Ross's "Diced Pineapples" and I slowly twirled myself around the pole, trying to imitate the professionals who did it before me. I got five dollars thrown at me. I smiled at the nerdy-looking gentleman who tossed the bill.

I had no idea what I was doing. Stripping was harder than I thought it was, from moving your backside to the beat, climbing the pole, spreading your legs and removing your clothes to put on a show and entertain these horny hound dogs. But show some flesh, caress your breasts, play with your nipples, and shake your ass with the beat or not, these niggas didn't care; they still paid to see.

And that night, I made $300. It wasn't much, but it was something and I was able to keep my lights on and buy groceries for the apartment. Niggas wanted a VIP with me, but I had my limits; stripping was already farfetched in my book, but to become a whore, nah, never. And since that night, I never looked back. Stripping in Crazy Legs became the normal for me. It was my income, because God knows Rico wasn't able to do shit to help me out.

Chapter Three

Mouse

When I walked into my room and saw a few of my things had been disturbed, I flipped out. Someone had the audacity to violate my things. I didn't have much in life, but what I did have was precious to me. What infuriated me more was seeing my notebook of rhymes and poetry ripped apart. My words, my heart and soul, my works, they were destroyed, ripped away from my spiral book and torn to pieces, then thrown everywhere in my room like a simulated snowfall.

I wanted to cry. I loved my words. I loved my writing and I put a lot of effort and soul into my writing. Every night I wrote in my book. Every night it was a pleasure expressing myself. My book of rhymes and poetry became my own personal journal, my teenage diary. I had platinum-selling stuff inside that book and one day the world was going to hear my words, my voice so loud and clear. But now I lost everything; my words were in shreds. It felt like I was a mute. I picked up what was left of my words and cried. When it rains, it pours; but my life was becoming a fuckin' downpour with a hurricane on the side.

I snatched up what was left of my works from off the floor and gripped them in my clenched fists. I stormed out of my room in tears. Someone had disrespected me on a whole new level and I had an idea who it was. There was only one person in this shelter who hated me: Dietra.

I marched toward her room looking for revenge. I wasn't putting up with her bullshit anymore. The bitch pushed me too far and I snapped. That was my shit she fucked with, and she might as well punch my daughter in her face, because you fucked with my daughter or my rhymes, and I was ready to kill you.

I heard Dietra talking to someone in her room. They were laughing and mocking someone, saying, "She's a dumb, bird bitch," and I assumed it was me. I appeared in the doorway suddenly, scowling, quickly catching Dietra's and her friend's attention. Dietra cut her eyes at me and exclaimed, "What, bitch? Your feelings are hurt?"

"You fuck wit' my shit?" I shouted.

"What shit, bitch?" Dietra retorted.

"That book, them words, they was my fuckin' life," I screamed out. "My fuckin' shit!"

"Bitch, you can't write anyway," she returned with attitude.

I heard enough and had my proof it was her. Hearing this fat, bird bitch insult me and my talent made me go temporarily insane. I was ready to take my chances, because I was tired of this bitch. I knew if I fought, there was a great chance of being kicked out of the shelter. But when you're upset, and when enough is enough, and you feel threatened, rational thinking goes out the fuckin' window. So I charged into her room and punched her in the face so hard she went flying off her feet. Her friend in the room was stunned, but pussy. She ran out the room while I viciously tore into Dietra.

She fought back, swinging at me. I gripped a fistful of nasty weave and tried to roughly pull out all of her tracks. We fought tearing her room apart, knocking shit over and breaking shit. I repeatedly punched Dietra in her face and took my nails and scratched her heatedly, drawing blood on the side of her face.

"Get the fuck off me!" Dietra yelled.

I was just getting started.

I was somewhat short, but I had the advantage over this trifling bitch. We tussled like wrestlers in the ring. I tore open her shirt, snatched an earring from her ear, and then cold cocked her in the temple.

"Fuckin' bitch! Don't you ever touch my shit again," I screamed heatedly.

I found myself on the floor, on top of Dietra with my hands entangled around her weave and banging her head against the floor repeatedly. Blood had spewed and she was clearly defeated, but I didn't care. I had gotten worked up into a vicious frenzy that I couldn't stop. I hated this bitch. I kept on going, punching her madly and viciously banging her head against the floor like a mad bitch. She became unconscious and I had her blood on my hands.

Suddenly I felt myself being pulled off of her by several pairs of arms grabbing me roughly. The staff had come into the room and broke it up. I had blacked out. I lost it. She pushed me to my breaking point and I snapped like a twig. I glared down at Dietra thinking that I went too far and killed her. She looked lifeless. The nurse in the building quickly went to her aid while they were dragging me out of the room. The chaos I created stirred up the place like a hornet's nest.

I heard someone shout out, "Call 911!"

Damn, it had gotten that serious so fast. Instantly, my daughter came to mind. I left her in my friend's room sleeping. Everyone was so busy trying to aid Dietra that the people who were supposed to detain me temporarily had forgotten about me. It gave me the chance to flee. I knew I was going to be kicked out of the shelter right away. I had broken their cardinal rule: no fighting in the shelter and definitely no trying to kill another resident.

But I figured getting kicked out of the shelter was the least of my worries; they were definitely going to call the police and have me arrested for assault. I fucked up Dietra really bad. I couldn't go to jail. I couldn't abandon and leave my daughter's side and have her in the care of some stranger.

I rushed to my friend's room and snatched up my daughter from her bed, saying to her, "Eliza, baby, c'mon, we gotta go," and hurried back to my room. I grabbed a black trash bag and hastily tossed everything I owned into the Glad bag, which wasn't much, just some clothes, personal items, and the notebooks I had left. With Eliza in one arm and the trash bag in the other, I hurried away from the threat of being locked up. My heart was beating like a hundred times per second. Panic started to set in, and the homeless shelter was in disarray over what I've done.

I hurried from the second floor down to the first. I walked briskly toward the exit and when I was near leaving, I heard one of the staff members shout, "Mouse, don't leave. We need to talk to you."

Of course I wasn't going to listen to their demands. I didn't even turn around to see who was calling me. I took off running toward the exit with my daughter clutched tightly in my arms and barely hanging on to my belongings. She started to cry, knowing Mommy was in trouble.

"Mouse, c'mere!" he shouted.

I bolted through the front doors and ran into the cold New York street not once turning around to see if I was being chased. I heard yelling and police sirens in the distance, which made me panic even more. They were coming for me. The winter cold hit me and my daughter immediately; we didn't have on any coats and the brisk air attacked us like we were in UFC match.

I ran for what seemed like an eternity. My adrenaline pumped through me vigorously, but I only covered about six blocks until I finally stopped to catch my breath and collect myself. I found myself what seemed like the middle of nowhere, though we were in Harlem. The cold and night made the streets empty. A few snowflakes started to rain down from the heavens, which made my predicament even more alarming. I was cold and my daughter was freezing. We weren't going to survive like this, out in the cold, hungry, and scared. I had to find some shelter for us promptly.

"We're gonna be okay, baby," I said to her. She was crying and shivering. I didn't want to panic, but thinking about my daughter getting sick with pneumonia and dying, I did what any desperate mother would do for her kids. I ran into the wide street with Eliza glued to me and tried hailing down a passing cab in this cold and wintry weather. The streets were sparse with traffic though, and barely any cabs were passing by.

I looked around frantically; every store was closed for the night. The streets seemed evacuated and there appeared not to be a soul around for me to cry out for help. I kept worrying that police were going to roll up and arrest me. The shelter wasn't that far away and I was desperate to leave the area. I wanted to go anywhere. I couldn't stay in Harlem.

I desperately tried to hail down any passing car in the night, but everyone seemed aloof to a woman in the cold with her one-year-old daughter. Every car that passed me by, not giving a fuck, it angered me so much that I wanted to pick up a rock and throw it at the next passing car. I would definitely get their attention then.

Fifteen minutes went by; my daughter wasn't looking too good. She was crying and sleepy. I was trying to keep her warm the best that I could. I was getting desperate.

I was tempted to hotwire and steal a car, go back to my heyday of when I used to steal shit to get paid. Maybe I could break into a parked vehicle to find some warmth for the night. I needed to do something.

Fuck it; to save my daughter's life, I was ready to go back to the shelter and turn myself in. Eliza didn't need to be out here this long in the cold because of something I did. She didn't need to suffer like her mommy. She was only one year old and so innocent.

The tears flooded my eyes; the panic settled so deeply in me that it was breaking me down like a building collapsing. The air coming from my breath was ice cold and I felt my fingers numbing up. I found myself in the middle of the wide two-way street desperately trying to flag down any passing car. I gazed at a pair of headlights approaching my direction. I was ready to jump in front of the moving car, taking the chance that it would strike me and my daughter.

The car was approaching slowly though, the headlights becoming blinding in front of me. I was so cold, I felt like a snowman.

"Please stop, please stop, please stop," I chanted uncontrollably. I didn't know what I was going to do if this car passed us by like so many others. New York was a heartless place.

Fortunately for us, the car stopped in front of us and I never felt so relieved. The driver's door opened up and a tall, lean man stepped out. It was a gypsy cab and the driver was Haitian. He looked at us and asked, "You need a ride somewhere, ma'am?"

I didn't answer him. I rushed his way and climbed into the back seat trying to clutch to the warmth of his car. I was shivering uncontrollably and my daughter was too. The heat blasting from the dashboard felt like paradise to us.

"Thank you," I uttered.

"Where to?" he asked.

Yes, where to? I asked myself. I didn't have too many friends out there and too many places to go to. I was alone. I was desperate to find somewhere warm and welcoming. The driver turned and looked at me, waiting for my reply. I uttered, "Take me to the Bronx, Edenwald."

He nodded and pressed down on the accelerator. I grasped Eliza tightly to my chest with my arms wrapped around her like a blanket and tried to nestle her with some warmth. My baby was suffering and she needed to be somewhere safe and warm. My breathing was labored and my hands were so cold that they felt like they were about to snap off like icicles.

The cab driver crossed into the Bronx borough and we getting closer to Edenwald. I didn't have any cash to pay him, so I only had one option: once he stopped, just run off. Maybe he would give chase, maybe he wouldn't. I had the disadvantage though; I had a baby and a trash bag to carry. But I was anxious to do something. The only location I could think of going was to my friend's place, Erica. She had spent some time in jail for drug use and violation of her parole, but I heard through the grapevine that she was home again. Erica was my only hope.

The gypsy cab came to a stop in front of the building on East 229th Street. He had the car idling and turned around looking at me, expecting payment. *Shit,* I thought. How could I run when I was tangled with so many things? There was no way I was going to outrun this muthafucka.

"That'll be twenty-five dollars," he said in his thick Haitian accent.

"Can you give me a minute? I have a friend in the building who's gonna pay my fare for me," I lied.

He looked reluctant to let me leave. We locked eyes; I was hoping he would believe my lie, but he didn't. "You go, the bag stays," he said. He wasn't stupid.

"I need my stuff, though," I begged. "I'm not gonna jerk you, yo."

"You get your stuff when I receive my fare," he countered.

I sighed with frustration. Everything I owned was in that garbage bag, and Eliza's things were also inside there. The driver was adamant though. He kept his eyes on me, knowing the scheme, knowing that people from my neighborhood always fled without paying their fare.

I had no choice. It was heartbreaking, but I removed myself from the back seat of his cab, leaving all my belongings behind, and went to see if Erica was able to take us in. I was so desperate that I was willing to do anything. I slowly walked away from the cab. The driver sat behind the wheel waiting for my return, but I knew I wasn't going to return. I had to take it as a loss; my shit was gone and he would be left with clothes and womanly and baby shit.

It was the middle of the night, and Edenwald appeared quiet for once. There was no one lingering anywhere. The frigid cold kept everyone inside; even the drug dealers and fiends looked like they retired for the night. I hurried toward Erica's building towering over the urban area. I rushed into the lobby and got inside the elevator. It was just me and my daughter, nothing else. I pushed for the eighth floor and the door closed, and the foul, pissy-smelling elevator ascending toward my floor. I stepped into the narrow, graffiti-scrawled hallway and walked toward Erica's apartment. I was so nervous. I hadn't seen or spoken to Erica in years, since we were fifteen years old. The bitch was always in and out of jail for numerous transgressions: drugs, prostitution, assault and battery, shoplifting, disorderly conduct, grand larceny, and more. She was hood and didn't give a fuck. But she was always a friend to Sammy and me.

I sighed deeply standing in front of her door and hesitated to knock. She could be a friend to me, or she could tell me to fuck off. I was in a bad predicament and had to rely on friends I hadn't spoken to or seen in years. I didn't even know if she still lived in the same apartment; everything was an assumption.

Eliza was falling asleep in my arms. I had the cab still waiting outside in the cold with my stuff in the back seat. I had nothing but the clothes on my back and not a penny to my name. I was hungry, cold, frustrated, and agitated all at once.

Fuck it, I thought. It was late and I knocked a few times on the door. I prayed this turned out well for me. If it didn't, I didn't know what I was going to do. My old apartment had already been rented out. I hadn't spoken to Sammy in months; my old crew, EBV girls, was in disarray. Tina was dead. She was stabbed in a club fight right after Eliza was born, and Meme and La-La were both incarcerated upstate on drug charges. They each had to do five years. The only one left was Crystal, but she was doing her own thing and hanging out with some heavy hitters in the game. She was also fuckin' with this notorious gangster named, Trice.

The Edenwald Blood Vixens, we were a dying breed.

I continued knocking, until I heard someone on the other end of the door shout out sharply, "Who is it?"

"Erica, it's me, Mouse." I was meek and praying.

The door opened and Erica stood in front of me wearing some boy shorts and a T-shirt. She had long, cascading cornrows and was swathed with tattoos on her curvy figure. She was hardcore, grew up rough like the rest of us, but she was a friend to me, someone I grew up with.

Erica smiled and greeted me. "Oh shit, bitch, Mouse, what's up. Damn, it's 'bout time you come by and check a bitch. I've been home for almost four months now."

I was glad to see her smile and elated to see me. I looked like a pathetic lost puppy in front of her. I tried to keep my sanity and composure. I truly needed her help. I needed someplace to stay, and if I had to beg, then so be it. I couldn't be proud.

"Hey, Erica," I replied with a frail smile.

"Oh shit, is this ya daughter, Mouse? Look at her. She's sleeping and she's so cute," Erica said.

"She's exhausted. It's been a really long day for us both."

"Damn, Mouse, you lookin' crazy. You okay?"

"Erica, I need help. I hate to ask, but I need a place to stay temporarily. I just got kicked out of the shelter." I had to be frank; it wasn't the time to be nostalgic or beat around the bush.

"Mouse, you ain't even gotta ask. I got you, you know that," Erica said with no hesitation in her tone.

She stepped to the side and allowed me and my daughter inside. She lived with her elderly grandmother who was in her mid-eighties and becoming senile. She came home after doing time and was fortunate to have someplace to stay; some of us weren't that lucky in life.

It was somewhat cozy inside the dingy and small three-bedroom apartment, nothing fancy, antique and tattered-looking furniture, worn-out carpet, narrow, long hallway leading to the three bedrooms, family pictures plastered all over the wall, and one small color television sitting on top of the broken wide-back forty-inch TV. The place was the epitome of a ghetto apartment. It reminded me of home.

I looked at the time and it was after midnight. I just wanted to put my head to a pillow and close my eyes and sleep for days. Erica had her two kids with her: Tracy, who was six, and Timothy, he was four. I put Eliza in the bedroom with them. They had bunk beds and Eliza slept with Tracy on the bottom. Erica's grandmother occupied the second bedroom, and the third bedroom was Erica's, but she already had company: some shirtless young buck male and it was obvious she was fucking him.

"You cool to sleep on the couch, Mouse?" she asked me.

Like I had a choice. If it was soft, warm and cozy, it was perfect for me. "Yeah, I'm good," I said.

Erica removed a blanket and a pillow, and made a place for me on her couch in the living room near the window. I happened to look outside just in time to see the gypsy cab drive off with my shit in the back. I could have asked Erica for the money, but I felt I was reaching. I had already asked her to take me and my daughter into her home. I sulked; the last that I owned, it was gone. Some of the stuff was sentimental to me and I could never get back.

I wanted to cry, but I didn't. I was so crushed that I felt my insides twisting up like pretzel. I lost everything, but I couldn't lose myself. I had a daughter depending on me. I sat on the couch with Erica keeping me company for a moment. Even though she had some dick waiting for her in the bedroom, she took time out to talk to me. I guessed she saw the stress on my face and was worried about me.

She rolled up a blunt and we smoked for a moment, chatting it up and reminiscing about the good old days. And then, after a few pulls later, we talked about our current situations. I told Erica about my circumstances, getting pregnant by Rico, the fame I almost had at the tip of my fingers, my pop's trifling ways, the crew, and so on.

"Yo, I heard you and Sammy ain't fuckin' wit' each anymore. That's crazy. Ya both were tight like that," she mentioned.

"Long story, we fell out over some dick," I said.

"I heard, fuckin' wit' that nigga Rico. He always been a trifling-ass nigga," she said.

Yeah, I learned that about him the hard way. But he was my past. I didn't want to talk about him, or Sammy and I falling out. Erica went on to tell me about her situation. She came home adjusting to the change, talked about her baby fathers—one was locked up, the other nigga was on the run from the feds—and then she mentioned the nigga she had in her bedroom.

"He a'ight and shit, provides when he can, and looks out for my kids when I need to work," she said.

I was happy for her. It must be nice to have a decent man in your life and someone to hold you down. I didn't have that. Thought I had that with Rico, but that turned out to be hell.

"Anyway, we can continue talkin' in the morning, I know ya tired and shit. But I got you, Mouse. You know you family," Erica said affably.

I smiled.

She went into the bedroom to be with her nigga. I lay across the couch and put my head to the pillow. I cried for a moment before I closed my eyes and went to sleep.

Chapter Four

Sammy

"Girl, use what you got to get what you want," Kawanda said to me. "I do it all the time. Selling this phat, sweet pussy pays my bills and you see a bitch ain't ever broke."

I listened to what she was telling me, and she was telling me a lot about stripping and tricking. It was a lot of money in the game, especially tricking; men were willing to pay handsomely for sex with a beautiful and curvy woman, but I still held on to my morals. I just couldn't go there like that. It was my pussy and to give it out so freely to make a dollar, it bothered me greatly. I was making good money just dancing. I wasn't banking heavily like the girls who turned tricks in the backrooms, but I was surviving, making my decent ends.

Kawanda had encouraged me to do a few out-of-club parties for groups of men: private parties, birthday parties, bachelors' parties, sex parties, and so on. I would be paid an upfront fee, and whatever I made there, it was mines to take home. She explained that there was good money in doing these parties, so I decided to give it a try.

I took a strong pull from the burning blunt between my lips, allowing the weed to influence me, and then I looked at my reflection in the outsized bathroom mirror, being in the presidential suite at the swanky Marriot hotel in Times Square. I was getting dressed and preparing myself to entertain a hotel room full of hungry men. I wasn't the only girl entertaining; three other girls, including Kawanda, were already scantily clad, perfumed up, high off haze, and maybe tipsy while in the extravagant room dancing and flirting with over a dozen mixed muthafuckas. I was the last to get dressed.

Kawanda and I had shared a cab from the Bronx to the city; we split the fifty dollar fare and strutted through the grand atrium pulling our rolling luggage behind us. I left Danny with my elderly neighbor, paying her twenty-five dollars a night to babysit my son. I figured this gig was going to be an all-nighter for me. Kawanda boasted that these niggas paid well and loved black girls. I was hyped.

As I got dressed, I could hear hip hop music blaring from the room and men shouting and yelling all kinds of obscenities to the dancers, hooting and hollering like a pack of wolves. They were having a grand old time with the girls. I got dressed in something truly sexy and eye-catching: a VIP minidress featuring a halter neckline with string ties and a silver weave for a glittery effect. Underneath the see-though outfit I wore a bright G-string and my dark nipples showing. I wore my bright red, six-inch stilettos with my platinum wig and my body glistening with glitter. I didn't have to borrow any of my friends' outfits anymore; over the weeks I had acquired my own stuff and my own taste.

I stepped out into the party with my flirtatious smile and long strut. The minute I entered the room, the lustful eyes and smiles were glued to me. Now, these Wall Street and white-collar businessmen had something new to ogle over and play with. There was a sprinkle of black men in the place, but it was these white crackers who were drooling a great deal with their hard, white dicks protruding from their tight slacks and khakis, and yearning to get them a piece of some blackberry.

I wasn't in the room no more than a minute, when two bushy-haired white males came rushing my way with fistfuls of money. They were wide-eyed at my beauty and my scrumptious figure. These white boys, they had money to burn, far more than niggas at the club were spending. I saw only twenties and fifty dollar bills in these crackers' hands and they were willing to spend it all on some black pussy.

The night got started in great fun, and then it got really kinky. Everyone was drinking and smoking, getting tipsy with the hip hop music blaring. The girls were all over these white boys like wallpaper on wall. Kawanda, looking almost buck-naked in a teeny-weeny string monokini with microcups and string thong back, was damn near fucking this white boy on the couch. He touched and groped her body everywhere as she ground against his crotch and tongue kissed him. Next thing I saw, he was pulling out his dick and she was jerking him off right there in front of everyone. He tilted his head back from the blissful pleasure and moaned. Just like that, it was turning into that type of party.

I was giving this chunky, pale-looking white boy a sensual lap dance as he stuffed one big face dead president after another down my G-string. I had my tender chocolate nipples mush in his face and felt his erection poking me intensely. I worked the room like magic, jumping from one customer to another, enjoying the big tips and flirting heavily to make my money. From my peripheral vision, I noticed Kawanda pull her customer up from the chair by having his dick in her hand. She was butt-ass naked with her heels in her hands and leading the man into a private bedroom where he could enjoy her a lot more. The girls were constantly in and out of bedrooms in the suite, fucking and sucking these white boys for a high price and they were coming back out with a fistful of money and a smile larger than anything.

An hour went by, and I was still just dancing, having them touch me anywhere they wanted to, maybe suck on my nipples and let them feel between my thighs, and touch this pussy, but the real money was having sex. I was offered the chance for a private session with a few white boys, but I would gently turn down the offer. I wasn't ready to prostitute myself like that. When I took a break to go into the bathroom, Kawanda boasted about making $1,500 already. I made close to $400, but at my rate, it was snail money compare to my coworkers sexing these white boys down.

The next hour, I found myself dancing for this cutie with blue eyes and what looked like a promising physique behind his stylish attire. He resembled Brad Pitt. He tipped me nicely and touched me so dotingly that I found myself getting wet and aroused. He was dressed in a sharp three-piece suit, sporting his gold Rolex and diamond ring. He looked smart and well established. I could tell by the way he looked at me that he was extremely attracted to me.

"I love black woman," he whispered in my ear with his hand on my tit.

I felt his bulge and he seemed to be packing some nice in his pants. He cupped my tits as I ground my pussy against his bulging crotch. Since I started dancing for him, he already placed $500 in my G-string and was willing to pay me a lot more.

"You're beautiful," he said to me, smiling.

"Thank you."

"What is your name, if you don't mind me asking?" He was such a gentleman.

Of course I couldn't give him my government name, and I gave him my stripper name. "My name is Bambi." Now I really don't know why I came up with the name Bambi, it sounded like a reasonable stripper name to me, and it was the only suitable name that I could come up with since so many other names were already taken. And it didn't hurt that I was a huge fan of the movie when I was young.

"I like that, Bambi. You definitely look like a Bambi," he said.

He played me close like liquor on a drunk man's breath as I ground on his lap and pressed my lovely breasts against his chest. His cologne was so alluring. The fragrance pleased my nostrils and made me feel high. He was the finest-looking white boy in the room and I had his undivided attention.

"And what's your name?" I asked him.

"Travis."

"Nice name."

"Thank my mother."

"I need to thank her for a lot more things than just your name," I flirted, feeling his bulging erection move between my thighs.

He chuckled.

He fondled me. He kissed my nipples softly and I reached down and felt his dick swelling more and more in his pants. He looked at me and I looked at him. And then the inevitable happened. "How much for you?" he asked.

Damn. I sighed and didn't respond.

"I mean, I don't want to offend you, but I really like you and I'll pay whatever you charge. I have money," he stated.

I continued dancing on him, and didn't know what to say. I guessed he took my silence for a no, but he wasn't giving up. "I'll give three thousand to have sex with you."

Shit! $3,000 could help me in so many ways right now. Usually any girl would jump at the offer, but I was shocked at it. He was so hard between my legs that I thought his dick was going to rip through his pants and penetrate me. It felt so big.

"Bambi, you're the only woman I'm attracted to in here and you're about to have me burst like a balloon because I want you so badly. How about five thousand for your time?" He upped the offer and I couldn't resist it. I damn sure needed the money. With the $900 I already made plus his five grand, it was going to be a very good night.

I took a deep breath and huffed out, "C'mon, let's have some fun," before I changed my mind. But I wasn't going to change my mind. It was good money. I stood up and took him by the hand and led him to one of the unoccupied bedrooms in the suite.

The party was still going strong, and I became the final girl at the party who was about to suck and fuck a man for money. I was about to contradict myself, but for $5,000, who wouldn't? I escorted him toward the bigger room down the hallway, and as I was about to enter the bedroom, the door swung open and Kawanda walked out still naked counting her money. A shirtless and big-bellied forty-year-old white man exited behind her looking like he had the best pussy ever. She had sexually pleased her umpteenth trick for the night and was still going strong. Her pussy had to be sore and her mouth had to somewhat numb, but she was a money-hungry girl.

When she saw me about to turn a trick, she smiled and winked at me. "You go, girl, get that money, and he a cutie. I ain't mad at you," she said.

I didn't respond to her remark. I hurried inside the room. I felt embarrassed that she saw me go into the room with someone. Travis walked into the room and I closed the door behind him. This was it. The bedroom boasted floor-to-ceiling windows, a plasma TV, a king-sized bed, an overstuffed sofa, lovely furnishings, and a few other luxurious amenities.

Travis stood in the center of the bedroom and smiled at me. His deep blue eyes displayed his eagerness to have me. I locked the door to make sure we weren't interrupted and strutted toward him in my sexy stilettos.

"You are truly beautiful," he said. "I can't wait to have you."

"I can't wait to feel you inside of me," I replied, touching him gently and fondling his crotch area.

I could tell he wanted to kiss me, but I didn't go there with him. He couldn't have everything from me; I had to save something for myself. He pulled me into his strong, masculine arms and held me close. I never been with a white boy before and was glad that he would be my first. He was too fine. He started to foreplay with me by undressing me slowly and admiring every inch of me. He lowered his lips to my nipples and tenderly took them into his mouth and sucked on them so pleasingly with his lips and tongue. I couldn't help but to moan from the wetness of his mouth sampling my flesh.

As he sucked my hard nipples with me in his grasp, my hands guided their way to his crotch area and I effortlessly unzipped his pants. I reached inside his trousers, searching for that magnificent piece of meat I felt poking between my legs when I was giving him a sensual lap dance. I didn't have to search with my hands too long. His dick seemed to gravitate toward my touch; and when I palmed it in my manicured fist I could feel his size growing so big between my fingers. Travis had to adjust himself at times to accommodate the raging erection that he couldn't control. He deflated the myth about white boys having small dicks. Travis was packing, and he was packing nicely.

I pulled his lengthy, big dick out of his zipper and stroked him lovingly. He moaned as my hand gladly glided back and forth against him, jerking him off satisfactorily. We were entangled in each other's bliss. He pulled me closer and showered my neck with kisses and the moistness between my legs was a strong signal of the passion and intense fucking that was about to transpire.

Things got hot and heavy. For $5,000, I was his bitch all night long. He finally pulled himself away from my black essence and started to undress, but before he continued any further in taking off his clothes, he uttered, "Oh, I didn't forget."

He reached into the inner pocket of his suit jacket and pulled out a $10,000 stack of bills. It wasn't the first time I seen money like that. When I used to hustle for Rico, I was stacking probably more then he was. But when a bitch is broke, it becomes impressive to see again. He peeled off nothing but hundred dollar bills and handed over the $5,000 that he owed me. I beamed. Now it was time to get this party started.

I got butt-ass naked for him, but kept my stilettos on. He couldn't help but stare at my body, my beauty, my poise, and enchanting curves. But the surprise came my way when Travis completely undressed and his body was phenomenal. His tan flesh ripped with lean, cut muscles, the six-pack on his stomach looked sculpted, his strapping chest looked like it could be on the cover of *Men's Fitness,* and between his legs was the nicest big dick I ever saw. It was already eight inches flaccid, and when it got erect, gotdamn, I was in for a workout.

I was ready to drop on my knees and suck his dick, but he didn't want that. He just wanted to feel the inside of me.

"You have a condom?" I asked.

If he didn't, it was easy to get one from the girls. But fortunately he did. He pulled out a Magnum condom from his pants pocket on the floor. He tore it open, rolled the latex back on his thick, long size, and was ready for me. He curved me over the bed and spread my legs in a downward V with my pussy exposed. He positioned himself behind me. I couldn't believe I was selling my pussy, but money talks. He shoved his cock inside of me with force, stabbing my womb with his weapon of flesh. I gripped the sheets and moaned. His flesh filled me completely. As he fucked me from the back, he reached around and underneath me and rubbed my clit furiously and shoved his fingers in my pussy. It was intense pleasure.

"Ooooh shit. Ooooh shit, damn, damn," I moaned animatedly from the extreme sensation.

My dark, sweet juices saturated the condom thrusting inside of me. He placed both hands on my shoulders and buried my face into the bed with my phat ass arched in the air. He shoved his cock in repeatedly, pushing, shoving, and ramming until every inch of him was embedded deep inside my glory hole.

"Damn, your pussy is so good, so fuckin' good, so fuckin' good. I love that dark berry juice. Give it to me, fuckin' give it to me," he raved.

He concentrated on making sure he drove every millimeter of his dick deep inside me and withdrew it all the way to the head before he rammed it in deeper and harder than before. He smacked my ass almost red from the spanking and my pussy gaped open like the Midtown Tunnel. White boy was a freak, but I loved it.

"You like that, don't you, girl," he said.

I grunted my affirmation and took a deep breath. He was all the way in and I was about to lose my mind. I pushed when he said push. I squeezed when he told me to; he gave the command and I followed. I trusted him to take care of me and he knew exactly how to control the situation so we both got maximum pleasure.

Twenty minutes later, he was still thrusting inside of me doggie style. It was his favorite position and he had complete stamina. I couldn't front; he made me cum twice with his big dick in and out of me. Shit, we were in the room for so long other girls started knocking, wanting access. But my date needed to get his nut off inside of me. I started grinding my phat ass back on him. He grabbed my hips, worked his dick in and out.

"Ooooh shit, you gonna make me cum again," I cried out. I buried my face into the pillow to keep the other girls from hearing how good the dick was to me.

I was chanting an erotic mantra.

"Oh shit, I love this black pussy. Ooooh, I love this black pussy," he chanted. "I'm almost there. I'm almost there."

He took a deep breath and gave me the last inch of his hard dick and both our legs started to tremble. I felt his dick swelling bigger inside of me. He was finally about to come. And when he did, he gripped my hips tightly, shivered uncontrollably, screamed out, "Fuuuuuuuuuuuuukk," and then he suddenly pulled out, snatched the condom off his dick and I felt his hot cum splash on my back. I didn't care where he came and how, as long as he didn't do it inside of me raw.

We both were breathing heavily and my hair was in somewhat disarray from his constant grabbing and my face being pushed into the pillow. Travis was exhausted and drained. He pulled up his pants and smiled gratifyingly.

"Was is good?" I asked.

"Yo, that was some of the best pussy I ever had," he complimented me.

"I'm glad you enjoyed it."

We both collected ourselves. My sexual servitude was done and I was happy to have five grand on me. He walked out of the room first; I made my exit two minutes later. I had to get right again. When I walked out the bedroom, there was Kawanda smiling at me. She was waiting to use the room again; the other two had just become occupied.

Standing behind her was a black man this time, and the look on his face said he was ready to have the time of his life.

"Damn, girl, you had some fun?" she asked jokingly. "Shit, as fine as he was, I woulda spent an hour wit' him. Did he pay you well?"

I smiled and walked away. It wasn't any of her business. I already made my money and I was ready to leave. But the party in the presidential suite was still in full swing and it didn't look like it was about to die down anytime soon. The men were drunk, horny, and having the time of their lives, and the girls, they were fucking and sucking everything moving in the room. It became a full-blown orgy when a few more girls showed up to get in on the action and they didn't care where they did their business at, as long as it got done. Pussy and dick was from wall to wall, hip hop music still blaring, and mostly white men with their pants around their ankles, and tiny, hard dicks showing, were eager to stick their wieners into anything wet and sloppy.

I was glad more girls showed up; it made me fall back and just chill. I still flirted and gave lap dances, but when it came to the hardcore stuff, I let the other girls get their shine on. I already struck gold with Travis, and I told myself he would be the first and only trick I turned.

Five hours later, it was five in the morning and I was exhausted. I made $7,000 that night, and I was all smiles. I felt I didn't need to dance at Crazy Legs anymore and degrade myself. I had enough money for rent, food, clothes, and other important things. But who was I kidding? $7,000 in New York would be gone in three, maybe four months tops, and since I didn't have a high school diploma or GED, and didn't have a baller boyfriend to spend on me, I was struggling.

The cab let us out on Laconia Avenue with dawn about to crack open the sky. Kawanda and I walked the block to our buildings feeling like we could sleep for days. I saw the police lights a half a block away and thought something happened, but when we got close, it was cops who pulled over a Chevy Impala with tinted windows and they were harassing the young hoods who had occupied the car. They had the three men handcuffed and lying face down on the ground as an officer thoroughly searched through their vehicle. It was obvious that they belonged to YGC. But it was crazy.

Kawanda and I minded our business and went into our building. The Bronx was heating up like an oven on Thanksgiving. I was sick of it. Gunshots every night, and niggas dying; this had been my world for so long that it felt I could never escape it.

When I got to my floor, I knocked on Ms. Wilson's door to pick up my son. The heaviness in my eyes showed very much and my pussy still felt stretched out from Travis's big dick in and out of me. I was paid a lot of money, but I felt dirty and used. The only thing I wanted to do when I walked into my apartment was take a long shower and sleep for hours. But that was going to be an impossible task if Danny was awake with his crying.

"Who?" I heard Ms. Wilson asked through the door.

"It's me, Sammy."

I heard the locks turn, and Ms. Wilson answered with the chain still on the door, glaring at me in her bedtime rollers and housecoat.

"Chile, you know what time it is," she hissed at me.

"I know, I'm sorry, I just lost track of time, Ms. Wilson and then coming from the city . . ." I apologized sincerely.

She continued to glare at me. I didn't want to keep explaining myself. I only wanted to pick up my son and just leave. "Is he still up?" I asked.

"He's 'sleep, and you look like shit, chile," she said.

"I just have a lot on my mind."

"We all do. But you still need to be here to pick him up at a decent time."

"I know." I was willing to pay her more than twenty-five dollars for the extra help. "Well, can he—" I started, but she cut me off.

"Look, you don't even have to ask me. He doesn't need to be woke up at this time in the morning, and with you looking like that. I'll keep him for the morning so you can go and get some rest."

It was music to my ears. "Thank you."

"But don't make this a habit, Sammy."

"I won't." I pulled out some money and handed her fifty dollars. Ms. Wilson wasn't shy in taking the cash. She may have been old, but like me, she was about her money.

She stuffed the cash into her housecoat and shut the door. I went into my apartment and left a trail of clothes from the doorway to the bathroom. I couldn't wait to get into the shower and scrub myself clean as the water cascaded down on me like a waterfall. In my mind, I felt like I traded in the drug game for prostituting myself. It had only been one date, but why did I feel ashamed?

I spent almost a half hour in the shower, cleansing myself after a dirty and wild night with millionaire white boys who saw black women as exotic and sexual pleasers for their limp white dicks. We sucked and fucked them for pennies compare to most of their net worth. We were a fantasy to them, and tonight, we made all of their sexual fantasies come true. I know I sure did for Travis.

I dropped all my cash on the bedroom dresser and stared at it for a minute. The heap of it sitting there, spilling over onto the floor, was very impressive. I worked hard to make it. I remembered what Kawanda had said to me: "Girl, use what you got to get what you want." And I did just that, used what I had between my legs to get what I wanted, or what I needed to feed and clothe my son. I would count it again in the morning.

The minute I climbed into my bed to sleep and dream of some alternative place to be, some slice of heaven for me, pretending I didn't spread my legs for a dollar tonight, the sounds of the ghetto brought me back to my reality.

Bak! Bak! Bak! Bak!

The gunshots echoed from the streets into my bedroom window at six in the morning, a clear indication that the streets never sleep and there was a war going on between two rival gangs.

Chapter Five

Mouse

I woke up on Erica's couch feeling a little better, but it was far from okay for me. I was wrapped up underneath the blanket she gave me so snugly I looked like I was in a cocoon. The warmth was so soothing that it made me not to want to get up. It was another cold day, and there was nothing I wanted to do more than just sleep all day somewhere comfortable. But I had to check on my daughter and make a plan for myself.

I got up and became startled at Erica's grandmother seated across from me in an ugly brown chair. She just looked at me stoically, like she was some zombie, her eyes black and aloof from everything around her. I remembered Erica telling me that her eighty-four-year-old grandmother was senile and had Alzheimer's.

I smiled and greeted her with a simple, "Good morning."

"Jackie, you still going to school this morning," her grandmother said out of nowhere.

Jackie? I looked around me to see if there was anyone else in the room, but I was the only one.

"I need to get ready for school, Jackie. Mama gonna get mad at us if we're late," she said. "Jackie . . ."

I was confused; she was talking to me, but wasn't talking to me. It seemed like she was in a different world, or a different time. Her thin, frail, and wrinkled body was clad in a blue housecoat and her thinning gray hair was in small braids.

"I'm not Jackie," I said.

The woman's toothless smile was aimed at me and she repeated, "Jackie, we gonna be late for school. I need to go."

Yeah, her memory was warped.

"Grandma, your sister Jackie has been dead for ten years now and you ain't been to school in forever," Erica said, coming into the room to care for her grandmother.

Erica kissed her grandmother on the cheek and buttoned up her housecoat to make sure she was warm and fine. She took her grandmother's wrinkled hand in hers and massaged it tenderly. "You hungry, Grandma?" Erica asked.

She looked up at Erica with her warm smile and replied, "Hey, Candy."

"Grandma, I'm Erica, your youngest granddaughter, remember?"

She nodded.

I never had been around anyone with Alzheimer's before. It was weird to me. She kept calling me Jackie. I just hoped I never succumbed to such a horrible disease when I got older. Sometimes I thought I wasn't going to see my next birthday. Every day to me was a blessing, because for me, it was survival of the fittest out here.

Erica looked at me and asked, "How did you sleep?"

"I slept fine."

"You hungry?"

"Very," I replied, feeling my stomach growling like a loud engine.

"I'll make some pancakes."

"Where's Eliza?" I asked, becoming concerned about my daughter.

"She's in the bedroom watching cartoons with my kids," said Erica.

The first thing I did was get up to check on my daughter. We had a horrible night in the cold and I had to make sure she was fine. I had no changing clothes for her, no food, diapers, toys, or a decent winter coat. We just had each other and the clothes on our backs.

I went into the bedroom and saw Eliza seated between Erica's daughter's legs watching cartoons. When she saw me standing in the doorway, Eliza jumped up and came my way with open arms. I scooped my daughter up in my arms and kissed and hugged her tightly. I loved my little girl and didn't want to let her go.

I said hi to Erica's kids, but they looked at me like I was some alien from another planet, especially the daughter; it looked like she caught an attitude with me because I interrupted the cartoons. So I went into the kitchen to see about breakfast. Erica was a hood bitch, but one thing for sure: she knew how to throw down in the kitchen. She was whipping up some blueberry pancakes and an omelet.

While she cooked, I sat at the kitchen table with Eliza still in my arms and we talked. Erica smoked a cigarette while cooking. I needed a cigarette too. I removed one from the pack on the table and lit up desperately, allowing the nicotine to seep into my system. I exhaled and didn't think twice about smoking around my daughter. She was used to it and I didn't believe in that secondhand smoke shit. Sometimes, Eliza would laugh and smile at the smoke I blew out and try to catch it with her tiny hands.

"How long has she been like that?" I asked about her grandmother.

"For years now. She's getting worse every day."

"That's crazy."

"What can you do? It's what happens when we get old," said Erica.

"I don't know about me. I might not even see old age. Shit. You know how we used to do," I said.

"Shit, there were times when I thought I wasn't gonna see my eighteenth birthday."

"But we did."

"Now I'm workin' on seeing my twenty-first birthday," she said.

While we talked in the kitchen, her boyfriend walked in on us. He caught my attention knowing he was far from my friend's type. He was shirtless and lean with no muscle definition at all. His cornrows cascaded down to his back and his upper body was swathed with tattoos. He had baby-face features, but devious-looking eyes.

He walked behind Erica while she was over the stove, threw his arms around her, kissed her, and said, "Good morning, baby."

"Good morning," she replied, smiling like a schoolgirl.

He looked over me and simply asked, "Who she?"

"A friend from back in the day," she replied.

"A friend, huh? What's ya friend's name?"

"Mouse," Erica answered.

"Mouse. That's a cute name, and she's cute, too," he replied. They talked about me like I wasn't even there. He removed the cigarette from Erica's hand and was going to finish it off. She didn't care. She continued cooking breakfast.

He smiled at me, I didn't smile back. There was something about him that I immediately didn't like. When he looked at me, it felt like he was undressing me with his eyes and thinking about some devious shit to do to me. He focused his attention back on Erica and said, "You gonna go and get that money tonight?"

"You know it, daddy," Erica replied.

Daddy?

"That's my bitch," he said and then smacked Erica on her ass causing her to giggle. "Call me when you get done up in here; a nigga hungry like a muthafucka."

He walked by me and winked. I didn't say anything.

It was crazy to see Erica looking so domesticated, especially for some man who wasn't even that cute. Back in the day, she ran through niggas like a pack of Newports and had a fierce reputation on the streets for robbing niggas if she wasn't moving weight for drug dealers. Like us all, she had a hard lifestyle growing up with her mother murdered when she was thirteen and then being molested, raped, and pregnant by her own father when she was fifteen. Of course she had an abortion and her father got fifteen years, but Erica's life ain't been sweet since her mother pushed her out her pussy inside of Rikers Island.

She was born in jail, and been going back and forth inside since she was fourteen years old. Like me, she was nothing to play with and a nuclear terror in the Bronx. This bitch was a pit bull in a skirt. But seeing her again, I saw a change in her. Maybe her last stint in jail reformed her somewhat, because the Erica I knew wouldn't be fuckin' with the lame nigga she had in her bedroom. She always loved them goon, muscular niggas who got it popping. The nigga in her life now, whose name was Cream, looked like he took advantage of a bitch and was sleazy in my eyes.

But it wasn't my business. I was living day by day, surviving and trying to lift my head out of the water, trying not to drown. And I didn't know if I killed Dietra and had a warrant out for my arrest. That night my temper got the best of me.

Erica made a stack of pancakes for breakfast. It was really good to see her home and looking good. She had gained some weight and looked so calm, and to see that she had her kids was great. A few years ago, the state threatened to take her kids away from her because of child endangerment. She had a few hood niggas over her place one night, and everyone was drinking, smoking, and gambling. Now you mix in those three combinations along with some thugs and pussy, and a fight ensued, with muthafuckas getting it popping and started shooting with her kids in the house. Her daughter was two at the time and was almost killed in the melee.

Six months later, she had gotten locked up.

I dined on her blueberry pancakes and omelet, and devoured them like I was Scooby-Doo and Shaggy. It was much better than the food at the shelter. I think I had like ten pancakes all together.

As we lingered in the kitchen with the kids in the bedroom watching TV and the day going by, Erica and I got to talking. We shared the last cigarette in the apartment, and while her nigga was locked away in her bedroom, I told her my situation, the fight, being out in the cold, and losing all of my shit in the cab last night.

"You were in a shelter, huh?" she said.

"I had to get away from that place, Erica. Fuckin' bitches in your business, the rules and shit, bitches hatin' on me," I griped.

She coolly countered with, "It beats being locked up, Mouse. At least you got to come and go when you pleased. Fuckin' upstate is hell. Missin' my kids, my peoples, and missin' some good dick in my life."

I laughed. I took a drag from the Newport and exhaled. Erica and I always connected. She could never replace Sammy, but she came close when she wasn't locked up. "I feel you. I just can't go back there."

"Shit, I can't get locked up again. I'm on like my third strike, and they gonna try and give me some crazy football numbers if I catch another felony."

"You ain't hustling and robbing niggas anymore, huh? You tryin' to become an old maid?" I joked.

"I'm tryin' to get this money a different way, Mouse, you feel me?" she returned.

"A different way like how?"

Erica took the cigarette from my hand and took a deep pull herself. And then she went off the subject we were talking about, saying, "When I was locked up, I heard you and Sammy were doin' ya thang, gettin' ya music out there. What happened? You still writing, right?"

It was a sad reminder of where Sammy and I were a year ago. We were like sisters, making things happen for ourselves, going to clubs to perform and having Search manage us. *Now look at us.* Fuckin' nowhere because everything went to shit so quickly.

"That's another long story," I said. "But I'm still writing."

"I wish I had your talent, Mouse. You and Sammy always been talented, fo' real," she said.

I didn't respond. It really hurts to know you had the talent to go places, to finally get out of the ghetto, but it doesn't happen. You come so far only to fail and then you find yourself in my predicament, reaching out to a friend for a place to stay with not a pot to piss in.

"You shouldn't give up, Mouse, fo' real. I still believe in you."

"Thanks," I plainly replied.

"But like I was telling you before, you need to make some money out there in the meantime, and I got you."

"What you talkin' 'bout?" I asked.

"Come wit' me tonight, and make sure you look really nice."

"With what? I have no clothes," I said.

"I got you. We the same size in everything, so you can borrow some of my clothes until you can buy your own."

"And who's gonna watch my daughter?"

"Mouse, you ain't gotta worry 'bout all that, I got you. Trust me," she said.

That was the problem; it was hard to trust her because she was always into some shady shit, and I do mean shady. She was telling me to look nice and willing to lend me some of her clothes. I couldn't help but to be nervous about what she wanted me to do with her or get involved in.

I looked at her apprehensively and Erica picked up on it.

"Why you lookin' at me like that, Mouse? You my bitch and I ain't gonna let nuthin' happen to you. I let you stay here wit' me, right? So trust me. I'm gonna get you back on your feet," she proclaimed.

I had no choice. I had nowhere else to go and no one else to turn to. All my friends were dead, locked up, or we weren't speaking to each other. I was caught between a rock and a hard place. Erica looked at me and smiled glibly. "You gonna be a'ight, watch."

I sighed lightly knowing me being a'ight was gonna be me doing something risky and stupid.

The duration of the day I spent watching television with my daughter. Erica and her man were in and out of the apartment running errands, and her cousin, who was a registered nurse, came over to look after her elderly grandmother. When evening descended over the hood, and another frostbite night dominated over the projects, Erica and Cream came walking back into the apartment. She instantly tossed me a shopping bag. I was surprised.

"What's this?" I asked.

"Go ahead, look inside."

I reached into it and pulled out a pack of Pampers, some clothes for my daughter, and some toys for her to play with. I was immediately overwhelmed. "Oh my God. You didn't have to do this."

"Yes, I did. You a friend, Mouse, and my goddaughter gonna be well looked after," she returned with conviction in her tone.

Goddaughter?

I didn't know what else to say. The diapers were truly needed. I was working with paper towels and an old tattered T-shirt I thought wasn't anyone's. Erica looked at me and smiled. Then she hit me with, "C'mon, let's hurry up and get dressed for the night."

"Who's watching the kids?"

"Cream's sister," she answered.

I was taken aback. "What?" I blurted out. I didn't know this bitch, never met her, and here she was supposedly coming over to watch my daughter. *Oh hell nah!* I threw my hand on my hip, shot an angry look at Erica, and expressed my uneasiness. "You serious?" I exclaimed.

"What's the problem?" Erica returned with a slight attitude in her tone.

"I ain't wit' having some strange woman watching my child. Are you crazy?"

"Mouse, she's cool, trust me. And besides, you owe me anyway," she countered.

"Owe you?" I was amazed by her reply.

"Yes, owe me. I let you stay here, and I bought ya daughter some stuff, and giving you clothes to wear and trying put money in your pocket. Bitch, I'm doin' you a favor."

She did help me out, and I couldn't argue. But I didn't ask her to buy Eliza anything, even though we truly needed it. But now if felt like she had my arm twisted around my back. Her favors, they cost, and how much they were going to cost me I was going to find out, because I was backed into a corner and didn't have a choice.

She continued with, "Mouse, I'm about my business, and you can either get down wit' me, or be on your own. It's ya choice. We friends, but money comes first."

Yeah, she definitely changed all right, and I thought that nigga Cream was brainwashing her. She looked at me, waiting for my answer. I had a hint of what she was about. It made sense to me all of a sudden.

"You turning tricks, ain't you?" I blurted out.

"And? You got a problem wit' it? I hope not, because it's mad money doin' it. I gets mines, Mouse, and I get plenty of it," she justified the behavior.

"Erica, I'm no fuckin' prostitute," I exclaimed.

She looked at me sideways and came back with, "You better be, because if you wanna stay here, then you gotta get that money out there on the streets wit' me."

"Wow, it's like that?" I said pointedly.

"Yes, Mouse, it's like that. Look at you, you ain't got shit right now. You is broke bitch wit' nowhere to go, and I'm being the friend I am because I got love for you. What, you turning ya nose up at me because you think it's foul? You sucked dick before, right? You fucked niggas before, right? And you ain't had a problem doin' it for free. So why all of a sudden a bitch gotta problem suckin' and fuckin' a nigga for that paper?" she frankly proclaimed.

Because it was disgusting, I thought. "And Cream, is he your pimp?" I asked.

"He just looks out for me while I'm on the street, that's all," she said, sugarcoating his role.

"And what, he gets a large cut when you the one spreading your legs and opening wide?" I was being sarcastic.

"He gets what he gets, okay!" she snapped at me. "You either in or ya out, it's ya choice, Mouse. Ain't nobody holding a gun to ya head."

She might as well have been, because it felt like she was extorting me.

I found myself in a critical dilemma. I couldn't go back out there onto them cold streets with Eliza in my arms. It would have been suicidal. Tonight it was going to be fifteen degrees and tomorrow night they were predicting snow. Erica stood right there in front of me, waiting for my answer.

Why me? And was this it for me? Was this actually what my life had turned into?

"Mommy," I heard Eliza call out to me.

I turned around and she was standing in the hallway, wearing the new clothes Erica had bought for her and had dressed her in: Baby Phat pajama sleepwear that made my daughter look so cute. It was little things like that that was getting to me. Seeing my daughter in something nice that wasn't hand-me-downs. She was warm and she was fed. She was somewhere comfortable, to some extent.

Eliza came trotting over to me so I could blanket her with my motherly affection. I wrapped her in my arms and said, "What's wrong, sweetie?"

She didn't say anything. She nestled her little head into my chest and only wanted me to hold her. And I did. As I held Eliza in my arms, I looked over at Erica, who was still standing there. She smirked and shrugged, waiting for my answer. With a steely glare focused on me, she said, "A mother would do anything to take care of her kids, I don't care what. My kids are good. I want yours to be too."

I sighed heavily. She was right.

Chapter Six

Mouse

I was the last to exit the cab in front of a closed automobile/mechanic shop on Oak Point Avenue. It was nearing midnight, and I, Erica, and Cream were in the Hunts Point neighborhood in the South Bronx, an area dominated by industry, and considered a "Red Light District," in many cases for its crime and prostitution. It also consisted primarily of older apartment buildings with a smaller number of semidetached multiunit row houses. It was a very dangerous area to be in after dark, suffering from crime and poverty for many years with many drug addicts and drug dealers residing in the dilapidated community, and here I was about to walk the track to flag down cars for a date.

Erica and I were both clad in Skhoop down miniskirts with insulation for sleek warmth, keeping ourselves warm with tights and winter boots. It was too cold out to try to look sexy in some heels and skimpy attire. I wore a Micro Puff Hooded Jacket, and underneath it a simple T-shirt. Erica wore something almost identical to me.

Cream was dressed in a leather jacket and Yankees fitted skewed across his head with designer Sean John jeans and beige Timberlands. He concealed a 9 mm in his waistband and was considered our protection. But he was nothing less than a young pimp. He was happy to see me out there with Erica. But I wasn't his to control. I was doing this for my daughter, until I was able to get back on my feet and get us our own place to live.

It was a cold night, feeling like it was below zero, freezing. I blew into my hands to keep them warm as we stood next to an abandoned and stripped automobile. Traffic was sparse, the area deserted like a ghost town. It was creepy. The wind cut bitterly through my coat and I felt like someone had shut the door and locked me inside a freezer.

Erica turned to me and said quickly under one breath, "Okay, it's fifty for a blowjob and a hundred for sex. You give a trick fifteen minutes to cum; if they don't cum in fifteen, you fuckin' leave or charge them extra. Time is money, and we can't be wasting our time on one trick for the entire night. You make him bust a nut as fast as you can and leave. But you always get paid first; no pleasure until you receive that treasure, you understand?"

I nodded.

She continued with, "Now you walk around always with a smile and flag down as many cars as you can. Get them to stop, flirt wit' muthafuckas; pull up ya skirt and show that pussy if you have to. It always gets their attention. If they ain't alone, don't fuck wit' it; that's how bitches get killed out here."

I continued nodding.

Cream was standing off to the side looking around as Erica lay down the rules to me. I could tell she was already a professional at this. She knew the do's and don'ts. Me, I was trying to keep warm, always blowing in my hands to keep them from numbing up and catching frostbite. It was so cold that it was painful. And we had to walk around in this frigid weather to make money. And speaking of money, Erica jumped onto that subject like she was reading my mind.

"Now when you get paid, you put that somewhere safe, 'cause believe me, these tricks out here can get grimy and shit, and try to take back what they paid you, either by sneaking it from you or taking it by force. So you gotta protect yourself. Here," she said, handing me a small razor to carry on me. "If niggas even think about tryin' sumthin' on you, you cut that muthafucka deep, and cut somewhere where they gonna definitely remember you. If they exposed, cut they dick off. They gonna definitely remember not to fuck wit' you then."

Just thinking about being put in a frightening situation like that had me thinking second thoughts. But it was too late to turn around. The cab was gone and we were at the point of no return.

"Also, I get sixty-five percent," Erica said.

"Sixty-five?" I uttered in disbelief.

"Yeah, bitch. Until you get on ya own, I gotta get mines. You stayin' wit' me, right? So that's rent, food, clothes, transportation. You ain't paid for shit yet."

It was highway robbery. Crazy!

"So sixty-five is my cut."

I couldn't argue with her. I could only bend over and take it in the ass roughly without any Vaseline to make it easier.

"And don't play me, Mouse, you understand? Don't steal from me, 'cause I'm serious about my money," she warned.

"I'm no thief," I said.

"Cool." Erica handed me over a dozen condoms, mostly Magnums, saying, "Keep them in ya purse, protect you from that HIV shit."

Just hearing her mention HIV had me like, *whoa, this is really serious.* I thought about Sammy's mother's having that treacherous disease and I prayed I wouldn't end up like that.

From there, it was about business and turning tricks. "I'm gonna work across the street and you stay here and work this block, walk around, but not too far, keep yourself in a certain perimeter, and watch out for five-oh and undercover, 'cause they be creeping."

"Y'all bitches have fun," Cream said to us with an unruly smile. He looked at me and winked, and then walked away from us, allowing us to do our thing. I guessed he didn't want to scare away any potential customers.

I exhaled noisily, still not sure about this. Erica strutted across the street and started to walk leisurely up the block, switching her ass left and right and having her eyes fixated on every passing car with a smile and a welcoming wave. She stepped out into the street and advertised herself for sale.

I went the opposite way, toward Tiffany Street. Traffic was so sparse that I didn't think any business would come my way soon. There was a part of me that hoped it didn't. Was I really ready to suck a stranger's dick and give him my pussy? But then it was getting so cold and I was so desperate to make some money that I prayed tonight didn't end up in a bust.

Ten minutes later, I saw headlights approaching my way. I continued walking slowly away from them, trying to keep warm and focus on my surroundings. It was a dangerous area. The car was approaching me from behind. I turned my head and noticed it was slowing down and moving closer to the curb. I stopped walking and turned completely around to see what he was about. It was a blue five-door hatchback. He pulled alongside me and rolled down the passenger window. He leaned across the passenger seat and called out, "Hey, what's up?"

"What you want?" I asked gruffly. I was nervous. I felt my heart beat a million times per second. He was a black male, looked to be in his mid-thirties. He was slim with glasses, and had a small afro and a mustache. I made it my business to screen everyone quickly.

"How much for you?" he asked promptly.

I just blurted out, "It's fifty." I didn't even know if he wanted a blowjob or sex. Fifty was the first thing that popped inside my head. *Shit,* I said to myself. I hoped he didn't think it was fifty for sex.

"Fifty for a blowjob?" he asked.

"Yes," I replied, being short with him.

I was tempted to walk away. Then I heard the words, "Get in."

For a moment, I froze. I stood there like the cold had frozen me to the concrete looking like a deer caught in headlights. He said, "Get in," but I didn't rush to the passenger door like I had seen Erica do just recently. She had spoken a few words to the driver and then trotted around to the passenger side and climbed inside this stranger's vehicle like he was an old friend giving her a ride somewhere.

I just wasn't that forthright about it, not yet anyway. I knew once I climbed into his car what would be expected of me: sexual favors for nothing more than a hundred dollars, if that.

"You gonna get in?" he asked loudly.

I took a deep breath and felt myself moving closer to his car. He unlocked the door and there was me reaching for the door handle, opening it up and getting into the front seat. Then I closed the door and he drove away. It was like I was watching myself in this vivid dream. But this was reality.

I was so nervous that I felt myself getting sick.

"You're beautiful," he said.

"Thank you," I replied faintly.

"What's your name?"

There was no way in hell I was about to give him my real name, so I quickly uttered a false identity. "Diamond." It came out all of a sudden because I remembered the character from that movie *The Players Club* with Ice Cube and LisaRaye.

"Yeah, you are definitely a diamond."

I displayed a fraudulent smile. He drove east, toward the more industrial part of the area where there was darker alleyways, parking lots, and dead-end streets. I could tell he'd done this before.

"Yeah, I want you to suck my dick. You pretty, too, with some nice lips. Damn, I can't wait," he said bluntly.

His callous comment made me even more nervous. He parked near the water, behind an uncoupled container at a shadowy dead-end street on East 149th Street. The block was industry, still because everything was shut down for the night. We had privacy. He had fifteen minutes.

He killed the ignition and looked at me hungrily. "Fifty, right?"

I nodded.

He reached into his pants pocket and pulled out a few dollars. He peeled away two twenties and a ten and handed it over. I took the cash and placed it into my bra strap. It was the most secured place I could think of. Now that I had the treasure, I reluctantly had to give him the pleasure.

He didn't hesitate to unbutton his pants and unzip his jeans. He pulled down his jeans to around his ankles and removed his erection for me to suck. His dick was average size, about six inches hard, with a thick, bulbous head, but not terribly long. He also had some girth and his privates were hairy. He gripped his dick, stroking himself and waited for me to put my lips to it. I grabbed a condom, tore it open, and rolled it back onto his small size.

"You got fifteen minutes," I told him.

With his pants down and legs spread he was ready for me, groaning as he pleased himself with anticipation for me to take over. I leaned into his lap, opened my mouth wide, relaxed my throat, and slowly wrapped my lips around the tip of his cock and took him deeply as I could into my mouth. He was hard like stone as I slid my mouth up and down on him a few times, sliding and popping him past the urge to gag. I knew how to suck dick. I was really good at it, pleasing the ones I loved and wanted to be with. But a stranger in the front seat, I had to close my eyes and pretend he was somebody I liked in my past.

"Oh shit. Oh fuck! Ooooh, that feels so good. Damn, girl. Ooooh," he cooed, "You really like this, don't you?"

No, I didn't, but the way I sucked him off, it seemed like I did. I kept my eyes closed for the oral duration. I didn't want to see him or even hear him. I just wanted him to cum quickly.

I bobbed my head up and down on him a few times, following my hand as I stroked him. I felt his hand on the back of my head, touching my hair, and he was shoving his dick farther into my mouth. It upset me. I stopped momentarily and warned him, "Please, don't do that. Don't grab the back of my head."

"I'm sorry," he quickly apologized.

I continued.

"Damn, your mouth feels so good. Ooooh. Oh fuck, you're going to make me come! Oh, fuck."

His breathing was already a bit ragged as he reclined in his seat and groaned loudly from my oral sensation. The feel of his dick was growing inside of my mouth, indicating he was about to come.

"Jesus, girl," he hollered. "Oh shit. Oh damn. Oh fuck!"

The tension in his body and the way his cock twitched as I felt him shoot inside my mouth was proof he loved it, and the condom barrier prevented me from tasting and swallowing his semen. I felt him explode like a volcano with my mouth on him and his body shuddering in the front seat wildly.

And just like that, it was over.

But for me, the latex taste from the condom lingered in my mouth and I wanted to gag so badly. I really felt the urge to throw up when he came inside my mouth. I couldn't believe I actually went through with it. The degrading feeling, it wasn't worth the fifty dollars he paid me and by the end, I was just an open, wet mouth for him to please himself and make him come.

"I really enjoyed that, Diamond," he said, pulling up his pants.

I didn't.

"You got a number so I can call you?"

"I don't have a cell phone."

"Do you be out here often?"

"I don't," I said, being brief. "Just drop me off."

"I was just making conversation."

I wasn't in the mood to talk. I wanted to scrub his taste from my mouth. I wanted to go home, but I had no home. It was going to be a very long night. He dropped me off at the same place he picked me up. I climbed out of his car and didn't want to look at him. When he pulled away, I saw Erica jumping into a black Accord across the street. She was working on her third date while I barely finished up with my first.

Cream was standing in the shadows a block away. He was on his phone and watching the block. The only good thing about being in that trick's car was the temporary warmth I got from the heat blasting. Besides that, it was the worst day I ever had.

I started to walk down the block and I couldn't even get a minute to myself when a second car pulled parallel to me, rolling down his window and vying to get my attention. This one was in a burgundy minivan, and he was a bearded white guy.

"How much for a blowjob?" he hollered out the window.

I told him my price and he told me to get in. Several minutes later, parked on a secluded block, my head was in his lap, with my lips sliding up and down his pink, little raw sausage. He came quickly. When I was done with him, I threw up on the street and continued walking the track. The third trick I turned, he wanted sex. So in the back seat of his SUV, I lifted my skirt, pulled off my tights, spread my legs, and he pumped himself into me so excitedly that he came inside of me instantly. The next trick, he wanted to fuck me doggie style in the back seat of his cramped car. He was well endowed and stretched my pussy out like it was a rubber band.

By three a.m., I sucked five dicks and fucked three men, and I never felt so dirty in my life. I was in and out of cars constantly. I was the main attraction. I wanted to cut my throat. I was in need of a long shower, something to eat, and some sleep. I braved the cold and worked hard to earn some cash for myself.

By the end of the night, I made $650. It came mostly from giving these men a blowjob. My mouth never felt so numb and disgusted. I met up with Erica and Cream, and I had to give this bitch 65 percent, which was over $400. After paying her, I had $228 for myself. It was better than nothing.

Before dawn, we jumped into a cab and headed back to Edenwald. We all were dead tired, and I just wanted to sleep all day. The minute I walked into the apartment, I immediately went to see my daughter. Cream's older sister was sleeping on the couch. I was anxious to get home to my daughter, not knowing what this bitch was about. I was so relieved to see that she was okay. Eliza was sleeping with Erica's daughter on the bunk bed. I went into the room and kissed her softly on her cheek. She was a sleeping princess. What I did tonight, I did because of her. My daughter wasn't going to live out on the streets, not if I could prevent that with all my power.

I gazed at Eliza sleeping for a moment. I couldn't take my eyes off of her. She was so beautiful. She came from me and she was going to be better than me when she got older.

I sighed and went into the bathroom. Erica and Cream went straight into the bedroom to sleep. I couldn't sleep until I took a much-needed shower and scrubbed every last bit of sex, funk, and the memory of what I did from my skin. With the shower cascading down on me, I fell to my knees in the tub and cried and cried. I spent an hour in the shower, yearning to cleanse myself fully. But then what was the point when tomorrow night I would have to go back out and do it all over again?

Chapter Seven

Tango

Tango stepped out of Attica prison a free man, but after doing ten hard years in one of the harshest conditions, he felt like a fish out of water and his freedom was something he thought he would never see again. The towering, steel gates to the notorious castle-like prison slowly closed shut behind him and being on the other side felt golden to him. He didn't even turn around, no last look or any fond memories. Tango walked forward to the idling fifteen-passenger bus waiting to take him into the rural town. It was for ex-inmates who weren't fortunate to have anyone pick them up after their release. From there, it was a one-way trip to New York City with the hopes of never returning again.

But where would he go from there?

Ten years was a long time to be away from home. He didn't have much family left, no job lined up, seven years of parole to deal with, and he had only $150 to his name.

Tango had enough of rural upstate and the cracker guards who were bred to keep a nigger in line with their billy clubs and racist attitudes. He just wanted to go home and live his life in peace, however that may be.

He got on the short bus with six other released men fortunate to see their home again. Tango sat in the back near a window and remained quiet like a mouse. He enjoyed the view of the countryside while traveling farther away from his hell. Riding in a vehicle and seeing the land was something mostly everyone took for granted. It had been years since he drove in a car. It had been years since he had seen or talked to his kids. It had been years since he cooked his own meal and came and went as he pleased. And it had been years since he had the pleasure of being with a woman, the feeling of pussy pleasing him. The first thing Tango wanted to do when he arrived in New York was adjust, see his aging mother, and get himself some pussy. He was long overdue for a good nut.

It took several hours to arrive in New York from Attica, New York to the Port Authority in Times Square. When the bus navigated its way through the bustling, big city, Tango was overwhelmed. He had forgotten how lively and dynamic the city could get. There was people and traffic everywhere, and the town was lit up all over like a Christmas tree. And the noise was deafening. The hustle and bustle of New York could become very startling for someone who wasn't used to it.

Tango looked at everything like a baby in awe. Though he was born and raised in the Big Apple, it almost all seemed foreign to him. He focused on the women walking by and felt such a craving for them. Being around men for so long, he almost forgot what a woman felt like: their glorious insides, their sensual touch, their warm smiles, and more. The women he did interact with were either butch-looking guards, older staff with graying hair and wrinkled skin, or married and aloof to any male inmates.

Times Square was flooded with various cuties who were wrapped up in their winter attire and moving about freely from point A to point B. Tango tried to fixate his attention on every last one of them. And so did a few other inmates who were sprinkled on the Greyhound bus about to pull into the bus depot.

The sun was gradually setting behind the horizon to bring about dusk over the city. Tango stepped off the bus behind so many others clutching only his small bag that contained a handful of items. He didn't have much to take back home with him. The state said he had been reformed and able to return into society believing he would live a conducive life. Ten years ago, the man was a menace to society. He was sentence to seventeen years for murder, drugs, kidnapping, and extortion. At one time in his life, Tango was hell on earth; violence and murder was his way. And once he was one of the most feared men in the Bronx.

Tango wanted to wander around the city like a bird soaring through the skies. There was so much to see and do, and most of all, so many women he wanted to meet. In his heyday before his incarceration, he had been a playboy with drug money to burn and he went through women effortlessly. And during his days of sowing his royal oats, he begat seven children from six different women. His oldest was seventeen and his youngest was eleven years old.

An hour after arriving into the Port Authority, Tango made his way home to the Bronx, stepping off the city bus in the cold. He gazed at Edenwald projects and instantly the good and bad memories flooded him. Feeling somewhat nostalgic, he lingered in front of his mother's building on 229th Street and sighed. The last time he saw his mother was when she came to visit him six years ago. But over the years her health had declined and she found herself wheelchair bound needing the help of a home aide. She had worked for over thirty years for the MTA and now she was a frail, seventy-year-old woman living off of her retirement pension and having decent medical coverage.

Tango was one out five children: three girls and two boys. He was the second youngest. He was the only one who was pulled into the streets; the rest of his siblings were hard and honest working man and women. His oldest brother was a doctor in Chicago. His older sister was a schoolteacher in Philadelphia. His younger sister was in college trying to attain her bachelor's degree. And his older sister was a housewife to a prominent business/entertainment attorney in California and they had four great kids. Tango was the black sheep in the family, the only failure. He was the one who stayed home while everyone else was scattered across the nation living their own lives. He was the one who stayed close to home, and stayed close to their mother. Each of them had different fathers, except for the two oldest.

Tango exhaled with anxiety and walked forward. He stepped into the lobby and looked around. A smile appeared on his face. "Home sweet home," he said.

He pressed for the elevator; it was taking too long to come. So he decided to take the stairs. He quickly ascended his way up the iron steps and onto the fifth floor. The walls of the narrow hallway were covered in graphite and graffiti. Most of the graffiti was gang markings and various symbols; BMB stood out, Bronx Mafia Boys. Tango had no clue who these new muthafuckas was. Back in his day, niggas got money and gangs were never his thing. The hallway was also permeated with the smell of weed-laced Purple Hazes and fresh urine. The floors were littered with empty beer bottles and other trash. Tango moved past it not paying it any concern. He had been living in squalor for years.

He took a deep breath and knocked on his mother's door. He knew she would be excited to see her son finally home. After a minute of waiting, the apartment door finally opened. A middle-age Latino woman with long black hair and wide brown eyes stood in front of Tango. She was a little overweight with bright red lipstick, and looked at him deadpan. She was clad in colorful scrubs and dryly asked, "Can I help you?"

Could she help him? This was his home and she was staring at Tango like he was some salesman at the door.

"Yeah, you can help me, by lettin' me the fuck inside my own gotdamn house," Tango rudely replied.

"Excuse me!" the woman snapped back.

She blocked the doorway with her arms folded across her chest. Tango had been gone for too long and came too far to be denied entry into the apartment he grew up in and have a bitch with an attitude greet him at the door. He was ready to react, shout out, "Bitch, move," and force his way inside, but he quickly remembered that he was on parole and one minor incident could send him back to prison. He quickly collected himself and said, "I'm Tango, where's my mom?"

"Oh, I'm sorry," the home aide replied. "She's asleep right now."

"Well, can I come inside? I just came home, ya know what I'm sayin'?" he let be known.

The home aide looked reluctant to do so. She gazed at Tango with some apprehension. Tango was a towering man with a muscular physique and an intimidating charisma. His eyes were black and cold; he was swathed with tattoos and had scars on his hands and neck, and a healed slash across his right cheek representing his rough life. His clothes looked old.

The home aide always heard Ms. Davis speak about her kids and she always talked about Tango, how one day her son was coming back home to her and he would get his life right this time.

Lingering in the hallway while the bitch decided to let him inside into the place he grew up in was slowly but surely making him upset. He wasn't going to keep his cool for too long. He needed a cigarette, a drink, something to eat, a place to rest, and, most of all, some pussy.

"I guess it's cool," she said.

"I know it's cool," Tango uttered.

She stepped to the side and allowed Tango to walk in. Tango walked inside and looked around. The place hadn't changed a bit with the antique furniture from the mid-eighties and torn plastic covering. There was an aroma of boiled cabbage coming from the kitchen. Dozens of family pictures and portraits taken over the years, three decades of pictures, plagued the walls in the living room and the narrowed hallway. And the bookshelf had rows of various books from top to bottom, mostly biographies and nonfictional reads. Ms. Davis was a voracious reader.

Yeah, nothing had changed in the ten years he had been incarcerated.

Tango quickly made himself at home and walked into the main bedroom to check on his mother. She was sleeping silently like the nurse aide had said. Her wheelchair was by the bed, his mother's only method of moving around. His old room was bare, just a sheetless bed, peeling paint, and a small, broken-down TV. It wasn't the Ritz hotel, but anything was better than his tiny cell in Attica.

While Tango was settling in, the home aide continued with her job, cooking in the kitchen, cleaning some parts of the apartment, and making sure Ms. Davis's medication was ready for her to take when she awoke. Tango sat on the couch smoking a cigarette and gazed at the slightly overweight Latino woman. She was somewhat attractive—not Beyoncé or Rihanna attractive, but easy on the eyes with her brown skin and long black hair. He fixated his eyes on her plumped backside as she moved around the apartment. She wasn't his cup of tea. He was used to dating women ten times better than her, models with curvy figures, golden smiles, ample breasts with booty to match, beautiful women who turned heads and could grace the covers of magazines. However, being locked up for ten long years, even the slightest piece of pussy made his dick hard, overweight or not.

"So what's your name?" he asked the home aide.

"Vanessa," she replied.

"Vanessa, that's a pretty name. How long have you been taking care of my mother?"

"Over a year now," she said, answering his questions and tending to her duties simultaneously.

Tango puffed out smoke and leaned back into the sofa. He studied her. He undressed her with his eyes. He could tell she had rolls on her sides and probably sagging tits. But at this point in his life, a woman was a woman. It was his first female interaction in a long, long time, besides the guards who ordered him around and escorted him in the vicinity of the prison.

He could feel an erection growing in his jeans while watching the Latino woman perform her job. He started thinking perverted thoughts: a blowjob in the bathroom, or a quickie in the bedroom. He was horny. He was desperate to feel the inside of a woman; it didn't matter what she looked like, as long it felt wet, tight, and pleasurable. Just watching Vanessa work and walk around made him tempted to slide his hand inside his jeans and stroke his dick.

"Where you from, Vanessa?" he asked.

"Puerto Rico, and raised in Bushwick, Brooklyn."

"You got a man, Vanessa?" he bravely asked.

"Yes, two years now we've been together."

"That's what's up," he replied.

He was making conversation with her. He wanted to try to get to know her. He wanted some action, pussy or some head, but the last thing he wanted to do was rape the bitch, especially in his mother's apartment and just getting out of jail. Also, he had to check in with his parole officer first thing tomorrow morning.

Vanessa kept her replies short and simple. She showed aloofness to his questions and lurking eyes aimed at her. Her only concerns were Ms. Davis's well-being, and not entertaining her horny son. It was obvious that she wasn't interested in him, or giving some ex-con a cheap thrill just because his dick was getting hard and he hasn't had any sex in years.

Tango was making himself desperate and showing his vulnerability, but Vanessa wasn't buying into his foolishness. Tango decided his questioning wasn't getting him anywhere and he retreated into the bedroom to lie down and chill for a moment. Despite his failure at his first attempt to get some ass, he felt good to be home finally. He had privacy. He had freedom. He had $150 to his name and was determined to use some of that money to satisfy his sexual need.

He closed his eyes and relished being back in his old bedroom. It was the same bedroom where he lost his virginity at thirteen years old. It was the same bedroom where he had a stable of girls coming and going, fucking his brains out. It was the same bedroom where he stashed drugs away from his mother's prying eyes and hid his first gun. It was the same bedroom where he conceived his first child, and it was the same bedroom where cops came rushing in to arrest him for drugs and assault.

Tango was a headache to his mother and the neighbors. He had been in so much trouble as a youth, that they nicknamed him the Problem Child. And then when he got older, he terrorized the neighborhood and was the most feared man in the Bronx.

Tomorrow morning, when he had to go check in with his parole officer, the question was, was he truly rehabilitated. Did serving ten years in prison change him? Or was it all a façade?

Tonight, Tango's mind wasn't on seeing his parole officer, or anything else. As he lay on his sheetless bed in the quiet, still room with his hand down his pants, he jerked off with the pleasing thought of being satisfied by a beautiful woman. The man was sex deprived and his first priority was fucking the finest bitch he could lay his hands on. It'd been ten years too long since he had a good nut.

Chapter Eight

Sammy

I wanted to make the $7,000 I earned account for something, and make it last. The first thing I did with the money was buy my son some decent winter clothes and an ample supply of Pampers. He went through them so fast. Then of course I took myself shopping, bought a few outfits, new shoes, some things for work, and treated myself to a spa treatment. It was much needed. At first I was tempted to buy some drugs with the cash and flip it into a profit, that hustle was in my blood, but I decided against it. One look at my son's beautiful and innocent face and I knew he didn't deserve to have both parents in jail, or maybe one dead.

It was another sunny but cold afternoon. Danny was asleep in his crib and I was in the living room smoking a blunt in my panties and bra while watching videos on BET. It was quiet for once, and relaxing. I hadn't been to work in a week. I took some time off for myself. It from time to time became tiresome working at Crazy Legs and having various niggas grabbing naked parts of your body, trying to stick their dirty fingers in special places and yearning to fuck you.

It felt good to get away, my mini vacation.

I didn't want to get too sucked into that lifestyle. I'd seen it suck bitches dry and age them ten years ahead of their time. And at the end of the day, after dancing continually and fucking and sucking niggas left and right, they didn't have a dime to their name and were left with stretched out and dry pussies and a stained reputation in the game.

Not me.

I had a plan for myself. I wanted to save money, and get myself back into music, maybe open up my own studio, possibly get signed by a label, start writing for a mixture of artists, or just produce something. I still had it in me, my drive and my talents. My brain couldn't stop; it was running twenty-four/seven with creativity and the next hustle.

I took a pull from the blunt and watched this new female rap group video premiere on BET. They called themselves Vixen Mistress, and I was in awe of the name. It sounded too much like our group, Vixen's Chaos. But then when I heard some of their lyrics, I was completely taken aback, because those were my words, my flow.

"You keep falling victim to things that really don't matter, addicted to the person who keeps shattering ya laughter, hooked on a love that's tainted like acid. It's blasphemy how you stay chasin' after an unwilling happening."

I stood up, aghast, blunt damn near falling from my lips, and screamed out, "Oh my fuckin' God, are they serious!"

Those were my lyrics, my words. It was the song I performed that night with Mouse at the Latin Quarters in the city. These two fake bitches weren't even on our level. One was skinny like a number two pencil with a long weave and bad makeup, and the second was thicker with short blond hair and trying to look like Eve. They weren't even original. I knew Search or someone in the studio had to be behind the theft. Just watching these fake bitches get their shine on with their own music video made me want to cry. I was crushed. It felt like I was about to have a panic attack. I wanted to contact Mouse so badly and tell her what I saw, but I didn't have a number to reach her by and we still weren't on good terms with each other.

When the four-minute video went off, I sat there dumbfounded. It should have been us on there, not them. I wanted to scream. I wanted to break something. I wanted to contact Search and shout out, "Yo, what the fuck! Really? Fuck you! Why you playin' us like that?" I knew he was still upset with the way things played out between us. He really liked me, but the feeling wasn't mutual. Search was only a friend in my eyes, and I never wanted to fuck him. But I felt he took us for granted. I had him beat down, which was a decision that I regretted to this day. Did he do this just to get back at us, be spiteful? He was out there, grinding in the hip hop scene, on the serious come up, making a name for himself while leaving us behind.

I couldn't do anything but cry. It was the ultimate disrespect. I was here struggling, dancing naked, spreading my business to strangers and having to turn a trick to keep from drowning in poverty.

"He ain't gonna get away with this shit," I said to myself.

I thought about hiring an attorney; sue his ass and that whack-ass group he was managing for copyright infringement. But then I had to think, with what cash? Even I knew better that lawsuits cost, and none of my songs were copyrighted. I wrote them, performed them, and wasn't thinking on the business level. I was the victim of music plagiarism. I fucked up.

So the tears fell as I dwelled on my mistakes.

For an hour, I sat there stunned and so hurt; it felt like I was becoming sick to my stomach. I kept saying to myself, Search or whoever couldn't get away with this.

I was so hungry to do something about it, that I even thought about getting a few homeboys who liked me to find him and fuck his ass up.

I was in a deep zone until I heard someone knocking at my door. I slowly got up, covered myself with a long T-shirt, and went to see who it was knocking. Through the peephole, I saw Kawanda in the hallway. I wasn't in the mood to see her at the moment, but I opened the door anyway. She walked into my place smiling and dressed like she was going to the club in the afternoon: six-inch heels, tight jeans, and her shirt tighter than her jeans highlighting her ample tits. She was always dressed like she was going out somewhere with tight clothes that looked painted on and accentuating her luscious curves.

"Hey, girl, what you doing?" she asked gleefully.

I forced myself to smile and returned, "Nothing, just chilling, smoking, and watching TV."

"Where's Danny?"

"Sleeping. I ain't complaining," I said.

Kawanda made herself comfortable in my place. We weren't best friends, but she was cool peoples. She took a seat on my couch and decided to smoke with me. She pulled out a phat dime bag from her purse and dangled it in front of me. "I know you ain't finished smoking yet. I just copped some of that good shit from my homeboy and I ain't tryin' to smoke alone."

"Yeah, I'm down. Let me go check on Danny first."

I walked down the hallway to see if my baby was still sleeping. He had been asleep for two hours now and I knew it was going to be hell trying to put him back to sleep tonight. For some reason, that boy loved to sleep during the day and keep his mama up at nights. I started breastfeeding him at first; like any nigga, pop a nipple in their mouth and they would shut the fuck up and enjoy. But since I started dancing and smoking weed, I stopped breastfeeding him. I didn't want my baby getting high too. Because I read online that if you smoke marijuana and breastfeed, the active chemical in marijuana is passed to your baby through your milk. So I felt it was better to abstain from breastfeeding than smoking. Yeah, I was the mother of the year for choosing smoking weed over breastfeeding my child. But a bitch was stressed the fuck out and weed was the only thing that soothed me and made me break away from my worries.

I left the door ajar to Danny's bedroom. I quietly glanced inside and saw he was still out cold, lying on his stomach probably dreaming about when he was born, or missing home when he was safe and sound nestled inside my stomach and going everywhere with Mommy. I smiled at my little bundle of joy. My baby boy was so cute.

"Sleep tight," I whispered to him.

I went back into the living room to join Kawanda. She had kicked her shoes off and was rolling up the dime bag on my secondhand coffee table. She had split the blunt apart, slid the tobacco out of the blunt from the mouth end down, and started loading up all the freshly ground buds into the blunt wrapper. Kawanda was a professional at rolling up. She was precise and fast, not like some of these nonprofessionals who rolled sloppy joints and had bad weed.

She said to me, "We ain't been seeing you at the club in a week, Sammy," as she started rolling the mouth piece in her right hand and the burning end in the left, rolling right to left. She tucked the bottom flap under the top flap using her thumbs and thumbnails.

"Niggas been askin' 'bout you and shit. They missin' you fo' real," she added.

I smiled. I was definitely becoming the center of attention at Crazy Legs. Kawanda continued putting together the blunt by licking what she got done so far and pressing it to the bottom of the flap. She kept licking it until it stuck firmly. Then she said, “Girl, you missed out on some money the other night. This young baller came to the club and just started makin’ it rain everywhere, throwing up money like crazy. I’m tellin’ you, he must have spent at least ten stacks that night.”

“Word,” I uttered.

“Word. Bitches were all over that nigga like sweat on skin,” she joked. “But you know a bitch had to get her money. I got to that nigga first, fucked and sucked that nigga so good in the backroom, made that nigga suck on his thumb afterward. His money might be long, but his dick sure ain’t.”

I laughed.

Finally, she was ready to light it up so we could enjoy a wonderful high. I sat next to her on the couch. I wanted to forget about what I saw on BET. I didn’t mention it to her because I didn’t want her to be in my business. Kawanda was a talkative person and sometimes she could say too much around the wrong type of people. She sat back and lit up the blunt and took a few strong pulls. I could already smell the Haze permeating through my apartment. She passed me the blunt and lounged next to me. I took my few pulls and passed it back.

“You must came up last week wit’ that fine-ass white boy at the party,” she said.

“What you mean?”

“I mean that one nigga you fucked in the room, he was on the news the other day, and yo, they sayin’ that muthafucka is paid!” she proclaimed.

“The news? For what?”

“They sayin’ he was part of some big time Ponzi scheme that netted over something like hundreds of millions of dollars and he was one of the main niggas running it,” she informed me.

"What?"

"Hells yeah, girl. They had that nigga on the news with cops escorting the nigga out some fancy downtown building in handcuffs. I was like yoooo, that's the muthafucka my homegirl fucked at the party last week," she exclaimed ghetto loud.

I was just glad it was just us two in the apartment. I didn't need anyone else knowing my business, especially if I was turning tricks on the low.

"Damn, Kawanda, can you say it any louder? You know my son is sleeping in the other room."

"I'm sorry."

I took a few more pulls from the burning blunt and felt my eyes getting seeded. The weed was good, had me feeling like I didn't have a care about anything at the moment. I just sat there and felt high like a kite.

"He was cute, too," I heard her say. "You never did tell me how much you came off wit' when you fucked him."

It wasn't her business to know. "And you never will know," I said.

"Oh, so you keepin' secrets from ya friend now."

"No, but you don't need to know." I chuckled. She laughed quietly too.

We continued smoking. My son was still sleeping. I thanked God he was giving me my moment to chill. I was too high at the moment to even hold him in my arms. Smoking also made me forget about what I saw earlier on BET, my rhymes being spit out of some other bitches' mouths, and the betrayal I felt.

"Sammy, what you doin' tomorrow night?" Kawanda asked.

"Why?"

"I know 'bout this bachelor party in Brooklyn that's supposed to pop off. I heard some heavy hitters are gonna come through and they want some fine-ass girls to dance and entertain them," she mentioned. "You can make some serious money there."

I wasn't fond of doing bachelor parties, especially in Brooklyn. Most times it was too many thirsty niggas and too little girls to please them, and it could be a hit or miss. You had no security to watch your back. And you left there with more regret than reward. At bachelor parties, especially the hood ones, niggas expected pussy and for you to suck their dicks; sometimes they could become a little too aggressive to get what they want. I wasn't the one to turn tricks, but I'd heard many horror stories from girls who did these bachelor parties, and it was scary. A few months ago, they brutally raped this one dancer repeatedly, at least ten niggas ran the train on her and no one wore a condom while they raped her, and unfortunately she caught HIV.

It scared me to death, knowing how my mother died from it. I refused to allow that type of problem into my life. That's why I always had been skeptical of who I fucked and sucked. I couldn't and refused to die like my mother. I wanted to be healthy until the day I died. I had my son to live for.

I hesitated with my answer. I thought about it. Out of the $7,000 I made from the other party in the city, I only had about $2,500 left over. It was enough for my rent, to pay some bills, food for about a month, and some knickknacks. But by next month, I knew I was gonna be struggling again.

"You need to come, 'cause you know I got ya back," said Kawanda.

My mind was telling me, *don't do it,* but my desperation was screaming out, *you need the money, bitch.* I looked at Kawanda and said, "I'll do it. What part of Brooklyn though?"

"Brownsville," she said.

Fuck me!

Brownsville was one of the most grimmest and worst neighborhoods in New York City. Niggas out there didn't give a fuck, with one or two murders every week, and it was definitely too far from home.

"Brownsville," I repeated with trepidation in my voice. "You know how fucked up that area is."

"Yeah, I know, but trust me, it's gonna be cool, Sammy. I ain't gonna take you to no bullshit. It's gonna be other bitches out there too."

"You know I don't do VIP like that."

"Yeah, I know."

The bitch talked me into it. I was reluctant to go, but Kawanda was a smooth bitch with words, even when she was high. She amped a bitch up about making that paper and how it was a rapper's party, and how he was signed to a record label and getting married to his high school sweetheart. And then she mentioned he was kin to Steele from the group Smif-n-Wessun, a well-known hip hop artist back in the nineties.

Kawanda spent an hour at my place. We talked, ate, and chilled. I truly needed the company. The minute she walked out, it was when Danny finally woke up from his nap. I heard him crying in the bedroom. Everything came to an end just in the nick of time.

I went to hold my son and feed him his bottle. I knew he was hungry. As I was holding him against my chest and feeding him his milk, I couldn't stop thinking about that fraudulent rap group and then thinking about taking this trip to the Ville. I looked around my cramped, shitty apartment and knew I needed to do better. For the reason that I saw myself becoming like one of these bitches who got sucked into that hole of misery and nothing more but dancing, and turning tricks for weed and rent money.

It was my worst nightmare to become a broke-down and bum bitch with nothing to show for all her hard work and sweat over the years; especially when you have kids.

Chapter Nine

Tango

Tango exited the division of parole office on 14 Bruckner Boulevard and quickly lit a cigarette. He truly needed the nicotine. It had been a stressful morning. His first meeting with his parole officer, who was a bitch named Rochelle Hammond, and she was already up his ass about the conditions of his parole. She was a black woman with a curly afro and bad attitude. She looked harder than stone itself and was already warning him how quick she would violate him if he violated any conditions of his parole.

"Don't fuck with me and I won't fuck with you," she had warned him.

He had been out of Attica for forty-eight hours, and even though he was a free man, he still wasn't free with having so many restrictions while being on parole. And there were too many restrictions for him to abide. He had to find a legal job as soon as possible and notify his parole officer of any new jobs. He had to tell his parole officer where he lived and worked, and if he moved, he had to tell his parole officer of his new address before he moved. He couldn't socialize with any known felons or criminals. He had to ask for permission to travel anywhere fifty miles from his residence and receive approval before he could travel. He couldn't carry a gun and a knife with a blade longer than two inches except a kitchen knife. He had to take mandatory drug test randomly. He had to abide all laws, not even run a traffic light. And if he broke any law, he could be sent back to prison even if he didn't have any criminal charges.

Being on parole sucked, but Tango was still happy to be home.

Tango puffed on his cigarette and looked around the bustling area. While sitting in the waiting area of the parole building he ran into a few familiar faces from back in the days. It was somewhat like a street reunion. One particular friend he was happy to see again was Sheldon, his longtime running buddy and partner in crime. They came up together in the mean streets long ago. Sheldon had been sent upstate before Tango for drugs and grand theft; he did his time at Clinton Correctional facility. He had been home for over a year and wouldn't max out until 2016.

The two men started talking and quietly reminisced in the waiting area as they passed the time until they were called to meet their parole officer. For Tango, it was good to see a friend again.

Tango leaned against the building enjoying his cigarette and enjoying every woman who walked by him, as he eyed them heavily and tried to holler at them.

"Hey, luv, can we talk?"

"Damn, ma, I like the way you walk."

"Beautiful, you need some company?"

Tango used every available pickup line he could think of, but to no avail. He was outdated and shunned by the passing women. The Bronx was like a whole new world to him after being locked away for ten long years. But he was going to continue trying.

He felt like a kid in a candy store with so many beautiful women walking all over that he was desperate to take one home to his mother's place and lock her in the bedroom for twenty-four hours and sexually have his way with her.

With the morning fading, Tango didn't know what to do with his day. He had ten years of time to catch up on. He was waiting for Sheldon to exit the building so the two could continue to catch up on lost time. While he lingered out front on the sidewalk, his eyes darted everywhere from the ladies, to the changes in the street, to the different cars that were out now. And then there were this new gadgets called iPhones and smartphones that everyone was carrying around now. Before his lengthy incarceration, people only carried around cell phones and most of them were flip phones.

Tango was in awe at how much things had changed, from social sites to the streets. Yeah, he definitely had a lot of catching up to do. But his first priority was sex. It had been on his mind from the time he stepped out of prison.

"I see your eyes lookin' around, all thirsty and shit," Sheldon said, stepping out of the parole building and catching Tango's eyes glued to a big-booty woman passing him by.

"Yo, I don't remember bitches ever being this fine in the Bronx," he replied.

"Yeah, a lot done changed," replied Sheldon.

"I see, I see."

"You got another cigarette?" Sheldon asked.

Tango reached into his coat pocket and pulled out his dwindling pack of Newports. He passed Sheldon one and lit it for him. The two enjoyed a cigarette in the thirty-degree temperature. Sheldon took a few drags, exhaled and asked, "So when did you get out?"

"Two days ago."

"How long they got you on paper for?"

"Seven years."

"Shit, I max out in three."

"That's what's up. This parole shit is a fuckin' bitch," said Tango.

"Man, you don't even know the half of it. My PO be itching to catch me slippin' out here and ready to violate my ass."

"I got this bitch named Rochelle Hammond."

"Yeah, I know 'bout her. Muthafuckas call her the Iron Lady," he joked.

"That bitch is hard and ugly like a muthafucka. Lookin' like a fuckin' sasquatch and shit," Tango joked.

Sheldon laughed.

"But on the real, nigga, I'm so fuckin' horny right now, I'll even fuck that ugly bitch in a heartbeat. Crazy," Tango let be known.

Chuckling, Sheldon replied, "Damn, you ain't break in no pussy yet? Shit, first day home and I fucked like three bitches the same night."

"Nah, yo. I just been window shopping, and bitches ain't showin' a nigga no love. I'm lookin' all ragged and shit."

"Yo, what happened to that bitch you used to fuck wit' back in the days? That Dominican bitch wit' the big tits. What's her name?"

"You talkin' 'bout Yvonne."

"Yeah." Sheldon smiled.

"That bitch wasn't ride or die wit' me. The minute I got sent upstate, she whoring around wit' the next nigga, got pregnant like four times and fell off and shit. Niggas was telling me she a crack fiend now, you kna' what I'm sayin'," Tango said.

"What, that's crazy, yo."

"Man, fuck that bitch."

"Yo, you need a ride back?" Sheldon asked.

"Hells yeah, I do. What you pushin'?"

"Sumthin' simple, nuthin' fancy. It ain't like back in the days when niggas had matching Benz wit' the chrome rims and shit."

Tango smiled, remembering what Sheldon was talking about. "Yo, we were doin' our thang."

They slapped five with each other.

"Yeah, we were, and ya lethal-ass couldn't stay outta beef."

"Who you tellin'? 'Cause niggas was hating on us hard 'cause we were 'bout that money and gettin' that money."

"We was," Sheldon agreed. Sheldon flicked away his cigarette, said to Tango, "C'mon, I'm parked around the corner."

Tango followed his friend. They approached a blue, '89 Volvo. The car was definitely a major step down from what they were used to driving: high-end foreign cars that attracted attention wherever they went. The men climbed inside the Volvo and Sheldon was driving on the Bruckner Expressway North, heading toward Edenwald.

As Sheldon drove, Tango said to him, "Yo, what's up wit' the strip clubs out here? Bitches still gettin' buck-naked and selling pussy?"

"My nigga, you don't want to fuck wit' these hole-in-the-wall spots. They too hot right now. They been gettin' raided a lot lately, undercover cops be lurking and too many eyes watching, and the last thing you need is to get caught up in a fuckin' raid and get violated. And, plus, these bitches be tryin' to overcharge niggas and ain't no privacy like that," Sheldon proclaimed.

"My nigga, I need to smash sumthin' tonight."

Sheldon chuckled. "A'ight, I got you. I got this bitch I know in Edenwald, sometimes she be knowing bitches that get down for their bread. I'll make that call fo' you."

Tango nodded. "My nigga. They cute right?"

"She don't fuck wit' no gorilla-lookin' bitches. You know I got you," Sheldon said.

Tango smiled like the Cheshire cat. He leaned back in the passenger seat, lit up another cigarette, and gazed out the passenger window. After his conquest of the pussy mission, he needed to look for a job. He needed to show his PO that he had some kind of employment. But the only thing he knew how to do was hustle, sell drugs, and kill people. He had no legal work history or a GED. The task seemed nearly impossible. Seeing that Sheldon was doing pretty good for himself, he asked, "Yo, how you makin' ya ends out here?"

"Every day is a struggle out here, my dude. But I'm workin' at this body shop on Jerome Ave. You know I was always good wit' workin' on cars. It pay a'ight, but when I want that extra bread, I sell weed on the side. I keep me happy and my PO happy," Sheldon stated coolly.

"I feel you. They hiring?"

"Nah, I wish they were. Niggas barely wanted to give me the job, but my cousin looked out fo' me," replied Sheldon.

It didn't hurt to ask.

They made their way back to Edenwald and Tango couldn't help but to think how much the neighborhood had changed. The gang activity increased heavily in the neighborhood. His first day home and there was a shooting outside his building; a fifteen-year-old kid was shot three times, but he survived. He noticed BMB scrawled everywhere from the bodegas to the lobby walls of his building. The young thugs were lingering all about, hustling, gambling, shooting, and beefing with their rivals, YGC. YGC claimed their territory too, and they were warring over buildings and corners, something major Rico used to control.

Sheldon gave Tango the rundown on what was going on in the hood.

"Yeah, it got more fierce out here, Tango, the wild, Wild West on steroids," Sheldon said. "These young niggas today, they ain't got no respect fo' anybody, killing everything movin' out this bitch, even got the OG's walking around on eggshells."

Tango smirked. He wasn't worried about anyone. "Sheldon, you know I never worry 'bout no fool. Shit, muthafuckas better be glad that I retired from this shit," said Tango with a pugnacious tone.

"Yeah, we already know 'bout ya lethal-ass, nigga. Ya name still rings out in these streets."

"Ring on, muthafucka, ring on," replied Tango humorously.

Sheldon chuckled evenly.

However, Tango planned on minding his business and trying to go straight, and live his life as a civilian. As long as they didn't fuck with him, then he wasn't going to fuck with them. They haven't seen a killer on his caliber or level. But that was over ten years ago. He was now in his early thirties and trying to retire from the street life.

Sheldon parked on East 225th Street and the two walked into his building together. Tango wasn't in any rush to go back to his place, so he decided to hang out with an old friend. Plus, Sheldon planned to make the phone call to his female friend to set up Tango with a date, or more like a booty call for some ass.

All day, they sipped on cognac, smoked cigarettes, and talked. Sheldon lived alone. Tango respected his bachelor pad setup and couldn't wait to get a place on his own like his friend: leather furniture, fifty-inch flat-screen TV, Xbox, cable, a shelf spilling over with DVDs, along with a fridge filled with beer and snacks, and a cabinet filled with liquor. It was a haven to him, especially after being locked in a small jail cell for ten years.

Lounging on the leather couch, Sheldon said to Tango, "Tonight, this bitch is on me. I got you. Consider it a welcome home gift from ya boy."

Tango raised his Corona beer in the air and said, "Cheers to that."

He smiled and felt his dick getting hard just thinking about getting some pussy after ten years of jerking off to adult magazines and abstinence.

Chapter Ten

Mouse

I heard the weatherman forecast snow tonight, at least seven inches with freezing wind, so I assumed tricking tonight on the track would be cancelled. I needed a break from Hunts Point. Night after night, Erica and I worked the blocks, climbing in and out of cars, sucking dick and fucking in whatever position the clients requested. Cream was also always around, watching our backs, proclaiming to be protecting us with his pistol in his waistband. Some nights were good, easy going; I would make $500, maybe more, and give Erica her 65 percent. And then there were nights where I would be wearing out the bottom of my shoes walking constantly, freezing my butt off, and not catching a date, barely making a hundred dollars that night.

I hate to say the words that I was getting used to it, but I somewhat was. I was feeding my daughter, buying her the clothes she needed, and actually able to take her to fun places like Chuck E. Cheese's, the movies, and the museum. And I was trying to save to get my own place and get from underneath Erica's wing. I didn't plan on selling pussy and sucking dick for the rest of my life. I didn't see myself doing this in the spring or summer. I was determined to find my way out somehow. I thought about going to school, but that cost too.

When we weren't out on the track degrading ourselves, Erica and I would be chilling, smoking, talking, laughing, and being friends. It was like night and day in that apartment. Sometimes she would cook a wonderful meal and I couldn't get enough of her cooking. We would watch movies and just be normal ladies with kids to raise. But the best times were when Cream would be gone all day, maybe a day or two. He proclaimed to be out on business, but I knew the truth behind his absence. He was fucking some other bitch out there. Erica was too blinded to see the truth. And Cream had a heavy influence on her. It had me thinking, *damn, is the dick that good?*

But it wasn't any of my business, so I kept quiet about it.

The evening was a good day. I was playing with Eliza and we all sat around the TV watching Disney's *The Lion King* and then we watched *Brave*. I always enjoyed watching children's films; the storytelling and the animation was utterly amazing. I looked out the window and saw the first snowflakes falling to what the weatherman predicted the city receiving at least six to seven inches over the night. I sighed with relief and smiled. Growing up, I always enjoyed the snow; and when it stopped snowing, I was ready to take Eliza out in it so we could play around and make a snowman and probably find a hill to slide down in a homemade snow sleigh.

"Look, y'all, it's snowing," I announced.

The kids immediately ran to the window to peer outside. They were in joy seeing the white flurries cover the entire projects trying to make the hood transform into some winter wonderland. I gazed out the window with them.

"See, Eliza, look, it's snowing," I said.

My daughter tried to reach to grab it, touching the window and smiling. I smiled too. While I and the kids were distracted with the snowfall, Erica's phone rang. She picked up and went into the kitchen to talk. I didn't think anything of it. I continued gazing outside. Five minutes later, Erica came back into the living room and said to me, "You wanna make some extra money tonight?"

I looked at her perplexed and replied, "How? It's snowing outside."

"Not on the track, close to home."

I felt reluctant in seeing a client close to home. I didn't respond right away, but Erica added, "He cool people. He lives close, on 225th Street. We can walk there."

"Who's watchin' the kids?"

"I can call a neighbor. But this can be an easy two hundred, Mouse, for an hour."

I sighed. "Fuck it, I'll do it."

She smiled. She got back on her cell phone to arrange the date. Erica was like the post office: rain, sleet, or snow, our clients were still going to get their service. I pulled Eliza into my arms and held her lovingly. If it weren't for her, everyone could kiss my ass, because my pussy was precious to me; now it was for sale like some groceries in the supermarket.

Erica and I hurriedly walked in the cold and snow to 225th Street. I was bundled up in a yellow North Face bubble jacket, tight jeans, snow boots, and a wool ski hat. It was snowing and too cold to try to look cute for anyone. I didn't know much about the apartment we were heading to, or the man who called, except he was a very good friend of Erica's and was cool peoples.

We entered the building lobby and took the stairs to the third floor. I had to get some warmth. It felt like negative twenty degrees outside. The snow was accumulating and we seemed to be the only two fools walking around in it. I followed Erica to apartment 3B. She knocked. I waited. Seconds later, a man answered with a smile and a beer in his hand.

"Damn, y'all came fast," he said.

"You know how I do, always 'bout my business," she told him.

The man's eyes looked past Erica and lingered on me and he nodded. "Yeah, your friend is cute."

"I told you."

He stepped to the side and allowed us inside his place. I immediately noticed another man inside. He was seated on the leather couch, smoking a cigarette, and the minute I came into his view, he smiled cheerfully and gazed at me like I was some sizzling prime steak that he was ready to devour. He couldn't take his eyes off of me.

"Ladies, this is my friend, Tango," the man at the door introduced him.

"Hey, Tango," Erica greeted him, with her flirtatious smile.

He stood up and walked over toward us with his attention fixated on me. I stood quietly in everyone's presence. Tango, he was tall and seemed to have a well-built physique underneath the T-shirt he had on. His eyes lingered on me with pleasure. It was like he was starstruck on me, making me feel like I was some celebrity.

"You're beautiful," he spoke, making me smile.

"Thank you."

"I mean you are a very beautiful woman," he repeated. His words were genuine, authentic. And he truly gazed at me like I was the most beautiful woman in his eyes.

I couldn't help but to blush in front of him.

"What is your name?" he asked.

"Diamond," I lied. It was my stage name.

"And you are a diamond."

"Well, it's good to see that everyone getting along nicely," Erica chimed.

She and her friend were getting acquainted with each other. I never got his name, but I had to admit, Tango and his friend were very handsome men. I instantly knew they were street, hood niggas with some charisma in them and looking to have a good time tonight, either with us on our knees or on our back with our legs spread. They offered us a drink and told us to feel at home. I knew what we came there for, but Erica wasn't in any rush to handle business. She and the man named Sheldon were laughing, flirting, and acting like they used to date each other. She was seated on his lap with him rubbing between her thighs and kissing on her neck.

I was seated next to Tango and he seemed cool. I nestled next to him sipping on some liquor and conversing.

"So, Diamond, I heard you speak Spanish. Where you from?" Sheldon asked.

"I'm from here; my pops is from the Dominican Republic," I told them.

"Spanish females are so sexy. Say something nice in Spanish," Tango said.

I smiled, and said to him, "*Usted es un hombre muy guapo.*"

He smiled. "What did you just say?"

"I said, 'you are a very handsome man.'"

"Oh shit, my nigga, I think she really likes you," Sheldon chimed.

We all laughed.

I felt Tango's hand run up my thigh and rest between my legs. He rubbed my pussy through my jeans. He was all over me like white on rice, trying to put his hand up my shirt, feel my tits, and kiss the side of my neck. I could tell he was hard already; his erection protruded through his jeans. He was so antsy he seemed like a child with ADD.

"I want you," he whispered in my ear.

I chuckled lightly. "You do."

"Hells yeah, I do. You so fuckin' sexy and beautiful, I would put a ring on ya finger right now," he said.

From his fanatical look, it seemed like he meant every word of it. He kissed the side of my neck again and fondled me. I allowed his touch to roam all over me.

Erica suddenly went from playful mode into business mode. “Tango, I know you feelin’ my girl and all, but this pussy ain’t free. You gotta pay to play.”

“Oh, I’m ready to pay,” said Tango.

Tango looked at Sheldon. Sheldon nodded and said, “I got my man tonight.” He gently pushed Erica off of his lap and reached into his pocket. He pulled out a wad of fifties and twenties. Erica’s and my eyes were glued to the bankroll he pulled out. He peeled off $300 and handed it to Erica. She happily took his payment and said, “See, now we can continue on wit’ our play.”

The minute Erica was paid Tango pulled me from off the couch and wanted to take me into the room. I saw the strong lust in his eyes and kind of got nervous for a minute. He looked like he was about to get rough with me. He couldn’t wait to have me.

“Damn, your boy is thirsty for some ass,” Erica said.

“Yeah, he is,” Sheldon replied.

“I’m gonna play nice,” Tango said, showing a lecherous grin.

Yeah, like his words comforted me. But reluctantly, I was there to perform a service so me and my daughter could eat. Tango escorted me into one of the three bedrooms and before I walked in behind him, I heard his friend say, “Y’all two have fun now, my friend really needs this. And don’t stank up my room.”

The door closed behind me and I found myself in this barren-looking room, a small bed, no TV, or any posters and pictures decorating the walls. I guessed it was used for only one or two purposes: sleeping and sex. I stood by the door suddenly feeling apprehensive. Tango sat on the bed and stared at me.

"I'm sorry, do I make you nervous?" he asked.

"No," I said.

He did, but I didn't admit it to him. The look in his eyes showed a man who could be cold and dangerous. But yet, he seemed gentle and caring toward me for some reason. He was ready for me, and I had to ready myself for him. He took off his shirt, revealing his strapping and chiseled physique. I was in awe at his body. He was cut up and muscular everywhere. His biceps bulged out like a small mountain. His stomach had a wave of abs. And his upper body was swathed with tattoos; some I recognized as gang related, some was art, he had biblical scriptures written across his chest and back, and a few demonic artwork on his arms, which to me, contradicted the biblical passages.

"I gotta be honest with you," he started to say.

When a man said to me "I gotta be honest with you" I tended to get a little nervous for some reason. Tango looked at me and said, "I just got out of prison a few days ago, and you're the first woman I'll be with in ten years."

Wow, I thought.

He continued with, "I just need to feel the touch, the smell, the affection, and the inside of a woman right now. I'm so fuckin' horny right now that I'm 'bout to explode. And you are the most beautiful woman I ever laid eyes on."

That right there, his lovely comment, made me smile widely.

"And if you speculating 'bout my sexuality, I ain't never been wit' no nigga in jail. I don't fuckin' swing that way. I spent my time reading, working out, and jerking off," he stated.

It was good to hear him say that.

"You really think I'm truly beautiful?"

"I think you're an angel, Diamond. I think any man who is in your life is a lucky and very fortunate man. I look in your eyes and I see a woman so pure and down for hers."

"You see that in my eyes," I replied. "You don't even know me."

My first impression was he was spitting some game at me, sweet talking; but he already paid me to fuck him. So I assumed his words were genuine. A man locked up for ten years, constantly around men and prison guards twenty-four/seven; maybe he could tend to change and found himself in a better place. I didn't know his history or his past and I didn't want to know it. I was simply a form of pleasure to him, not his parole officer.

"I wanna get to know you," Tango said.

"You wanna get to know me huh?" I walked toward him, undoing my shirt and unfastening my jeans. Yeah, being inside me was one way of getting to know me.

He stood up and undid his jeans. That thirst for sex continually lingered in his eyes. He removed his jeans and boxers and showed me what he was working with. No lie, I was impressed with his size, not too big and not too small, but very right: eight inches long and with girth. His penis stood at attention, looking like a black steel pipe.

I came out my clothes and was buck-naked. His eyes lit up and his dick was so hard that it looked like a SCUD missile ready to launch inside of me.

"You have a condom?" I asked.

"Nah," he said.

Luckily, I did.

I pulled out a Magnum, which looked like it would fit him snugly in that area. I approached him and rolled the latex back on his hard dick. I got down on my knees and was ready to give him some head. But for some strange reason he stopped me.

"I wanna taste you," he said.

"You wanna eat me out?" I asked, somewhat confused.

"Yeah."

He pulled me down onto the bed with him and positioned me on my back, spreading my legs. This was a first, a nigga—a trick at that—wanting to please me. It was his money, so I didn't argue. His chin rested against my pussy's lips and pressed a little into them. His kissing lips were just a breath away from my clit. He placed his tongue against me below; I breathed easily. His hands were strong against my thighs; it felt like he could easily rip me apart with his strength, but he was gentle like a feather.

I gasped when I felt his lips against me, his tongue digging inside of me. I placed my head back and closed my eyes. My mind drifted off somewhere as he ate me out. I had entered somewhere and wasn't about to leave it, lying in an open glade with this thuggish and gorgeous specimen of a man devouring my pussy like if he needed it to live.

"Aaaah, ugh. Aaaah," I moaned and gritted my teeth.

His tongue invaded me deep, instantly finding my G-spot. My mind spiraled into a touch of bliss as it felt like he was about to bring an orgasm to me. I kept my body arched and opened, and stop my knees from simply collapsing in sheer, trembling bliss. Tango ate and ate, and ate, like a starving offering. I shuddered in his grasp, playing the carnal tune with my voice. One moment his touch was like feathers, and then it would feel like a wriggling snake with his breath tickling my every nerve.

I clawed his backside as his mouth and teeth nipped at my flesh and in doing so, his hands reached up for my nipples, pinching them softly and cupping them. His full lips supped and suckled my pink folds, tugging, licking, flicking, and teasing without end. He kept my unsuspecting body on the edge of breathless shivering when he fingered both places, and then having his tongue flick back and forth inside of me, and across my throbbing clit. My whole body shook trying not to cum. I was his toy to play with and he was playing well.

"I just wanna taste you. You taste so fuckin' good," he said between licks and sucks.

"I'm gonna cum," I cried out.

I was soon lost in this rapturous haze of a mind-blowing orgasm that never seemed to end. I quivered against the sheet and near him like I was having a seizure. My eyes fluttered and Tango worked me in a way that I had never been worked before. As I was coming down from my orgasm, my legs began to release his head, they became like vise grips around him when I was about to explode, and I could feel his tongue lapping up my juices. This man was a freak. I loved it.

He wasn't done with me yet. Before the last drop of me came out, he tossed me into the doggie style position and thrust himself inside of me roughly. His big dick penetrated me like a hot spear. He moaned and grunted as his balls slammed against me and my good pussy almost having him reach the point of no return.

"Damn, ya pussy is so fuckin' good. Oh shit, ugh, ugh!" he grunted.

I had him arched over me, weakened and clutching the white sheets, his dick at full staff with my glorious insides pleasing every inch of him to full throttle. He fucked me, and fucked me, grabbing my ass, cupping my tits, his rhythm dancing inside of me.

From there, he pulled out and wanted me to ride him cowgirl style. I straddled his nice physique with my fiery descent, slamming my pussy down on his dick and fucking him crazily. He gripped my hips as I rode that dick, trying to milk the cum from his nuts.

"Ooooh. Ooooh, shit. Ooooh, shit, ugh, ugh, ugh," his feral grunts echoed out.

With my hands placed against his strapping chest, I felt this nigga's dick cemented in my stomach. He was about to make me cum again, as I was about to do him the same way.

"I'm gonna fuckin' come," he cried out.

We both were nearly there to heaven, once again, reaching the point of no return. He had me creaming and dripping wet. I came on the dick, saturating the condom thrusting inside of me. Moments later, he detonated himself inside of me with so much force, I feared he tore through the condom and came inside of me. He was ten years backed up and I couldn't have any more mistakes.

When he was finally done coming, which took like forever, I pulled him out of me, quickly checking to see if the condom was still attached, which it was, thank God, and I fell against my back, breathing hard and sweating. He nestled against me and held me in his arms like I was his.

"That was so good, thank you," he said.

I was taken aback. It was the first time any man thanked me for sex and held me close afterward. This rough-looking muthafucka was more than met the eye. For a moment, we cuddled in that bare room like a couple. I didn't know him at all, but there was something about him that was truly comforting.

While he held me, he talked to me. I mean, he just literally opened up and started telling me about himself. His name was Tango, but his real name was Andre Clark. Tango was his street name, his nickname. The more he talked, the more he grew on me. He was warm and generous; he was even willing to pay me extra for more of my time.

He asked me about myself. I told him a few things, but not all of my business. I told him about the music career I tried to get into. I even spit a poem/rhyme for him. He was impressed. I mentioned my daughter, my likes, and dislikes. I told him about the shelter and why I started prostituting myself. The funny thing was, Tango looked at me and didn't judge me at all. Most niggas wouldn't be caught dead nestling against a prostitute and catching feelings for her. Tango didn't care at all.

We talked for an hour, until Erica knocked on the door and said it was time for us to go. He didn't want to let me go, but he understood.

"I wanna see you again," he said.

I smiled.

He added, "I'll pay you. I don't care."

He was sweet.

"Where do you be at?" he asked me.

"I work Hunts Point," I told him.

"Okay."

I got dressed. He didn't. He just sat there at the foot of the bed, remaining buck-naked and looking at me. His eyes lit up. His body was sharp. He was really infatuated with everything about me. Erica continued knocking. "Diamond, c'mon, let's go."

"I'm coming," I hollered.

Tango stood up from the bed, dick swinging and all. He reached into his pants pocket and removed a few bills. He handed me a twenty and said, "I ain't got much right now, but you deserve a tip."

I took it. "Thank you."

I walked out the room feeling cool. He pleased me and I pleased him. And I wondered if it was all just talk with him, or would he come and see me again.

Erica and I footed it back out into the snowfall with two inches of snow already on the ground. My pussy was still tingling from the experience and I couldn't wait to get back home to my daughter.

"Was he good?" Erica asked me, as we entered into the lobby covered in snow and cold.

I smiled at her.

Tango, he was more than good; he was different.

Chapter Eleven

Sammy

Brownsville was the worst, and will always be the worst in my eyes. I didn't even know how I let Kawanda talked me into this. I was in the heart of Brownsville, Rockaway Avenue, near the Van Dyke houses. The bachelor party was at this seedy-looking lounge/bar. It was spacious, but it was hood, too hood for my taste. It made Crazy Legs look like some rich white club. Every nigga in the bar/lounge had a blunt to their lips or a bottle in their hand, and everywhere reeked of weed, cigarettes, and funky-smelling niggas. It was only rap music blaring throughout the place; the bitches were ghetto and whack with majority of them having bullet holes or stab wounds, and bad weaves and trashy outfits that they kept off. Nearly a dozen bitches strutted around the party butt-ass naked trying to fuck and suck niggas for one hundred dollars or less. Some bitches were tricking for fifty dollars.

I shook my head at these trashy, low-class looking bitches.

Unfortunately, all eyes were on me. I was the baddest bitch at the party and didn't want the attention. But these hood and thirsty niggas were all over me like I was a star. I strutted around the place in a sexy minidress with a halter neckline with string ties and silver weave for a glittery effect and my clear stilettos. My style was original and I stood out. I was too shapely for these bitches who had stomachs and guts, and sagging tits and weak skin.

I sipped on a drink and chilled by the bar. Three hours in this place and I only made $200. I wanted to go home, but Kawanda and I shared a cab together. I was the only girl in the place who wasn't disappearing into a room with a nigga to sexually please him. I simply made my money by dancing and flirting with niggas. It was supposed to be a bachelor party, but the groom-to-be was so drunk and disrespectful to the dancers and niggas at his party that a few fights broke out with him, and his homeboy had to cool him down and seriously talk to him. This was the man who had the contract with a record label. He wasn't much to look at in my book. He was short and stocky with fuzzy cornrows and dark skin. Everything about him was off. He was also belligerent. When he would look my way, I would turn my head. I didn't want anything to do with the man of the party.

The other thing that pissed me off was there weren't any big-time ballers or rappers at the party. Steele didn't even show up and I heard he and the husband-to-be were supposed to be kin. It appeared to me that all these niggas at this party had struggling pockets. They wanted to have tons of fun on a shoestring budget. And I wasn't a shoestring budget bitch. I had these niggas coming at me left and right, yearning for my attention, craving to see my body in the nude, wanting to touch me in places to get their dicks hard. I was repulsed by everything. The place was nasty and the men were corny.

Kawanda was doing her thang though, making her paper, pleasing these niggas and doing what she did best: sex and being enticing. I watched her grind against someone in the dark corner in the nude and standing erect in a pair of red pumps. She had him against the wall, allowing his hands to touch her everywhere, one hand cupping her tit and the other between her legs. I assumed he was finger fucking her right there in public and she didn't care. She had money spread about on the floor: one-, five-, and ten-dollar bills.

I was glued to Kawanda's freaky actions until I heard someone say to me, "What's wrong wit' you, ma?"

He took a seat next to me at the bar. I glanced at him. He was tall and lanky with a nappy 'fro and looked like he didn't have a dime to spend in his pockets.

"Nothing's wrong with me," I replied.

"You look nice though. I like ya style," he said.

"Thank you."

"Can a nigga get a dance wit' you?"

"You got money?"

"Shit, ma, it hurts that you even have to ask a nigga that shit. Yeah, I got paper on me. I know you ain't no free ho," he said. "You one of them stuck-up bitches 'bout that money and you gonna hit a nigga's pockets to fuck."

"What?" I replied, screwing my face at his comment.

"I'm sayin', I got eighty on me fo' ya time."

"Eighty?" My face twisted up with a serious attitude.

He was serious.

"Nigga, you can take that eighty and find you some other thirsty bitch. I don't turn tricks."

"What? Then why you here, ma?" he asked.

Yeah, why was I there? I should have been gotten dressed and left. But I didn't want to leave Brooklyn by myself. It was late and paying for a cab was too costly from Brownsville to the Bronx.

As if things couldn't get any worse, the drunken groom came walking over with his eyes fixated on me. I noticed him watching me all night, and now I guessed he had the nerve to come over. I wanted to walk away, but I didn't get the chance.

"Yo, B, what's good, my nigga? What this bitch talkin' 'bout?" the groom said to him like I wasn't standing there.

Bitch?

"She actin' brand new, my nigga. She here, but she ain't tryin' to get that money like the rest of these bitches."

"She actin' brand new," the groom replied. "What?"

I sucked my teeth out of frustration and rolled my eyes. The husband-to-be looked at me and asked, "Yo, ma, what's ya name? I've been watchin' you all night. You the baddest bitch up in this spot. You know a nigga 'bout to get married soon and I'm 'bout to get put on."

I wasn't impressed. I felt sorry for the bride. "I'm good," I told him.

"What?" he replied with attitude, "What you mean, you good?"

"Fats, I told you this bitch is stuck-up."

"I told you, I'm good."

"Bitch—"

"I ain't ya bitch," I spat at him.

"Bitch, you better start actin' right, 'cause this my fuckin' party. I run this shit, bitch," he hollered.

These fuckin' Brownsville niggas, doesn't anything ever good come out of dealing with them. I shouldn't have come. But I wasn't about to let some short, drunk, ugly, and punk muthafucka scream on me and treat me like shit.

"Your mother's a fuckin' bitch!" I cursed.

The groom done started shit with everybody in the party, so I guessed it was my turn. He stepped to me; I towered over him being in my six-inch stilettos. He twisted his face at me and started becoming belligerent.

"Yo fuck you, bitch! I'm Fats Money; you know who the fuck I am!" he screamed, creating unwanted attention on me and him.

Kawanda noticed the heated incident ensuing and hurried over to have my back. She came between me and him buck-naked with her clothes in her hands. "This my homegirl yo," she said.

"I don't give a fuck!" he shouted.

"Well, you better," Kawanda warned him.

"Fuck you too, bitch!" he screamed heatedly.

I was ready to smash a bottle over his head. The problem was, Kawanda and I were the only girls who weren't from Brooklyn. We came from the BX, and these bitches already hated on me and my girl because we stood out. I was ready to fight though, not giving a fuck. I hated when someone disrespected me for any reason at all. And Fats Money, he was the rudest and foulest nigga I ever met.

I felt everyone glaring at me. Fats Money was big time in the Ville. He was an upcoming rapper with a violent street reputation. He was get a money nigga and didn't have any shame on putting his hands on a female. Kawanda and myself, I felt we were outnumbered and predicted coming here was going to be a mistake.

Fats Money continued being belligerent toward us at the bar, but then I heard someone say, "Yo, Fats, you need to chill the fuck out, fo' real, my nigga. Them girls ain't do shit to you."

Fats turned his aggressive attention to the voice commanding him to be easy and when he saw who it was, his whole demeanor changed. "Yo, fo' real," Fats started, but the man approaching us looked at him like he was food to eat.

"You already know, Fats, calm the fuck down. I don't wanna embarrass you at your own bachelor party."

Fats didn't respond. He stood quietly, easily being punked by this towering man who walked with a tiger's stride in the room and his persona manifesting respect and authority. He shut down the problem before it escalated.

"Go fuck with somebody else, Fats, not these two ladies," the man said.

Fats scowled, but he didn't respond. It was obvious who the real boss nigga was at the party. Fats and his friend walked away, defeated and embarrassed. I was thankful. I gazed at my peacemaker and had seen him before. He was a large man, well over six feet tall and probably over 300 pounds, but neat and well put-together for his size. There was an air of power about him with his ink-black eyes, glistening bald head, and thick goatee.

I noticed the tattoo inked on his neck: YGC. Young Gangster Crew. I immediately assumed he was from Edenwald and a gangster. They all were. Why was he in Brooklyn, I had no idea. But it seemed he had clout there.

"He more bark than bite," he said to me.

"Thank you," I said.

"They call me Power," he introduced himself, with a friendly handshake. "I be seeing you at Crazy Legs. You're a beautiful woman and a great dancer."

"Thank you," I replied dryly.

He saved me from a whirlwind of trouble, but I wasn't interested in him. The way he looked at me told me he was very interested in me; not to be conceited, but everyone was. He was trying to make conversation, but I was ready to leave. I didn't care if I had to leave alone. It was just too much going on around me.

"Can I buy you a drink?" he asked.

"No, I'm good. I'm 'bout to leave anyway."

He lit a cigarette and replied, "Yeah, I understand, I don't fuck with the Ville like that either. It's just business out here for me."

He blew smoke out his mouth, looked at me, threw up his left hand with his middle finger crossed over his ring finger, indicating an X, and said, "I'm BX for life."

I smiled, but it was more forced. "It ain't nothin' like the Bronx," I said, just to be nice.

"Word up, fuck these Brooklyn niggas," Power said recklessly around Brooklyn niggas. Nobody said a word; not a soul rebuked his rude comment. It indicated how heavy his status was.

I looked around for Kawanda. I was leaving. Power was cool, or seemed cool, but he wasn't my type and I was done dating gangsters. Rico was the Antichrist who ruined it for everyone.

"Listen, it was nice talkin' to you, but I gotta go," I said.

"It's cool, I'll see you around,' he replied.

Maybe he would, maybe he wouldn't, and I didn't care. Power let me walk away without any hassle or trying to get my number. I respected that. He was the classiest nigga in the place, if I said so. I went looking for Kawanda and when I couldn't find her, I figured she was doing VIP or was in the changing/storage room switching up outfits or counting her money. When I didn't see her in the changing room, I immediately knew where she was at. That bitch probably sucked and fucked more niggas than Heather Hunter.

I quickly got dressed and dialed a cab from my cell phone. The way these bitches were glaring at me in the room, I knew I wasn't wanted there. Every bitch was a Brooklyn bitch, and the fact that I was pretty they hated me like I was some Nazi German.

Clad in my jeans, sweater, winter coat, and winter boots, and rolling my small suitcase, I hurried through the growing crowd and rowdy-ass niggas toward the exit. I noticed Power eyeing me from the bar. He smiled, I didn't smile back. I exited the building without even telling Kawanda I was gone. She was taking too long in VIP for me. I already had the cab idling outside. I decided to call her cell phone and leave a message, or somebody would tell her that I left.

I climbed into the back seat and told the driver I was heading to the Bronx. He looked skeptical driving that far at this late in the night. He charged me extra: sixty-five dollars. I had no choice. That fee came out of the $200 I made that night. Pissed wasn't even the word I felt. I wasn't fuckin' with Kawanda or Brooklyn anymore. The night was a complete bust.

The duration of the ride to the Bronx, I pouted and thought about another source of employment because this couldn't be it for me. I refused to keep living like this.

"Open number two," the guard shouted.

The thick gray door opened up in front of me and I stepped into the visiting room of Attica prison, walking single file behind so many other women who were there to see a loved one. The spacious gym that had been turned into an inmate visiting area was teeming with inmates enjoying their family: girlfriends, husbands, brothers, and sons, and so on. I gave the female guard my ticket and she pointed to my assigned seat, farther in the back. I walked toward the seating area feeling the eyes on me. I came alone, choosing to leave Danny with my neighbor. It was a constant headache bringing a seven-month-old baby with me.

I was dressed simple in some stylish blue jeans, white sneakers, and a black gathered bust flutter top, which I must admit, did draw attention to my tits a little more. I didn't come to look cute for Rico; I just liked to look cute wherever I went.

I sat in the chair and waited. I wanted to be home with my son, but Rico called me collect the other day and said he needed me to come visit him. It was an emergency. Reluctantly, I was here once more. The chatter in the room wasn't noisy, but it was tiresome to hear, especially when you're alone and waiting. I noticed the fleeting looks my way, some from inmates already seated with their girlfriends and some came from other visitors. I caught even a few male guards staring my way. I ignored the attention and looked at the floor.

Rico and four other inmates were escorted into the room by a single guard. Rico was the first to walk in, leading the pack like he always did. I stared at him. His stature was still demanding even while incarcerated. His eyes scanned the room in search of me. He soon found me and smiled. I exhaled noisily and rolled my eyes. He came marching my way with this confident stride, and as handsome as he was, he was the ugliest person in the room.

"You look good, baby," he greeted me, with open arms and a grin.

"Thanks," I dryly responded, still seated.

"What, I can't get a hug and kiss?"

"It ain't like that wit' us," I frankly told him.

"Then make it like that wit' us," he said seriously.

I stared at him, knowing he was trying to make an impression in front of his fellow inmates. He couldn't be seen being disrespected and dissed by a beautiful woman like me—his woman. I stood up and halfheartedly hugged him and then gave him a quick peck on the lips. Rico looked for more, but there wasn't any more coming from me. We took our seat next to each other and I crossed my legs opposite his way.

"How you been and where's my son?" he asked.

"I didn't bring him."

"Why not?"

"Because I didn't. It ain't like you be playing wit' him or paying him any attention while he here like that," I said.

"Sammy, why you be trippin'?"

"'Cause you make me trip," I spat.

"Listen, I ain't got time to argue wit' you," he said.

"*Puede ser un idiota,*" I cursed in Spanish.

"You better watch ya mouth," he uttered.

I waved him off.

"Anyway, you thought about my proposal?" he asked.

"Rico, I'm not marrying you."

"What? Why not?"

"Seriously, you think I wanna marry you, after everything you put me through and you being in here for how long? *Debes estar loco.*"

"I wasn't asking," he warned.

"You know what, you can threaten me all you want, and if you're that cold to have the mother of your son locked up, then go to hell," I told him angrily.

"We can talk 'bout that some other time, but I want you to become my wife."

The muthafucka was impossible to talk to and reason with. It was like trying to squeeze water from a rock. I sat there with him and listened though. He asked me a few questions, about Edenwald and Danny. I told him what was going on in the Bronx. Then he asked me about Mouse.

"You seen or talk to her lately?"

I was dumbfounded. He knew Mouse and I didn't talk to each other at all. I had no idea what was going on with her. He ruined that relationship between us. He tore our friendship apart. He instigated shit and looked proud at his work.

"You know I don't talk to her," I said.

"I been tryin' to reach her, but she ain't nowhere to be found," he told me.

I sat there deadpan, not caring what he had to say about Mouse.

"I want her to come visit me. I wanna see my daughter," he had the nerve to say.

I chuckled lightly at his twisted reasoning of having Mouse come to visit. I guessed he wanted to control her like he was trying to do me. But Mouse, even though we weren't speaking, I give it to her, she completely cut Rico out of her life: no letters, no phone calls, and not any pictures of his daughter, nothing. He had no clue where she was. I only wished I had that same luxury she had.

"Don't talk to me 'bout Mouse," I rebuked him.

"You need to see what's up wit' her fo' me," he had the audacity to say.

"Are you fuckin' kidding me?" I said through clenched teeth. "You must have lost ya damn mind."

"I didn't lose anything."

He could have fooled me. He sat there, stern face aimed at me. I was silent. He added, "I just need to talk to her."

"And I'm the messenger," I replied.

"If you see her around, tell her I want to see her."

I wasn't telling her shit and I wasn't trying to look for her either. But I didn't tell Rico that. I straightforwardly replied, "Whatever."

Rico continued talking and I was barely listening. I thought about the hourly trip I had to take back to New York by bus. It sucked not having a car. It sucked to visit a man you despised, but he had this black cloud lingering over my head that I was almost like a puppet on a string.

As the visit moved forward, Rico leaned closer to me and said in a low tone, "Look, I'm gonna need you to do me a favor in a few weeks."

I frowned at doing him any favors. Doing favors for Rico was risky and I knew what he was about to ask me wouldn't be any different. I didn't reply. He continued running his mouth. "I'm gonna need you to sneak some stuff inside for me."

The look I gave him, he already knew my answer.

"Don't look at me like that," he said.

"You must be stupid," I spat through gritted teeth.

"Listen, the show don't stop wit' me being locked up in here, *entender*," he said. "I got a connect outside who needs to bring a small package inside. I thought about you."

"I'm glad to be ya first choice," I replied sarcastically.

"Don't get fuckin' smart."

I wanted to smack him. But there was no way I was going to risk my freedom by helping Rico sneak in drugs, I assumed. But he didn't care; he was a self-centered prick who thought about himself.

"I'll talk to you 'bout the details later," he said.

I didn't say yes, but he was already scheming and involving me.

The visit was finally over and I couldn't wait to leave his side and head back home. He wanted a hug and kiss before my departure, but I refused to show him any affection that I didn't have for him. I walked away without a good-bye and left him there in awe. The farther I got away from him, the better.

I had to do something about Rico, because if I didn't, he was gonna be like herpes: no matter how many times you treated it, it was always gonna come back.

Chapter Twelve

Mouse

It was a warmer night than usual with remnants of the last snowfall on the ground melting every day. Hunts Point was quiet tonight, traffic was light, and clientele felt like it was drying up. I strutted up and down Oak Point Avenue watching and waving at every passing car, but they weren't stopping. Erica was on one side of the street and me on the other. Tonight, I decided to look cute since it was fifty degrees and mild. I had on a pair of black pumps, tight jeans that accentuated my curves, and a leather jacket, with my sensuous long hair falling down to my back. I smoked a cigarette and couldn't believe I was still out here. I wasn't trying to get used to sucking dick and fucking strangers, but it became a job.

I turned the corner and started to walk down Longfellow Avenue, near the small park. It was dark and I was bored. My last date was an hour ago, and he only wanted a blowjob. I sucked his dick so good, I made that white boy's forehead cave in and had him coming like a geyser in the condom. He was nice, came fast, and his dick was average. I still hated turning these tricks, but I found a way to cope with it. I would close my eyes and think about something else pleasing, like playing with my daughter and finally doing for her, or recite a rhyme or poem in my head, maybe think about a future with prosperity, a loving man, living in the suburbs, something to make me forget that my face was in a nigga's lap with his dick down my throat or spread out in the car with stranger's dick inside of me.

I walked down Longfellow Avenue and the second I hit the corner, I noticed a red Honda Accord hastily pull up next to me with the windows rolling down and hearing rap music blaring. Instantly, I got nervous and was ready to flee. Stick-up kids, I thought, or was it the police? I couldn't outrun anyone in these heels and felt I should have worn my boots or sneakers. I stood there feeling my heart pound rapidly inside my chest and my eyes stuck on the car.

"Diamond," I heard him call out.

Fixated on the passenger door opening, I took a few steps back. If it was any danger, I had two choices: either fight or flee. I quickly removed a sharp razor from my pocket and held it in my hand. I was ready to protect myself and give whoever it was a very rude awakening.

But then I felt a little relief when I saw it was Tango climbing out of the car. He was all smiles, very excited to see me. "Diamond, I been lookin' fo' you," he said lively.

He had me nervous at first, but I never saw anyone so happy to see me. I mean, the look on his face looked like he had just won the lotto or something. It was all because of me. He approached and said, "I wanna date."

I looked inside the idling car and he didn't come alone. The driver behind the wheel was watching me too, and creeping me the fuck out. "I don't do doubles," I told him.

"Don't worry 'bout my man, he ain't gonna fuck wit' you. He just my ride out here, that's all," said Tango.

I was still worried. I didn't know him like that either. "Still, I feel uncomfortable getting in the car with two men," I let it be known.

"A'ight, I got you, beautiful," he said. "I'ma take care of it."

Hearing him always call me beautiful, it made me smile inside and blush. The way Tango looked at me, like I was more of a queen than some whore working the blocks at Hunts Point, it was the way every woman wanted to be looked at. His eyes spoke volumes toward me.

I watched Tango walk back to the car and climb inside. He started saying something to the driver. The driver glanced back at me and then turned his attention back to Tango. A few more words were said, and next thing I knew, they were both climbing out of the car. Tango waved me over. "C'mon, let's go."

I was confused.

"He gonna chill out here fo' a minute, while we do our thang," said Tango.

I walked toward the Accord skeptically. The driver seemed aloof about the whole thing. He stood on the sidewalk while Tango got behind the wheel and had me get in on the passenger side. I looked back at the male; he was average height with dreads and black as coal.

"You sure he's cool 'bout waiting out here? I mean, this is Hunts Point and it ain't that warm," I said.

"Yo, you ain't gotta worry 'bout my nigga; he ain't worried 'bout nuthin' out here. He a 'bout it nigga fo' real and he can handle his own. Besides, he owes me," Tango said.

I shrugged.

Tango put the car in drive and we slowly drove away. I sat back and for some strange reason, it felt good seeing him again. It had been a couple of days since our last sexual encounter and I would be lying if I didn't say he came into my mind since then.

"I miss you," Tango said to me.

"You do?"

"Hells yeah, since you left, I've been thinkin' 'bout you every day."

"You lying."

"Nah, I'm serious. Yo, just being next to you right now got a nigga feeling all jolly and shit."

I chuckled.

"And you lookin' so fuckin' sexy, beautiful. When you gonna marry me?" he asked as a joke.

"When you put a ring on my finger," I joked back.

"I can do that tomorrow."

"You know I was just playin' right?"

"I wasn't," he let be known with a serious face.

Wow. Tango was very forward and rough around the edges, but once again, he made me feel wanted and beautiful. It was crazy. I knew what I was about to do with him, suck his dick and fuck him, but the way he went about it, not making me feel trashy and used, it stirred something gushy up inside of me.

He parked somewhere secluded. He killed the ignition, looked at me, and said, "I know your time is money, so how much do I owe you?"

"What do you want?"

"A half hour of your time. I just wanna be wit' you; we ain't even gotta fuck right now."

"I charge a hundred for that," I said.

He reached into his pocket and pulled out a few twenties. He handed me a hundred dollars in twenties. I collected my fee and placed it somewhere safe. I could feel Tango's eyes all over me, admiring my nice body in the attire I wore and yearning for me. I smiled. He was really making me smile and it was nothing fraudulent about it, like how I did my other dates.

"You got a nice smile, Diamond," he said.

Diamond. I had him thinking my name was Diamond. I was tempted to be honest with him, but then common sense came to me and warned me that I still didn't know this man. I just met him a few days ago and it would be idiotic to tell him my government name.

I leaned toward him and kissed the side of his neck while my touch fondled his crotch. I felt him growing hard. I felt the blood rushing inside of him. I felt his eagerness to have me. He undid his pants and whipped out his pleasure. It stood full staff, ready for me to please it with whatever tool, mouth or pussy.

"You missed me, huh?" I whispered sensually in his ear.

"I did."

"You missed my good, tight, and wet punani?"

"I wanna feel every bit of you, Diamond. You turn me the fuck on."

This time, he pulled out the condom, Magnum of course. He tore it opened and put it on. I lowered my lips to his big, fat and black dick and engulfed the mushroom tip with my full lips. He moaned the minute I tasted him. He reclined in the chair and allowed my lips to work his flesh. I sucked and sucked, feeling his penis throb inside my mouth.

"Ugh, ugh," he moaned, as he massaged my backside.

My head bobbed up and down in his lap. I cupped his balls and worked my magic. I gave him good head for several minutes and then removed my jeans and panties and straddled him in the front seat, feeling his dick speared through me. Tango held me close and passionately, he kissed me all over with affection as he fucked me like a Mandingo warrior. I couldn't help but to melt and coo in his grasp. He opened my pussy up with his big dick like a doorway.

When he came, it felt like the ground shook underneath us. He shuddered and thrust upward inside of me, releasing every bit of man juice into the latex. He huffed and puffed, feeling sexually satisfied. I didn't climb off the dick right away. He held me in his arms, not wanting to let me go. Then he said, "I never wanna let you go."

It was sweet, but this wasn't the place or time to be romantic. He paid me for sex and it's what he got. I wasn't his boo and he wasn't my man to cozy with. For a moment, he sucked on my nipples with his dick still rooted inside of me. The thrill was gone and I felt the dick becoming flaccid. I finally got off the dick and got dressed. I still had to make some money. Tango pulled up his jeans and said, "I wanna continue to see you."

"You know where I'm always at," I said.

"Nah, I mean, I wanna take you out."

I looked his way. He was serious. "I don't date my clients," I frankly replied.

"Client? I'm not tryin' to be ya client, luv. I wanna see you."

"Look, Tango, ya sweet and all, but what's the catch? The game you playin' wit' me?" I replied sternly.

"Ain't no game, I'm always fo' real. I like what I see and I want sumthin' more. I just came home after doin' a dime and I need sumthin' real in my life," he countered.

"And you think I'm real?"

"What, you ain't?"

I sighed. "This is me, a whore, a fuckin' prostitute workin' Hunts Point. I ain't got shit to my name. I just came out a shelter; I got a one-year-old daughter, no degree, and an uncertain future. This is what you want? A bitch suckin' and fuckin' niggas night after night, that's the type of bitch you want in your life?"

"Ain't nobody perfect, Diamond," he firmly countered. "I'm fresh home tryin' to make it and survive. I got several years of parole wit' a dyke-ass parole officer up my ass just itchin' fo' me to fuck up so she could violate my ass. I got kids I don't even see like that or know where they at, 'cause my baby mamas snatched them up and left the state. And what you do out here, it don't faze me, 'cause you know why? If you wit' me, I'ma make sure my woman is okay and taken care of. It's what I do."

He words were touching, but I heard it all before, especially with Rico.

"So I guess we both fucked up, huh?" I said, smiling.

"I guess we are. And one thing, Diamond, you ain't no ho. I see it in ya eyes that this ain't you. You just doin' this to live, take care of ya seed. I don't knock anybody's hustle, 'cause at the end of the day, ain't nobody tryin' to pay our bills and take care of us. You do what you gotta do for you and yours," he proclaimed.

I nodded. "You ain't lying."

"I been through hell and back, and I'm still here, still alive and tryin' to climb this steep fuckin' hill."

I looked at him. He was attractive and into me. His eyes weren't lying about his feelings for me, I assumed. When Tango looked at me, it was with intensity and passion. We talked and somewhat connected.

"I have to be honest wit' you," I started, hoping I wasn't going to regret admitting this to him. "My name really isn't Diamond; it's Mouse."

"Mouse. That's cute. I like it."

"Yeah, that's my name."

"Well, I'm still Tango." He laughed.

I laughed too. It was always great when a man makes you laugh.

I felt something with him. Our chemistry was mixing strongly, and before I knew it, an hour had almost passed with us still talking in the car. He forgot about his friend on the corner and I forgot about working the track.

We hurried back to where he picked me up at, and his friend was still loitering on Longfellow and Drake Park Street. He was smoking a cigarette, talking on his cell phone, and didn't seem to be upset that we took really long to come back.

"You sure he ain't mad?" I said to Tango.

"That's my dude; he ain't mad. The nigga owe me a lot," Tango replied.

"A'ight," I said.

I was about to exit the car, but Tango gently took a hold of my forearm and gazed at me. He said to me, "I want you in my life, Mouse."

It all sounded nice, but it needed to be more show than tell. "If you want me, make it happen," I said to him.

"And I will."

I got out the car with his friend walking our way. He looked at me and didn't grimace or complain not one bit about standing almost an hour on the corner and in the cold. He actually smiled at me and got in on the passenger side. It was strange, but I didn't object. I guessed Tango had it like that. He seemed like a boss nigga before he was locked up and still now when he was home.

I watched the red Accord drive away and didn't know what to think of it. Was Tango really for real? Did he really like me that much? Would I be a fool to let an ex-con into my life? There were so many questions spinning around in my head. It was going on one in the morning and the night had been slow. Tango was the only live point of the night.

It would be another forty minutes until I caught another date. He was an ugly Hispanic looking for a blowjob. Like routine, he parked somewhere secluded, the parking lot of a mechanic shop closed down for the night, and I threw the condom on and wrapped my lips around his small dick and pleased him. I didn't want to do this anymore. I didn't want to continue degrading myself over and over again. I didn't want to feel trapped and burnt out in a year or two doing this. So if Tango was for real, which I hoped he was, and would be a man and rescue me from this world, I swore on everything I would be his loyal fuckin' bitch until the day I died. That's if he was man enough to become a one-woman man. I was tired of being lied to, used, and abused.

I just wanted to be loved.

I wanted to escape from this hell.

Chapter Thirteen

Sammy

Crazy Legs was so swelled with people on this particular night that I thought the place was going to explode due to overcapacity. It was a Friday night and lively from wall to wall. Every bitch was butt-ass naked and in some long heels in the place and the DJ had the place cranked up playing "I Luv This Shit," by August Alsina:

And I luv this shit
It's 2 o'clock and I'm faded
This kush feelin' amazing
Got a voice mail on my phone
From a li'l breezy feelin' X-rated

I worked the stage scantily clad in a three-piece set, a striped bra, tie side thong and matching stockings, with my black six-inch platform sandals. I had some silver glitter sprinkled on me and was well oiled up. I worked the pole like a professional, climbing all the way to the top and twirling myself around with my legs spread until I reached the bottom. I did gymnastics on the pole, being upside down, sideways, parallel to the stage, and contorted around it like I was a snake, having these niggas in complete awe. I moved my ass hypnotically. I had money thrown at me because I was entertainment. While these bitches did VIP in the back rooms, I learned to dance and entertain these niggas and money still came my way.

"I Luv This Shit" was one of my favorite songs to dance to. I would move my ass and hips to the beat and recite the lyrics while dancing. I had a crowd around the stage and they were aching to see my body nude. I undid my top and let my tits show and then I came out my side thong and showed my shaved pussy. These niggas were thirsty and ready to touch me in all kinds of places.

One face caught my attention in the crowd. It was Power. He stood there clutching a wad of money, at least three grand mostly in twenties and fifties and gawked at me intensely. I didn't forget how he saved my ass in Brooklyn and I was very grateful. He had been coming to the club regularly and watching me dance and tipping me big time. He would make it rain on me; I'm talking about it would be a downpour of cash on the stage, money flying everywhere. He would only tip me hundreds of dollars and give me his undivided attention, making some of the girls jealous in the club. He was persistent in wooing me. He thought I was playing hard to get, but I really wasn't interested in him. All the strippers in the club were on his dick, ready to fuck Power in a heartbeat; but myself, I was aloof to his status and reckless spending.

"Bitch, you crazy, you better get wit' Power. That nigga is a boss muthafucka and he sweating you," Kawanda had advised me. "That's a type of nigga who will take care of you. Shit, I wish I had a nigga like that chasing me."

She was a paper chaser; she wouldn't understand.

I already had a boss nigga in my life, Rico, and he fucked it up for everyone. I was just too scared to date that type of nigga again. And I was stressed; Rico would call me collect at all kinds of crazy hours and steadily harass me. He wanted me to sneak drugs into the prison. I was against it. He wasn't giving me a choice, something had to be done. And there was more shit adding on to my stress.

The other day, I got the scare of my life. One evening two homicide detectives came knocking at my door to ask me questions about Macky's death. Detective English and Detective McGowan, two suit and tie white boys with a hard on for solving murders that were going cold case. It seemed that some new information had emerged from some new witness testimony and, out of the blue, my name came up in the investigation. My heart literally stopped beating for a minute. I'd allowed them inside my apartment for a minor interrogation.

"Your name is Sammy, right?" Detective English had asked me.

"Yes, it is," I had replied.

"How did you know the victim, Macky?" he had asked.

I told him the truth. "We met once, in the studio in Manhattan. I was introduced to him by a friend of mines," I had said.

"Search?"

"Yes. I was doing a recording session."

"With a friend named Mouse?"

Damn, they knew everything and the more he kept bringing something up out of the blue, the more nervous I became and was sure they were going to charge me with murder and take me out of my apartment in handcuffs. But I kept a straight face and had answered their question as normal as I could.

"Yes, Mouse."

"Do you know where we can find her?"

"We had a falling out and I haven't spoken to her in months."

Detective English was jotting everything down in his small notepad while his partner just stared at me. I didn't know what to do with myself. Macky had been dead for months now, and only four people, including myself, knew who killed him. Why was my name coming up?

"When was the last time you saw or spoken to Macky?" Detective McGowan had asked.

"I told you, the day I first met him, when we were doing a recording session."

"Well, from information given to us, did you go out on a date with him a few weeks before he was killed?" Detective English had chimed.

I wanted to gasp, but I had kept cool. "I told you, I didn't know the man at all besides that one night in the studio, and it was only business between us." I had lied.

They gawked at me, having their suspicions, but I knew if they had any hard evidence on me then I would have been arrested and charged right there on sight. The only thing the detectives had was suspicion and even I knew that wasn't enough to indict anyone on. They had to leave my place. I answered their questions with the best of my knowledge. I wasn't a stupid bitch. I wasn't going to crack over a badge being shown to me and being asked about a murder.

"We'll keep in contact," Detective McGowan had said with his doubt about me showing on his face.

When they left my place, I had fallen to my knees and broke down in tears. Knowing it had to be Rico probably running his mouth, I couldn't put up with his blackmail or his shit anymore. The nerve of him taunting me the way he did. He owed me everything because he took away everything. But I quickly collected myself and was ready to plot his downfall. I didn't have the solution yet, but it was going to come to me.

I had to get my mind off the murder and I did that at work. I had to make money and Power was helping me with that; for a week straight, he showed me love and tipped me handsomely, also buying me drinks and talking to me.

After my routine to "I Luv This Shit," before I could take one foot off the stage, Power was standing right there to greet me. I had a fistful of money and my scanty outfit in my other hand. I was getting used to being butt-ass naked in front of dozens of men. I needed to refresh, but Power wanted to holler at me.

"You the best, luv, for real," he said.

"Thanks."

"Can I get a minute of your time and let me buy you a drink?" he suggested.

I did need one. Between the detectives questioning me, Rico blackmailing me, taking care of my son, niggas constantly trying to fuck me, and putting up with shit that went on in this club, it was enough to drive a bitch crazy.

"You remember my drink?" I asked.

"Cîroc Peach and Sprite. I can't never forget that," he said.

I smiled. Sometimes it was sweet when a man remembers the simple things about you. "Okay. Let me go freshen up and I'll meet you at the bar."

He smiled. "You do that."

I strutted toward the changing room. The minute I walked inside all eyes were on me and they weren't trying to be my friend. It was all hate. I had Power's attention. It was something these bitches been trying to do since the day he walked into the club. But these bitches didn't have any class like me. They were whack. Power was a kingpin in the Bronx and his reputation preceded him. He was known in Brooklyn, Harlem, and most likely out of state. See, bitches run their mouths and always got the 411 on a nigga, especially a nigga with major paper and major street credibility. He was moving at least twenty to fifty kilos a week, making close to half a million a week. He was heavily affiliated with YGC and they say he had a house in the Poconos, Upstate New York, Long Island, and a penthouse in the city.

Parked outside the club was a black-on-black Bentley Continental GT with the black rims. It was one of the many cars he owned. Power wasn't the finest man around, he wasn't exactly eye candy or a teenage heartthrob, but he had status, he had clout, he was well known and rich. In a way, he was like Biggie Smalls: overweight, black, but his charisma, his style, and sense of humor made a bitch's panties wet.

I was the envy of every bitch and here I was, not even liking Power like that, and it pissed bitches off knowing they wanted to be me.

I changed outfits, slipping my curvaceous body into an off-the-shoulder, pink fishnet minidress with long sleeves and a silver metallic bikini set with a triangle and G-string back. I was the shit. I looked good in anything I wore. I took time putting my outfits together. I wanted to stand out and I did.

I heard these bitches whispering, "She think she cute."

"I don't know what Power sees in her anyway, I'm the better bitch."

"Fuck her!"

"I heard she stabbed Mouse in the back, fuckin' her man."

"I know right, fake bitch."

I heard enough, I spun around on my heels with attitude, glared at every bitch in the changing room and exclaimed, "Y'all bitches got a problem wit' me, then say it to my fuckin' face. If not, then shut the fuck up and keep my fuckin' name out y'all mouths."

The room suddenly got quiet and now all of a sudden bitches ain't had shit to say. They knew who I was and what I was about. I was still EBV in the house, had a reputation that stretched for miles, and was still connected to dangerous people. I was nobody to be fucked with.

Bitches averted their attention from me and continued doing what they were doing: nothing. I marched out of the room needing that drink. They looked but they didn't say shit. I met Power at the bar and took a seat next to him. He smiled. For a goon, a thug, he had a really nice smile and a warm personality. He had my drink ready.

"Thank you," I said.

"You know I got you. Damn, you change up nice. I like that outfit."

"Thanks."

"You the baddest woman up in here," he complimented me.

He didn't have to tell me that. I already knew it. But it was nice to hear him say it. He was dressed nicely himself, sporting a leather jacket, dark jeans, and beige Timberlands. He wore a diamond-encrusted pinky ring along with a diamond-encrusted big-face watch and earring. And his head continued to be as bald as a baby's bum.

He looked at me and said, "Why you don't like me? I'm not ya type?"

It was unexpected. *Should I be honest with him?* "It's not that I don't like you, I just have a lot of shit goin' on in my life right now," I said.

"Like what, beef?"

I didn't know what to call it, but it was situations. "I have a son, first off."

"And, I love kids. I don't have any myself right now, but I would love to have kids of my own someday."

It was nice to hear.

"What else? What don't you like about me and I'll fix it," he said.

I smiled. "It's not that simple."

"Try me, and I can make it be," he said wholeheartedly.

It was nice to hear once again and he seemed believable, but I dealt with guys like Power my whole life. At first, they seem charming and caring, willing to give you the whole world, make you their queen, or pretend to be, and then suddenly, it all changes. They can become overbearing and controlling, and they think because they have money, bought you some nice things that they own you. I didn't want to be owned by anyone anymore.

So I didn't trust anyone. I wasn't picking on Power; he just came at the wrong time in my life.

"You're a beautiful woman, you know that, and you ain't gotta be so standoffish all the time," said Power. "Someone made a mistake with you; it don't have to rub off on the next man. Everybody's different. I'm different."

"It's what they all say," I countered.

"Well, it's what I say. Get to know me and see for yourself."

I gazed at him. He was intelligent and able to hold a conversation. I couldn't say the same for most of these niggas who frequented the place. If it wasn't about drugs, pussy, weed, or sports, then the men were left clueless with stumped faces.

"Give me a chance, let me take you out somewhere nice, somewhere different," Power said, continuing to woo me.

I sighed. I continued gazing at him fighting my better judgment. He was an intimidating man, but he spoke like a humble man to me. He drank wine instead of hard liquor. It was a first. But I knew in his eyes what this man was about, the type of life he lived: a gangster's life, possibly a hardcore killer and violent man who didn't get his savage street reputation by being humble in these mean streets. He wore one face around me, but in the game, he was someone different. Rico was the same way.

Power fixed his eyes on me, my beauty, and smiled. His teeth were white as pearls and his trimmed goatee was cute. “If you say yes, I’ll let you rub my head and make a wish,” he joked, rubbing his head for the fun of it.

I chuckled. *Say yes,* I told myself. What would it hurt? “Okay, one date,” I remarked.

“One date is cool. I can’t argue with that.”

“You can’t,” I said.

“I see ya sassy.”

“You don’t know what you’re gettin’ into,” I told him.

“I’m willing to take my chances.”

He ordered me another drink and we continued to talk. He made me smile and laugh, and for once, he took my mind off of the troubles in my life. It was a good thing. I needed the talk and laughter he gave me.

Time went by with us talking at the bar. That night, he put over $1,000 in my pockets and offered me a ride home. I had to admit, he was an interesting guy. I prayed that going out on a date with him didn’t backfire on me.

Chapter Fourteen

Mouse

Erica was living her life, being comfortable, but I felt that I was simply surviving. With me giving her 65 percent of every dime I made every time we hit the track, it wasn't any real money. It would take me forever to save for a place of my own at the rate I was going. Meanwhile, Erica had other schemes going on with Cream and she was buying nice clothing, jewelry, and doing her in pleasing ways. I felt like the wicked stepchild, me and my daughter. Whatever my daughter needed, I paid for it. Erica only did us that one solid when I first arrived to appease me, to get me to work for her. But now, she wasn't buying my daughter shit. I did for Eliza with my blood, sweat, and tears. It made me rethink and evaluate my whole situation.

I wasn't going to be able to come up on my own while I was still living with Erica and owing her all the time, and with Cream steady trying to fuck me while Erica wasn't looking. The nigga was a creep. The way he would look at me and come on to me, I wanted to knock his teeth out. I wasn't about to degrade myself that low; it was bad enough strangers got a piece of me on the track, but it wasn't about to happen where I slept, shit, and ate, and especially with Erica's man. He thought he was a pimp, but he was nothing but a lowlife, a disgusting pig who took advantage of women.

Cream was one of a few pimps who tried to persuade me to come under them, to choose them for protection in the streets. See, I may have been living with Erica and Cream, but I wasn't his bitch. I was too stubborn and boorish to have that muthafucka brainwash me into slaving me into lifetime prostitution. He was trying to acquire a stable of hoes to work for him. I wasn't about to be one of them.

However, Cream was the least of my problems. It was a pimp named Cat Head I strongly felt I needed to worry about. He was a gorilla pimp in the game who frequently saw me working the track. When the warm weather started to come around, more and more girls started to come out to the track. I got into a few conflicts with a few of Cat Head's bitches in Hunts Point. We fought over territory like drug dealers; like in the game, working the right territory mattered and Cat Head and his bitches tried to drive us away from the prime real estate. But Erica and I were the ones working Oak Point Avenue from top to bottom when it was freezing cold, and we weren't about to be run off like some scared bitches.

However, Cat Head took a serious liking to me. He would approach me when the chance came around and he would try to smooth talk me into joining his stable. He would mention how all of his hoes were well taken care of, from clothes, money, food, having a nice place to stay, to traveling around the country. He took his bitches to Vegas, Miami, Atlanta, Chicago, L.A, and Houston and so on. They were area code hoes. He was pimping some beautiful women and he wanted me.

Cat Head made Cream look like a bitch. Cream was all talk, trying to play a part that he wasn't meant to play, where Cat Head was nothing but bark, a fierce muthafucka who buss his gun and could be extremely violent. Whenever Cat Head came around, I noticed Cream was never around. He would disappear like Houdini, and then come back around whenever Cat Head was done talking to me. I had no respect for a bitch-ass nigga. Also, I wasn't about to join Cat Head's stable. I barely liked working with Erica, and the reputation Cat Head had was a whirlwind of trouble coming my way, no matter where he took his girls and how much he spent on them. Word on the street was it was hell in his camp if you disobeyed any of his rules or if he felt you disrespected him. He was a gorilla pimp, and those the niggas any bitch would stay away from. He was known to use brute force, excessive head twisting and arm breaking, and some of his bitches be looking rough and beat up.

But the nigga was persistent in trying to snatch me up and it was becoming scary. It got to the point where I felt he would try to kidnap me.

"You's one fine-ass bitch, Diamond. You and me, we would kill this game and make so much money. Shit you'd be straight fo' the rest of ya life," Cat Head said to me. "I would definitely make you my bottom bitch."

No matter what he said or how he said it, I wasn't interested. But gorilla pimps are excessive and relentless. The word no wasn't in their vocabulary.

The Juice Bar was a place where everyone went to unwind, get their drink on, listen to good music, and mingle. The pimps came to the place to show off their stable and solicit their women. The ladies came to display their sexy attire and maybe catch them a baller, and the ballers came to flaunt their wealth and probably snatch up a juicy booty call for the evening. Everyone came to the Juice Bar on East Gun Hill Road. It was a decent spot in a mutual location.

I was there with Erica sipping on a cognac and Coke. We sat at the bar talking, enjoying the evening, and chilling. She was buying and I was drinking. I needed the break. However, Cat Head walked into the place with two of his whores. He was dressed in a pricey leather bomber, a Yankees fitted, and bejeweled in white gold and diamond, looking excessive with his wardrobe.

The minute Cat Head noticed me seated at the bar with Erica, he grinned and came my way. He looked at me like I was some object of his desire. His dark eyes became fixated on me like a fat kid seeing cake and he strode my way leaving his two hoes behind and rubbing his thick goatee like some smooth cat daddy. He was bad news.

I sighed. Erica saw him coming and she looked annoyed too. He was upsetting her. In her mind, Cat Head was a threat; him desperately trying to snatch me away was like taking food out of her mouth. I was temporarily under her thumb until I came into my own and taking 65 percent from me every night did add up into a healthy profit. I was a bad bitch and everyone wanted me, for pleasure and profit.

"Ladies, good evening," Cat Head greeted us and invited himself into our personal space. "Diamond, you look lovely tonight, like always, but I can make you shine like brand new every day, you hear me. I'm like Robin Hood, I take from the rich, the poor too, and I keep it and my bitches prosper from it too," he added. He pulled out a wad of hundred dollar bills and flossed in front of us.

"Drinks on me tonight, ladies, I can afford it," Cat Head boasted, peeling off two hundred-dollar bills and dropping it on the bar.

Yeah, it was ladies now, but bitches later. He was a wolf in sheepskin clothing, the devil in disguise. And I wasn't impressed with his flaunting. He placed his arm around me and continued his flattering pimp talk like I really cared.

"You know when all the buildings fall pimpin' gon' still be tall, you feel me, and a woman's legs are her best friends, but sometimes best friends have to part, ya feel me? 'There are two types of people: those that talk the talk and those that walk the walk. People who walk the walk sometimes talk the talk but most times they don't talk at all, 'cause they walkin'. Now people who talk the talk, when it comes time for them to walk the walk, you know what they do? They talk people like me into walkin' for them.' You feel me?"

What the fuck? What was he talking about? And I swear he got that from some famous movie. But he was preaching to me this pimp talk as if I was listening. He was intense with his words and wasn't gonna give up on me. He talked to me like getting down with him was going to fix all of my problems, seducing me with fortune and moving to some utopia.

I wasn't sold and I was never gonna be sold.

I wanted him to go away. He wasn't. He invaded my world like an alien invasion. No one in the place wanted to mess with Cat Head because of his reputation, but when I saw Tango walk into the Juice Bar I felt it was all about to change.

Cat Head was still talking to me while I was looking at Tango. Inwardly I smiled seeing Tango. I admit I liked him. I liked the way he talked to me, and even better, the way he would look at me, like I was the last woman on this earth and he was going to cherish me. It made me feel good, especially now with the hell I was going through.

He came alone, clad in a leather jacket and Tims and looking finer than ever. He had this image about him that screamed bad boy and I was attracted to him. He noticed me and smiled, but that smile was short-lived when he saw Cat Head cozying next to me and being in my ear. The look that shifted in his eyes said he was fuming. He must have felt that Cat Head was trying to snatch his dream girl away from him, because I suddenly saw hell in his eyes.

He marched my way with a scowl. In my gut I knew it was a storm coming. Cat Head and Tango mixing with each other, it was like a tornado meeting with a volcano. It could get ugly, become a natural disaster, and affect everyone around them.

"Hey, beautiful," Tango said to me coolly.

He hugged me right in front of Cat Head and smiled. He didn't even acknowledge Cat Head. His attention was fixated on me like Cat Head was invisible. I could tell in Tango's eyes that he was annoyed by this pimp talking to me. But he gave me my love and attention first like he was claiming his woman. But I wasn't his woman, not yet anyway. He glared at Cat Head almost daring him to say something. And Erica stared at them both like she was waiting for the main event to happen.

"Let me buy you a drink," said Tango.

"She already got a drink, nigga," Cat Head chimed.

"Nigga, I wasn't talkin' to you," Tango barked. "And who is this muthafucka anyway?"

"You fuckin' wit' the wrong pimp," Cat Head rebuked him. "Don't worry who the fuck I am."

"Nigga, get the fuck out my face and stay the fuck away from my woman."

"Nigga, ya bitch chose me!" Cat Head exclaimed.

He was now talking crazy. I chose no one. But right now I had these two thugs ready to fight over me. I sat in between them and felt like I was in a tug of war match. They weren't physically pulling me, but the way they went back and forth with harsh words about me, it was dizzying.

"Y'all need to fuckin' chill," I chimed. But my statement was nothing but a whisper from a mountaintop and they were down at the bottom. They didn't hear shit.

"Nigga, she don't need ya fuckin' kind in ya life. You fake-ass pimp," Tango insulted him. "Step the fuck off!"

"My kind? Nigga, my kind make five to ten grand a night, you broke-ass nigga. I can give my bitches whatever they fuckin' want and travel the world. What can you give her, muthafucka?" Cat Head retorted.

By now both men were in each other's face, glaring at each other and shouting heatedly. The entire place took notice. I didn't know what to do. The inevitable was about to happen. Tango continued to be very disrespectful toward Cat Head. He said words to the pimp that would get any man killed. But the challenging look in Tango's eyes told me it was about to get uglier and their argument continued to ensue right there.

It came out of nowhere, the attack on Cat Head. The beer bottle smashed against Cat Head's head shattering to pieces and staggered the man. I stood aghast. It was so sudden. Shards of glass from the broken beer bottle got on me. Tango was all over Cat Head, pummeling the man down to the ground with his fists. He hit him and hit him, and hit him, not missing, and every punch coming from Tango seemed to echo like an explosion happening in the room.

"Don't fuck wit' me, nigga," Tango screamed out.

Cat Head was on the ground trying to protect himself, but Tango was a beast. It looked like a housecat trying to fight a lion. Tango was too strong. He hit Cat Head so bad I thought he killed him. And then he punched and stomped the man viciously into the floor. Tango raised his Timberland boot almost like fifty feet in the air and they came crashing down on Cat Head like the sky was falling. He howled from the pain and looked completely helpless.

"You a bitch-ass nigga!" Tango shouted.

It was almost like he zoned out and attacked and attacked like his own life had been threatened. I was afraid Tango was going to kill this man.

I just stood there and watched. I admit, I was part turned on and part scared at the brutality. It took a few workers at the bar to pull Tango off of him. He roughly resisted, but they finally pulled Tango off the man; it looked like they had to lift a concrete slab off a crushed man. He was adamant to finish what he started. It took hordes of security to pull Tango away. The man was difficult to control, but eventually they did and the beating came to an end.

When I finally got a look at Cat Head, he looked like he had been mauled by an animal. He was bleeding profusely with his face bruised and swollen, and he couldn't get off the floor. Tango demolished Cat Head's vicious and gorilla pimp reputation. He embarrassed the man in front of everyone.

Tango looked at me and then shot his eyes down at the man he had severely beaten, and then he suddenly took off, leaving the bar like it was on fire. I assumed the realization suddenly hit him that he was on parole. And that fight would have been a straight violation.

"Damn, he fucked him up," Erica said, smirking.

She hated Cat Head. I kind of felt sorry for him.

There was a part of me that wanted to go chase after Tango and make sure he was okay, but I didn't. I figured he would be long gone by now and maybe he wanted to be alone. I watched two of Cat Head's whores help their pimp off the floor. They both looked traumatized by the ass whooping he received. When Cat Head was finally on his feet, he flipped out. He roughly pushed them away, screaming, "Get the fuck off me, I'm okay! I'm fuckin' okay."

No, he wasn't. He looked like chopped meat.

He placed his hand on his face and it was coated with blood. He used the bar for support, still looking dazed and confused, bleeding from everywhere. I hadn't seen an ass whooping like that in a long time. It was almost humorous to witness, but insane to watch. The man was in terrible shape. His edgy and flashy persona was tainted now.

Cat Head turned and looked at me deadpan. We locked eyes but he didn't say a word to me. He was trying to tend to his injuries but the nigga needed a hospital. I didn't know what he was thinking, but I had a clue; he probably blamed me and wanted to know everything about Tango. It wasn't about to end with them.

His two whores went back over to attend to their pimp's injuries, but once again he heatedly shoved them away and cursed at them. His pride had been bruised just like his face. I felt it was time for us to leave. Erica and I removed ourselves from the bar with Cat Head licking his wounds and trying to put his pride back together, shouting, "I'm gonna find that muthafucka. He's dead. He's fuckin' dead!" but not even a skilled surgeon could piece that back together. What was done was done.

As we exited the Juice Bar, Erica said to me, "You must be like the Helen of Troy, got these two beasts fighting over you."

I wasn't amused by her statement. I was worried about Tango. I looked around for him outside but he was nowhere around.

Erica hailed a cab; I was also concerned about Cat Head storming out of the bar to confront me. I kept looking back at the entrance thinking the worst, this mean pimp taking his anger and frustration out on me. He definitely wasn't a stranger to putting his hands on women. I knew Erica and I weren't any different and we were vulnerable outside. It also only took one phone call for him to make and he could have his goons on the hunt. I had a daughter to go home to.

Thank God a gypsy cab stopped for us. Erica and I quickly climbed inside with me feeling like this was the chariot to heaven. I wanted to get home.

"We goin' to Edenwald, 233rd Street," Erica told the driver.

He drove away with me gazing through the back window seeing if there was going to be any activity bursting out from the Juice Bar. But nothing; my view faded the farther he drove. I finally turned around and felt relieved. But this wasn't about to be over. I knew it deep in my heart. Tango assaulted a man who was known to shoot muthafuckas even though he was a pimp; he was a dangerous man. And I couldn't help but to think what was going to be the outcome with me and him when he saw me on the track at nights. I already had static with his bitches, but since Cat Head had a thing for me, the confrontations didn't get that serious. Would that now all change?

But still, I thought about Tango and couldn't help to be worried about him. He was on my mind, from the time he stormed out of the bar up until I climbed into bed and closed my eyes to get some sleep. It had been a hectic evening.

Two days later, I saw Tango lingering in my lobby. I walked out of the elevator and was startled to see him standing there. I was alone, heading toward the bodega to pick up a few snacks and some drinks for the night. It looked like he was waiting for me, but how did he know where I lived?

"Tango, what are you doing down here?" I asked him.

"I came to talk to you," he replied.

"How did you know what building I lived in?"

"It wasn't hard. I got peoples who know you."

I looked at him. He seemed cool, stoic. He wore a leather jacket and stood some distance from me. The look in his eyes appeared that he was upset about the other night. He had his hands in his coat pocket and fidgeted in front of me somewhat.

"I'm sorry 'bout the other night, Mouse. It shouldn't have gone down like that," he said.

"You put that man in the hospital."

"I just lost my temper. Seeing that nigga up on you like that, it made me snap."

"But you put my life in danger too, Tango. Cat Head, he's not gonna forget about this. He's gonna come looking for revenge when he get out of the hospital. I know for a fact he got goons on standby," I told him.

"I got ya back, Mouse. I can take care of you. I can protect you."

"How?" I barked out. "How you gonna take care of me, Tango? You just came home. You don't have a job and you live at home wit' ya mother, if I'm correct."

"I'm workin' on sumthin'."

I sighed. It was good to hear a man say he was going to look out for me, but I had to come to my senses. Tango wasn't even in the position to take care of himself. He may have been the man back in the days, but now it was different; times had changed.

Tango stepped closer to me. He stared at me with his drunken eyes of passion and said, "I'm gonna make sumthin' happen, Mouse. I promise that you won't have to work the track any longer or worry 'bout Cat Head."

"Why, you planning to do sumthin' to him?"

"Nah," he drawled out.

"Then what?" I wanted to know.

"It's just sumthin' I'm tryin' to come up wit'."

"You just came home, Tango. Don't do anything stupid to get locked up again," I said.

I was starting to care about him. I really wanted something to happen between us, but in the back of my mind, I doubted that a relationship could actually work with him. He was an ex-con, and from my experiences with ex-cons, they always find a way to get sent back to prison and leave their woman alone, probably pregnant. I already had one baby daddy inside. I wasn't about to make the same mistake again.

"Trust me, Mouse; I have a friend who's lookin' out for me. He's trying to get me this job in construction. It pays thirteen an hour, and after six months of probation, I can jump on their benefits. Once I get put on, you get put on. I'll find us a place and take care of home. I'm tryin' to do it right this time. I need to do it right. I can't go back inside. I did ten years and I'm gettin' too old for the same ol' shit," he proclaimed.

I smiled. It sounded nice. He sounded genuine about the job. I could see Tango doing construction. He had the build for it. He always seemed like he could be a hardworking man. We both wanted a way out of the hell we lived in, and if Tango was the man for me, then I would follow him wherever.

"When do you go for the job?" I asked.

"Next week."

"Good luck."

He smiled. "Thanks, 'cause I'm gonna need it."

"You'll get it."

"You think?"

"I know you will," I said with conviction.

He gazed at me. Once again, the way this man looked at me, it was every woman's dream. He stared at me like I was his queen and the most beautiful and wonderful woman on the planet. He came closer and pulled me into his arms. Tango hugged me lovingly; his firm arms were wrapped around me like a blanket. He was strong, but always gentle with me. Next thing I knew, we were kissing each other passionately and I found myself not wanting to be let go from his arms.

Was it possible that I was actually falling in love with him so quickly? I didn't know what it was, but I didn't want it to ever end. I wanted to be taking care of and treated right. God knows that my last relationship ended up in chaos and regret. Rico did me so dirty and foul, that I swore off men forever. But Tango, he felt different. He didn't have much right now, but he felt so real and bold.

I kissed him and found myself drifting into this utopia. I had my eyes closed and daydreamed about the suburbs, living like the Cosbys and finally leaving the ghetto for good. Did I believe Tango could actually make it happen for me? I didn't know. I wanted to believe it. I needed to believe in something. Every night that I was on that track degrading myself for little cash, allowing strange men to ravage my body, it took something away from me, piece by piece.

We finally stopped kissing each other and I exhaled. Tango still held me in his arms and I wondered when this started to happen: a relationship. But it crept up on me. He didn't care about my past, or my ways; he cared about me and my daughter. I couldn't push him away. I couldn't be scared of the uncertain. I just had to go with it and believe this one was going to work out.

Chapter Fifteen

Tango

Tango took a few pulls from the cigarette between his lips and exhaled. It was a quiet and cool night as he heard his friend Mike say, "You know she used to be Rico's girl."

Tango didn't know Rico, but he heard niggas inside speak his name. Rico was supposed to be the new heavyweight on the street before his untimely incarceration on numerous RICO charges.

"Rico?"

"He used to hustle for Red back in the days, came up under the Bronx Nation Crew," Mike explained.

Tango didn't care for the man or his reputation. He had his own hardcore reputation, one probably fiercer than Rico's. His only concern was his future with Mouse. He thought about her a lot and wanted to be with her in so many ways. It was bad that Mouse had to witness the ugly side of him, but when he saw the pimp making moves on the woman he was crushing on, it made him snap with rage. He hated to be a jealous man, but he was, undeniably.

But Tango had other issues on his mind. He didn't get the construction job. They turned him away like a bad habit. He didn't have the courage to tell Mouse the bad news, so he stayed away from her for a day or two and needed to think about other alternatives to make some money. She needed help, an escape from her hell, and he was determined to give her that.

Tango and Mike lingered on the building rooftop with the view of the sprawling projects looking ghetto and picturesque in the night. The projects were quiet tonight, no gunshots and no police sirens crackling in the dark. The two men had their privacy to talk. Mike looked swallowed up by the puffy winter coat he had on. His style and jewelry were an indication of his wealth. He was a heavy hitter in the streets, well known and high ranking with Bronx Mafia Boys.

Tango looked nonchalant. He gazed at the Bronx glimmering with lights that stretched for blocks and seemed endless. Literally, it felt like he was on top of the world again, peering down at the cold Bronx street with admiration for his hood. He reminisced about his past for a moment and shared a cool conversation with a good friend.

"I don't give a fuck 'bout any Rico; nigga name don't ring bells around me," Tango replied.

"Well he did wit' Mouse. That used to be her boo. The nigga got her and her best friend pregnant at the same time, and that's her baby father now and when that nigga had it, she had it. You feel me?" Mike said. "He spoiled her, gave her whatever she wanted."

Tango didn't respond, he continued smoking the Newport and listened to his friend for over twenty years drill in his head about Mouse being used to having the finer things in life. He had to open his eyes to his realization: he was an ex-con on parole, no job, no cash, and probably an uncertain future; and he liked a woman who was used to having the best. So he thought.

"And her pops was straight loco, Hector was a straight lunatic out in these streets back in the days."

"Yeah, I remember that nigga. He used to run wit' Latin Kings back in the day," Tango said.

"Yeah, you know 'bout the nigga, and a shorty like that you know the only way to hold her down is having that bank nigga," said Mike.

"I'm on parole, Mike, fo' a minute; and I gotta get my paperwork up, something to show my PO. A nigga need a fuckin' job, my nigga. You know what I'm sayin'. I'm used to always havin' money in my pocket and this struggling shit, I can't get wit' it," Tango proclaimed.

"What type of work you lookin' for?"

"Anything, my nigga. I just need some real bread in my hand," Tango replied.

"I mean, I got some shit fo' you, my nigga, if you ready to put in that serious work."

"What kind of work?"

Mike didn't reply right at that moment. He took a few pulls from his cigarette too and gazed at the lively borough. He kept his look away from Tango and said, "You hungry right?"

"Nigga, I'm fuckin' starving right now. So what kinda work you talkin' 'bout?"

"A few 187 needs done," Mike replied coolly, like he was talking about mechanic work on a car.

Tango didn't say anything for a minute. He took one final pull from the cigarette and flicked it off the rooftop. He blew smoke out his mouth and nostrils and looked pensive. He turned to look at Mike and asked, "How much?"

"Five thousand a head."

"Y'all banking like that?"

Mike reached into his coat pocket and pulled out a wad of hundred dollar bills. He showed it to Tango and said, "It's a new day, Tango, and ya lethal-ass could get this money out here. You was no joke back in the day, and we could use a hitter like you in the crew."

"Y'all beefin' wit' YGC, right?"

"Man, fuck them *putas.*"

Tango was indecisive. He just came home, and ten years was a long time to be away from home. But times were hard. He felt lost. He wanted a change but society still labeled him a menace to society. It felt easy to pull up his old roots and plant what he knew what was going to grow best for him: putting in that work on the streets.

Tango locked eyes with his old friend and had to ask again, "Five thousand a head, huh?"

"Five stacks, my nigga. It's easy money to be made for easy work, especially for a killer wit' ya skills."

"Yeah, it's easy work until a nigga get caught."

"Tango, you too smooth and skilled to get caught," Mike replied.

"Then explain the ten years I just did."

"Nigga, we all pay our dues in this game, just chalk it up as the cost of doin' business out there," Mike replied.

Tango chuckled. "The cost of doin' business huh?"

"Hells yeah."

"Then business is gettin' pretty expensive out this muthafucka," said Tango.

"Nigga, who you tellin'?"

Tango felt reluctant in taking the job, but hard times were crushing down on him and he had a beautiful woman and her daughter to take care of.

"You do this for us and we got you, my nigga. You ain't gonna have to worry 'bout a dime ever," Mike assured him.

Tango sighed heavily. His mind was telling him no, but hard times was pushing him to say yes. "Who y'all want got?"

Mike smiled. "This *puta* named Dodo."

"I want half right now and another half after the job is done. And I do it on my terms," said Tango.

Mike nodded, approving to the stipulations to the deal. "Whatever you need, Tango. Welcome back."

Tango didn't respond; instead he lit another cigarette and looked aloof. He had to do what he had to do, even if it meant shaking hands with the devil again. A man had to survive somehow and support the ones he loved.

Chapter Sixteen

Sammy

I rolled over in the bed and didn't find Power lying next to me. He had gotten up earlier I assumed and went somewhere. It was quiet. And it was early in morning and the bright sun was percolating through the floor-to-ceiling windows in the master bedroom. I was buck-naked in Power's king-sized bed, relaxing on silk sheets, and was still recovering from last night's sexual tryst. My pussy was still throbbing and still hungry for some dick. Power had put that dick down inside of me and I admit it was good. He weighed a ton and fucked like a rhino, and the fact that he ate my pussy out for almost an hour, I came like a fountain.

His place in Upper Manhattan on the west side was superb: giant flat screens everywhere, plush furniture, pricey artwork and historical pictures displayed everywhere indicating Power had some culture, and a chandelier so big it looked like it came from a concert hall. I felt like a princess in his small kingdom. We started dating, and quickly started fucking. I found myself becoming very fond of Power and catching feelings.

He took me shopping in the city on Fifth Avenue, and I was in and out of high-end stores carrying a handful of shopping bags and couldn't wait to show off my new outfits. We had dinner at a few five-star restaurants and toured the city in his Bentley. Power spent money on me and I paid him back by being with him, becoming his woman. He didn't want me to be with no one else and urged me to quit stripping at the club, which I planned to do. I hated the job anyway and with Power willing to help me out, I was going to quit soon.

I crawled out of bed and walked to the floor-to-ceiling windows. I gazed out at the city coming alive in the morning. I remained naked while gawking at the Yellow Cabs below swarming the city streets and walls of peoples heading to work via the subway or public transportation. It felt good waking up somewhere new and plush. I didn't want to leave the master bedroom. I wanted to enjoy it all day and take advantage of what his money had to offer. The place was so comfortable, it made me feel secure. My son was staying with Ms. Wilson again. She was watching Danny so much that the babysitting money I was paying her was paying her rent. I did miss my son, but I also had to do me so we could both eat. The club was paying my bills, but getting intimate with Power was my opportunity of a lifetime.

I lingered by the window with my naked frame pressed against the glass and thought about so many things. Where was my life going? I thought about Mouse and our fallout. I wondered what she was doing because I hadn't seen her around lately. I did miss her. I thought about my music career and wondered if it would ever spark again. After seeing that shit on BET, it broke my heart. Then Rico came to my mind on a beautiful morning like this. He was steadily calling me collect, pressuring me into sneaking drugs into the prison. He needed to make some money and wanted to use me as his mule. I was totally against it. He came with his threats and I felt I was being backed into a corner.

I knew I had to do something about that nigga and do it soon. He was becoming a serious problem. The man was a virus and he was about to spread if I couldn't find the cure for that muthafucka very soon. I couldn't get sick off this nigga. I couldn't allow my past to destroy me. I had Danny and myself to worry about.

The bedroom door opened and Power walked in. He was clad in a long house robe and talking on his cell phone. I turned and looked at him. He acknowledged me with a smile and wink of the eye. I smiled back at him. He was talking business. I was ready to be with him again. I remained standing by the window and watched him take a seat on the bed and curtail his phone call.

"Yeah, make sure you do that for me, 'cause you know I got you. But look here, I got other important things to take care of; call me later tonight," said Power.

He hung up. I now had his undivided attention.

"How did you sleep?" he asked me.

"I slept really good. Your bed is so soft and last night was great."

"I'm glad you liked it."

I went over to him and straddled him. He wrapped his huge arms around me and held me snuggly. I pushed my breasts into his face and he started sucking on my nipples. He undid his robe and I slid it off of his shoulders. He had nothing else on underneath. He was completely naked. Power was tall and heavyset with stocky legs and a wrestler of compact build. His upper body and arms was swathed with tattoos. His physique resembled Rick Ross, but he was much more handsome and probably had money as long as Rick Ross, too. The only thing missing was the thick black beard.

As Power sucked on my nipples, I cooed and rubbed his glistening bald head. I loved touching his head. It was so smooth. He was also so neat. His charisma was fulfilling, and his generosity was unforgettable.

"You miss me?" he asked.

"Yes, baby," I replied, kissing the top of his head as he had one of my tits in his mouth with his tongue lashing against my hard nipple. He was hard again. He was a big man down below. I felt all eight inches of him rising between my thighs. I wanted to feel him again. He made me cum like a geyser and was about to have me go off the wall like Michael Jackson's first album.

"I wanna fuck again," Power said.

I wanted the same thing. I was ready for another round. Last night we used condoms, but this morning I allowed him to penetrate me raw and when I felt him inside of me, I hoped I wasn't going to regret it. But I was so horny that I just wanted to feel the dick in me. He thrust upward inside of me, clutching and squeezing my ass. I rode that dick; he continued sucking on my nipples and fucking the shit out of me.

I moaned into his ear. He grunted into mines.

We moved like a wave of water. I felt him balloon inside of me with his big dick cemented into my stomach. The room started to heat up. We locked lips, kissing fervently. Power raised his hand up to my hair and tangled his fingers in it. His other hand he pulled up to my face and cupped my cheek in his hand. His breath was warm. I started to breathe heavily as his dick went in and out of me. My breasts were crushed against his thick, hairy chest. I was so damn tight and dripping wet with his dick sliding up in my pussy with its full length.

I gasped as I felt the full magnitude of his big dick thrusting inside of me. The way he fucked me I felt my legs turning into jelly. He flipped me over onto my stomach and decided to hit this pussy from the back. I felt my legs spread wide like Pac-Man's mouth and he slid into me, but was careful not to press all of his weight onto me, knowing he was a big dude and I was a petite but busty female.

I couldn't control my body and my voice and started to moan out, "Oh Power. Ooooh, fuck me. Ooooh fuck me. Faster, faster, oh shit!"

I felt shivers go through my spine and I held on to the sheets feeling my pussy opening up like a good book to read. He fucked me harder and faster. I felt my body ready to come which was inevitable while feeling every inch of Power's dick thrusting inside my pussy. I was pressed between the bed and him, feeling the dick ravish me. I came hard and raised my head in the air and howled, feeling my white creamy liquid saturating the dick inside of me. I moaned with delight. Power continued fucking me. I got mines now it was time to get his.

"Shit, your pussy is so fuckin' good," he cried out.

He continued to hit this pussy from the back. I felt him about to come soon. I was on my hands and knees now, legs spread, gripping the headboard and trying to prevent myself from going through it. He fucked me hard and fast, vigorously. He gripped my hips and screamed out, "I'm gonna fuckin' cum!"

"Pull out," I told him.

I couldn't chance getting pregnant. It was bad enough I let him fuck raw, but I didn't want to feel his fluid inside of me. I prayed that he would pull out. He fucked me hard, slamming his balls against my ass and the more he remained inside of me, the more worried I became.

"Pull out," I repeated.

He didn't say anything, but moaned and groaned and was caught up in the sexual haze of pleasure my pussy gave him. He continued gripping my hips and slamming his dick into me. Then, it happened: he came inside of me, his white cum dripping out of my pussy; and it was running down my shaking legs.

He finally pulled out after exploding inside of me and released a satisfied, "Ah, now I feel so much better." He was still hard, his dick glistening with white cum and my pussy liquids.

"Why didn't you pull out like I asked you to?" I griped.

"Baby, you felt too good to pull out," he replied.

I was somewhat perturbed, but I didn't dwell on it. There was always the morning after pill and I prayed he didn't have any STDs. I could only curl against him and look up at the ceiling. My mouth was open in a beatific smile. I hadn't been fucked like that in a long while. I closed my eyes and stretched out, the sheepish smile lingering about my lovely lips.

Power got up after ten minutes of lying with me and started to get dressed.

"Where you goin'?" I asked him.

"I got some business to take care of."

He was a busy man. I couldn't complain. He allowed me to stay at his place until he returned but I had to get back home to my son. I got dressed along with him and he took me home. Power stopped his Bentley in front of my project building. I kissed him good-bye and I stepped out looking like a superstar, sporting a wrapped miniskirt in glazed leather with my matching jacket and a pair of stylish heels. All eyes were on me and it felt good. Power drove away and I walked into my building with my head up and ready to start a new day. It was a beautiful day and spring was right around the corner. After a cold and brutal winter, finally the leaves on the trees were budding and the flowers were starting to blossom and I was ready to blossom right along with them.

It was going to be my last week working at Crazy Legs. I wanted to make some extra money and even though Power was willing to support me, or help me out, I was a bitch who was used to making her own money. I admit I was a bit skeptical in quitting because I didn't want to depend on any man doing for me and my son. But I needed a change in venue. Despite Kawanda, I had the rest of these bitches hating hard on me. I had snatched me a baller, and not just any baller, one of the most prominent men in the game. Bitches spent years dancing in the club trying to snatch them up a hustler who would take care of them. I did it effortlessly, without a sweat. And then these men were wolves, hungry for my pussy and willing to do whatever. It was becoming too risky working at Crazy Legs. Just the other day a stripper was raped and beaten while trying to make a few extra dollars to support her daughter. And then there were the continuing raids from police officers rushing into the club to make noise. When the owner didn't pay them off, the police came knocking and they came knocking hard, arresting underage girls and anyone with warrants. And then between the drug use, the thievery, and the fights in the place, it felt like I was working on a battlefield. I needed to get out.

I got on the stage scantily dressed in a red fishnet camisole and thong set. It was a very sexy set with long sleeves, fence-net camisole top with cutout front and back detail, with matching laze trim thong and leg garter and my six-inch stilettos. The DJ started to play my song, "I Choose You" by Keyshia Cole. I closed my eyes and started dancing seductively to the song.

If it ain't you, it's not worth it
No matter what I do, nothing's working

I started to twirl myself around the stage pole and work my body for the men who crowded around the stage. I came out my top, tits showing, and bounced my booty to the song. It was a love song but I worked magic to it. I had these niggas hypnotized by me and only me. It was my last week there and I planned on going out with a bang. Money was being tossed at me; it was only singles, but they were adding up.

Ten minutes into my act and I caught the shock of my life. I stood there in awe, taken aback when I saw Search had come into the building. He was with a small entourage. We locked eyes and I didn't know what to say or do. I knew recently he had signed a deal with Def Jam and he and his peoples probably came into Crazy Legs to celebrate. He smiled at me. The club gave him and his entourage the VIP treatment. I realized that the show must go on no matter who was in the building. I continued with my exotic routine, trying not to be embarrassed. I got nude on stage and Search gazed stoically at me. He liked me for years; I wanted to tease him. Shit, I wanted to hate him for giving that whack group my song and seeing the video on BET. I yearned to have a few words with Search. I felt ambivalent about seeing him in there. I didn't know if I wanted to curse him out or apologize to him.

I still wanted to become a music star. Search was well on his way to becoming the next P. Diddy while I was working hood strip clubs. The scales were tipped lopsidedly. I was talented and beautiful; there was no way I shouldn't be on the top charts and gracing my beauty in front of millions of fans. I wanted a second chance. I ached for it.

Search left the VIP area and walked over to the stage. He had a fistful of cash and fixated his eyes on me. I was nervous. We used to be best friends; now it felt like we were the worst of enemies. I was hoping he come over and apologize to me, maybe talk reconciliation in my ear and was willing to get me back on track. But he didn't. The muthafucka looked blankly at me and tossed a wad of money into the air my way, like I was some regular, buck-naked bitch on stage he didn't know. He smirked while making it rain on me. It was an insult to me. He treated me like I was some slut. I couldn't hold my tongue any longer.

"So it's like that, Search! That's how you fuckin' do me?" I exclaimed.

"It's how you did yourself," he retorted.

"Fuck you," I inadvertently shouted out in front of everyone.

"No, fuck you! You a grimy bitch, Sammy, no lie. I was willing to give you the world and make it happen, for you and Mouse, but what you did to me, it's unforgivable," he heatedly replied.

"You and Macky are both fucked up in the head and I hope you end up just like him," I exclaimed. The minute the words escaped from my mouth, I regretted it.

"Macky?" Search uttered with a raised eyebrow. "Yeah, I heard you went out on a date with him, and now he's dead."

I said too much and said it around too many people listening. *Did I just dig my own grave?*

"You were fuckin' Macky?" Search asked. I could hear the rage in his voice.

"Yeah, I fucked him," I lied. Why did I lie, only to get him jealous? Search had a thing for me and the way he hurt me, I wanted to hurt him right back. Even if it risked exposure of the crime I committed.

"You were always a fuckin' slut," he snapped.

We started to argue heatedly in front of everyone. My customers stood aghast at what was happening. Search now became suspicious of me probably being involved with Macky's untimely death and it was the last thing I needed in my life.

I got so mad that I hurriedly collected my money and my things and rushed off the stage. I wanted to get away from him. I didn't want anyone to see the tears that started to shape in my eyes. I was hurting and it was deep. I went into the dressing room to change into my street attire. I was done for the night and wanted to go home. Search had disrespected me in front of everyone and I couldn't tolerate it. I was so angry with him that I wanted to see him dead, but I wasn't thinking rational. Search was still bitter about everything I put him through over time, from ignoring his romantic feelings for me to the drama and the embarrassment I put him through; and now the shoe was on the other foot and he was the one having the last laugh.

Chapter Seventeen

Mouse

I couldn't help but to notice how good and stylish Crystal looked as she climbed out of her boyfriend's burgundy Benz that sat on twenty-two-inch chrome rims. She was Gucci the fuck down from her shoes to her expensive handbag and looked like she was ready to hit the red carpet at a Hollywood event. Hair done up, nails done, Crystal was my bitch, EBV for life. But now she moved on to better things. She was dating Dodo, a major muthafucka with the YGC. He was a heavy hitter moving serious weight in the Bronx and making a name for himself. She was in love with him. I wanted to be in her position, being with a man who was financially stable and in love, but I refused to deal with that hustler's lifestyle. It came with too much drama. Tango and I were sort of working out, but we both were still struggling and learning about each other. The good thing though, he told me he had gotten the construction job, so things were starting to look up.

Crystal spotted me exiting the bodega and we both became jovial. "What up, bitch," she screamed happily my way.

"Crystal, what up," I hollered with a smile from ear to ear. I hurried her way and we hugged each other like sisters. It was so good to see her again. "Look at you, looking like a star," I said.

"My man takes really good care of me," she replied.

Dodo climbed out from the driver's side and walked our way. He was tall, at least six foot one with a lean build, narrow face, and intense hazel eyes. He was light-skinned with no facial hair and a pretty boy who was tatted up with gang literature and bejeweled in gold and diamonds indicating his wealthy status. It was all street money.

He looked me up and down and then said to Crystal, "I'll be in the store, babe. You need sumthin'?"

"Yeah, get me a pack of Newports and some chips."

He nodded and left her side. He was very attractive, I admitted that, but he reminded me of Rico all over again: trouble. However, I kept my feelings about Crystal's man all to myself. It wasn't my business to let her know how I felt about him. We all had to learn on our own. I sure did. It was about reconnecting with an old friend and not creating any drama with a friend. I already was not speaking to Sammy; I didn't want to burn any more bridges.

"So what you been up to, Mouse?" Crystal asked.

I wasn't ready to tell her my business. My life was harsh. Her life was peaches and cream, for now anyway. "You know, just tryin' to do me and make it happen."

"How's ya daughter?"

"Eliza is doin' good," I replied pleasantly. "She's getting big."

"I bet she is. I gotta see her."

"You do."

"You look good though, Mouse. I see you gaining some weight, and in the right places. Look at you, bitch, all thick and shit," Crystal said, eyeing me up and down. "Damn, ya booty got big, too."

"Me, I see you all styled up and shit. Gucci."

"Mouse, you always knew I loved my Gucci, and my man is taking very good care of me. He's spoiling me and I'm spoiling him, if you know what I mean."

I chuckled. "Yeah, I know what ya mean."

"You still beefin' wit' Sammy?" she out of the blue asked me.

It was a question I didn't want to hear or answer. My facial expression told her the truth: we weren't speaking still. I hadn't seen Sammy in months.

"Damn," Crystal uttered. "I hate to see y'all not talkin'. Both of y'all were tight like sisters."

"Yeah, we were," I chimed. "But everything comes to an end."

"Y'all didn't though."

I started to get upset that Crystal brought the bitch up. I didn't know what she was trying to resolve, but it wasn't going to work. And if she continued bringing Sammy up, then we weren't going to be friends anymore either.

"Sammy is yesteryear," I said. "I'm tryin' to move forward and do me."

"I feel you, Mouse. I got a good man and we got a nice spot of our own in Yonkers and he gonna buy me my first car soon. I'm doin' good, yo. I feel good, I look good and me and my boo comin' up," she proclaimed affably.

"That's good to hear, Crystal. I'm so glad to see you happy."

"I am happy."

I wished we all could say the same. Seeing Crystal looking like a million bucks reminded me of the time Rico had me looking like that. It was all a dream nevertheless, an illusion, something very transient, smoke and mirrors, because when it comes to an end, crashing down, which it will eventually, the wifey, the girlfriend of that hustler, gets hit the hardest. Really hard. It almost felt like I was underneath the Twin Towers when they collapsed and I became trapped underneath the rubble. Yeah, it sounded like I was hating on my girl, but I wasn't. I knew the future and I wanted to warn her, but I knew she wasn't going to listen. We never do.

Crystal and I talked briefly, catching up on old or lost time. Her smile was golden and the bling she wore could purchase a small house. Dodo had his woman shining like a gem. She was riding around the hood in his chariot and feeling like royalty. It's what hustlers do: make their woman feel supreme so we could be blinded by the bullshit coming soon.

Dodo stepped out of the bodega with his lips pulling on a Black & Mild. He looked around his surroundings briefly and I could tell he was packing heat underneath his jacket. He screamed danger. He looked our way and hollered to Crystal, "Babe, let's go."

Crystal jumped to his command. She quickly said to me, "Mouse, we need to definitely link up and talk. I'll call you."

I watched Crystal accelerate her way toward the parked Benz and get into the passenger side. Dodo gazed at me briefly and climbed into the driver's side. I wondered why he was looking at me like that. Did he think I was telling his woman something? I wasn't. But I wasn't about to worry myself. I had problems of my own.

The Benz ignited and Dodo slowly pulled away from the curb with Crystal looking my way, waving magnanimously at me. It was the end of a generation, the EBV girls: Edenwald Blood Vixens. We were nothing to play with back in the days; now it felt like we were a dying breed. Tina dead. Meme and La-La locked up, and a few others dead too. I felt like the last bitch standing.

I walked away feeling nostalgic. What happened to all of us? We used to be tight like a mayonnaise jar. Now we were all scattered in different directions, most of us struggling, surviving while few of us were making it.

I really hoped to see Crystal again.

I had this rhyme inside my head that I was ready to spit. It was about old times:

There was a time when we used to shine like Chicago crime

Thought we were gonna age together like fine wine, we were so lifted

Too high to ever come down, the stratosphere was our mile high

BX we rule, the streets we moved . . . any beef comin' through

We devoured like cooked food, we were the five points on a crown

It's hard to see time split us by, when we were solid like concrete

Unbreakable like Alicia, platinum like Keyshia.

Tina was the beast; La-La and Meme were dynamic in these streets,

Crystal was the prettiest to be, and Sammy and me,

We ran like kings, fuck queens . . . now things are no longer what they used to be

Time made us enemies; distance made us a memory, damn,

I want things to go back the way they used to be

When EBV was forever on the scene.

Chapter Eighteen

Tango

Tango remained hidden in the dark like a shadow, being still and quiet like a church mouse. But he was no mouse. He was a killer on the hunt. He was armed with two twin 9 mm's fully loaded and cocked back. He remained obscured in a rundown Chevy up the block, watching the area like a hawk.

For a week he stalked his prey and planned to execute the hit very soon. He needed the money and couldn't afford to make any mistakes. The man he planned to hit was a dangerous figure in the underworld. One mistake could cost Tango his own life. Tango needed the money badly and had to execute the kill just right. It was do or die. He wasn't thinking about his parole. He was concerned about survival.

Clad in all black, wearing latex gloves to conceal his prints, and keeping his identity a mystery with a ski hat pulled low over his eyes, he watched Dodo climb out of his pricey Benz and walk into the legendary Tosca Café on East Tremont Avenue. His Benz was parked across the street. The area was populated with people, but it was the one chance Tango had to strike. Traffic was sparse. It was 11:00 p.m. and everybody was either where they needed to be or on their way there soon.

Tango departed the rusty Chevy and made his way toward the burgundy Benz. He pulled out a Slim Jim from his jeans and looked around to see if anyone was watching; there wasn't a soul in sight. He proceeded to break into the Benz using his skills and within seconds, he popped open the locks and broke into the car. His plan wasn't to steal the car, but to lay low in the back seat. It was dark and the back seat of the car was roomy enough to conceal himself inside without anyone noticing. The black he wore helped his cover.

Hours passed and Tango was a very patient man. He didn't move an inch. He was like a statue lying on the floor cloaked by darkness and feeling the cold seeping through. He refused to move. He wanted to have the element of surprise. Dodo wouldn't see it coming. It would be unexpected. His breathing was labored and his eyes wide open.

After several hours of waiting and hiding, finally there was some activity. The driver door opened, but unexpectedly, the passenger door opened too. A young woman climbed into the seat while Dodo slid behind the wheel. There was laughter and conversation.

"You my number one bitch, right?" Tango heard Dodo say to the female passenger.

"You know it. I love you, baby," she replied.

"You better. I take care of my woman."

"Yes, you do, and I'm gonna take care of my man."

The ignition started. The people in the front seat were unaware that they had unwanted company lurking in the shadows of the vehicle so closely. Tango remained undetected and cautious. They couldn't even hear him breathing. The radio was playing and the Benz started moving. As Dodo drove, the female passenger, Crystal, unbuckled her seat belt, smiled seductively, and leaned her face into his lap. She unzipped his jeans and removed the growing thing she desired to place between her full lips.

"You always know how to treat ya man," Dodo said.

"Sssshhh, baby, and just drive while I do me," she whispered.

Crystal jerked his dick with her manicured fist and then wrapped her lips around his erection and sucked him off. Her head bobbed up and down in the driver's seat while Dodo cautiously navigated his prized Benz through the Bronx Streets. The slurping sounds of dick sucking echoed to where Tango hid. He wasn't moved by it. He had a job to execute and he figured now was a better time than never.

Abruptly, Tango popped up like a jack-in-the-box, emerging from the back seat and startling Dodo and Crystal. He thrust the gun to the back of Dodo's head. Crystal popped up with her eyes widened with fear.

"You move and you die," Tango said coolly.

"Oh my God. Oh my God," Crystal exclaimed frantically.

Tango pointed the second 9 mm at her head and she panicked. "Chill out, bitch."

"Please, don't kill me."

"I said shut the fuck up!" Tango advised her to do through clenched teeth.

Crystal muted her whimpering and looked like she was ready to pee on herself.

"You know who the fuck I am?" Dodo exclaimed.

"Just drive where I tell you to," Tango calmly said to him.

"You a dead man, muthafucka," Dodo continued to taunt him. "You're dead!"

Tango smirked. He knew Dodo's threats were empty to him. He had the advantage. He had the gun. He had the upper hand and harsh, threatening words didn't scare him easily. They didn't scare him at all.

Tango instructed Dodo to drive to a secluded and dark area in the Bronx, a street named Edgewater Road. It was a place not too far from Hunts Point. It was an industrial-looking place by the Bronx River with scrap metal yards, truck routes, and dozens of industrialized businesses stretching for several blocks. It was late and everything was closed down for the night. It was a ghost town until dawn cracked the sky.

Tango made Dodo park on a barren block, in front of Sal's scrap metal yard. The Benz sat nestled between a cement truck and a rundown box truck on the block meager with cars. He still pointed both guns at their heads. He made them shut off the engine and sit. Dodo was fuming, but the barrel of the gun pressed against the back of his head made him vulnerable.

"Who the fuck are you?" Dodo demanded to know.

Tango didn't answer him. He glanced at the frightened woman. She was beautiful but teary-eyed. She sat frozen in the passenger seat refusing to take her eyes off the man who held her at gunpoint. Tango leaned closer to Dodo and lowly said to him, "This ain't personal, but only business."

Hearing that, Dodo knew what was about to come next. And before he could cringe for impact or react, multiple shots went off, lighting the car up in a flashing, bright light.

Bak! Bak! Bak! Bak! Bak!

Five shots in the head and point-blank range made Dodo slump over the steering wheel with his blood and brains spattered all over the dashboard and windshield. Crystal madly screamed from seeing her boyfriend's murder. She tried to eject herself from the car, but she was too late. Tango aimed and fired, striking her multiple times also in the back of the head and back. She hardly managed to get the car door opened, but her body lay drooping from the passenger seat toward the cold pavement. The entire front seat was coated with blood and decorated with death, as two bodies lay contorted for homicide to investigate.

Tango exited the car in a calmly manner. He looked around; there wasn't a person in sight and no security cameras watching. He had picked the right area to kill them at. He didn't want to kill the girl, but she was at the wrong place at the wrong time; he considered it a casualty of war. She was an unforeseen dilemma. The bitch had to go.

Tango made his way up the block like he was taking a walk in the park. He tossed both guns in the Bronx River and planned to burn his clothes. They had specs of blood on it, and anything involving that night it was going to be incinerated. Today, DNA and forensics could incriminate the sharpest criminal. The good thing, he was $5,000 richer. He already had plans for the money: get himself his own place and have Mouse and her daughter move in with him.

Chapter Nineteen

Sammy

I could hear Power cursing and ranting in the next room. He was furious about something. Something bad had happened. He had been on the phone for an hour talking to various people while I was in the bedroom doing my nails and watching cable. We had just finished fucking when his cell phone rang. He saw the name on the caller ID and immediately picked up. It was one of his trusted lieutenants on the other end.

"What?" I had heard Power shout out. "When the fuck this happened? Dodo!"

He had sprung up from my side and gone into the other room. I minded my business, but by the tone of his voice, I knew he was upset and angry. I heard the name Dodo. I had no idea who the fuck he was. My assumption was he was killed last night. I put on my panties and bra and was about to get dressed when Power burst into the room with this sullen look about him.

"Everything okay?" I asked.

"No, everything is not fuckin' okay," he snapped at me.

"I was just asking. I'm sorry to even ask."

"You getting smart with me?" he barked.

"No, I wasn't."

He glared at me. He looked like a changed man suddenly. Whatever happened last night he took it to heart and was trying to take it out on me. I didn't want to argue with him. The past few days had been good with him. I had quit dancing at Crazy Legs and he was taking care of me. But I was also looking for other means of employment/income. I was trying to get back into the studio and record my demo. Power promised he was going to manage me and take me to the top. I heard it all before and I wasn't about to get caught up in the hype. I wanted to believe him, but when niggas get in their foul moods they start acting funny and promises start to vanish.

Power was in this nasty funk. His attitude became ugly. He started tossing things around, breaking shit, and cursing loudly. He was extremely angry. I figured it was best to stay out of his way. I was leaving. He saw me getting dressed and barked, "Where the fuck you going?"

"I'm leaving," I spat back.

"Leaving where?"

"It's obvious you are in a foul mood, but you ain't gotta take it out on me. Look, I'm sorry whatever happened to ya friend, but don't blame me," I said to him.

"You were listening in on my conversation?" he exclaimed.

"No, but you was speaking loud enough for the whole neighborhood to hear."

He scowled. He charged my way. I braced myself, but he didn't attack me. He came in my face. "You know what, bitch, get the fuck out then! Leave, bitch!" he shouted heatedly.

"Gladly," I screamed back.

I started to grab my things in the bedroom and rushed to get dressed. Power started tossing my clothing at me. I swear, Dr. Jekyll and Mr. Hyde, a case of bipolar at its worst. My shit was scattered all over his bedroom. I snatched up my jacket and shoes, and rushed toward the door with an armful of clothing. I was heated. I was done with him. But the minute I got to the door, Power came running behind me. He was now apologizing.

"Baby, I'm so sorry. I didn't mean to take it out on you," he said with a look of regret aimed at me. "I got some bad news."

I didn't want to hear it. He cursed at me. He disrespected me. He called me out of my name and I was supposed to take his bullshit? No!

"Baby," Power cried out. He grabbed me by my arm trying to stop me from leaving. I jerked myself free from his feeble grip. "Sammy, I need you right now!"

I stopped my exit. I sighed and slowly spun around to face him. This man was over six feet tall and weighed a ton, but the look in his eyes was sincere like a little puppy. He was a notorious figure in the underworld, but yet, he could be as warm and cozy like a teddy bear and funny and intelligent, and he had me opened. I was falling in love with him. When he shouted "I need you," something came over me. I needed him too.

He stepped forward with his body action looking apologetic. He reached for me; I hesitated in walking toward him. He continued with, "I'm sorry; it's just some serious shit went down last night and I overreacted toward you. My nigga Dodo was murdered brutally, shot five times in the back of his head."

"Oh my God," I uttered.

"Shit is hectic right now. They found him dead with some bitch in the car," he informed me. "Niggas is ready to retaliate."

My man needed me. I accepted his apology. It was me now reaching for him and pulling him into my arms to console him. It was no doubt Power was a gangster and a coldhearted killer himself, but the murder of a man named Dodo had him teary-eyed and distraught. I didn't get it. I was sure Power had seen death before, probably many times over, it came with the game, so why was he so upset about this one?

Power was on his knees in front of me. I was standing over him. He had his arms wrapped around my legs and he let the tears flow. He was crying like a baby.

"Who was Dodo?" I asked.

"He was my cousin and we were close," he explained to me.

Now I was really saddened.

Power grieved briefly while he kneeled down in front of me. It was a thing to see. I knew he didn't cry much, and if so, it was definitely not in front of people. It would be considered being weak in front of the wolves. But he let himself go in front of me. I respected him for that. He proved to me that he wasn't just a coldhearted and emotionless man; he had feelings too, feelings that he displayed in front of me.

I was pleased. And I was going to be there for him.

I spent the morning with Power, but when noon came around he left to handle his business in the streets. I was left alone in his Manhattan apartment, but I needed to get back home to my son. I was worried about Power, but Danny needed me too. Power was on top of the food chain and his clique, the Young Gangster Crew, was at war with the Bronx Mafia Boys. It was bloodshed on the streets and shootings were occurring every day. The police had their hands full; the neighborhood was besieged with violence and terror and they were calling Edenwald "Eden War."

I couldn't wait around Power's place worrying about him. He was a grown man doing grown-man business and he was able to take care of himself. I left and took the train back to the Bronx. If Power needed me, he had my cell phone number. I had other priorities to take care of.

When I got home, the streets were talking heavily about the murders. Dodo was well known and respected and YGC was out in full effect ready to avenge their fallen homeboy. The police were out too, trying to maintain order in a place that felt lawless.

The minute I walked into my building lobby, I was greeted by Kawanda and her friend, Brandy, stepping out of the elevator. The minute Kawanda saw me she hit me with the news.

"Sammy, you heard?" she said.

"Yeah, some nigga named Dodo got killed," I replied nonchalantly.

"Crystal too," she said.

I thought I heard her wrong. "What?"

"She was shot in the car wit' Dodo," Kawanda told me.

It felt like I got hit by a Mack Truck. The news came so sudden that it almost knocked me off of my feet. Crystal was my friend, my bitch, EBV. We grew up together and now she was dead. My nonchalant attitude suddenly altered into tears of pain and disbelief. I couldn't believe Crystal was dead. I couldn't believe someone murdered her. But then again, I could believe it. She wasn't the first friend murdered and, it was sad to say, I knew she wasn't going to be the last.

I cried. It was a coincidence that she was murdered with Power's first cousin. But by who? Whoever killed them both, they had a world of trouble coming their way.

Chapter Twenty

Mouse

Tango was so good with her, my daughter, Eliza. He played with her and treated my daughter like she was his own. I smiled. I could tell my daughter liked him too. She laughed, he laughed, and I smiled broadly. I loved every minute of it. It was a great thing to see, my daughter looking like she had a father in her life. Tango was also coming through with his promise. He had money coming in, and with it he took me and my daughter out to eat at Olive Garden. He told me to order whatever I wanted, and I did. I ordered the shrimp Alfredo and their well-known bread. We had wine. We talked. We were celebrating his new job. He was making me feel like a whole new woman. I haven't eaten dinner this good in so long that when it went into my mouth, I almost came from the cuisine.

Like promised, Tango moved me out of Erica's place and we stayed at his mother's home for a week until we got our own place. Erica was upset; she tried to persuade me to stay, telling me that we made a good team together, but we didn't. It was all bullshit. She was the one making money, not me. I was being paid peanuts, and it was my legs spreading and my lips sucking. Cream had nothing to say. He was too pussy to intervene and I didn't know what Erica saw in that bastard. It was clear as day that he was using her, and it was even clearer to see that she was using me.

I met Tango's mother and she was sick. She reminded me of Erica's grandmother. We stayed in his small bedroom, but it was comfortable. Tango made sure of that. If we were hungry, Tango fed us. He bought a bunch of DVDs for us to watch, and some kiddy movies to entertain my daughter. He was doing a lot for us. He was showing me that he really cared and wanted to be with me. I fell in love with him. And when my daughter would fall asleep, we fucked on the floor while Eliza had the bed to herself.

The first three nights we used condoms, but after that, I let him inside of me raw. The feel of his flesh penetrating me had me ready to explode. He loved every minute being bareback in the pussy and we fucked in every position. I cooed in his ear as he would grind between my legs. I did everything I could to please my new man. I promised I was his only. My life on the track was over with. The few months that I did it, it made me feel ugly, but Tango loved me for who I was and he wasn't concerned with my past but only our future together. I was ready to believe in him. He was trying and it actually felt like it would work out. He even had an apartment ready for us to move into soon. It was a two-bedroom in the West Bronx, away from Edenwald.

For once in my life, I was happy.

Yes, I was genuinly happy. But with that happiness there's always some bad news lurking, some tragedy ready to ruin your day.

I was out with my daughter in the park. The weather was finally breaking and spring was coming. It needed to come faster. I felt it in the air and in my mood. The leaves was trying to sprout in the trees and the flowers were starting to blossom. It was a fifty-five-degree day and I wanted to cherish every minute of daylight and warmth we had. It had been a brutal winter for everyone: snow, freezing rain, cold wind, and trials and tribulations. I did the unthinkable this winter, prostituting myself to survive. But I survived; we survived, Eliza and I. After abruptly leaving the shelter for whooping some bitch-ass and freezing in the streets with my daughter, begging for shelter, and hungry like an Ethiopian, I felt it in my bones that I was going to make it. I had a good man in my life with a good job doing construction and we were about to move into our new place soon. Tango talked with the rental office and the landlord and through grace, favor, and my man having the gift of gab, we were finally approved to move in.

I was ecstatic.

It was going to be great getting away from Edenwald. With all the violence happening around there, it was becoming a dangerous place to live and I didn't want my daughter around it. Ironic though, I remembered a time when Sammy and I were a terror in the projects, not giving a fuck. Shit, we helped the crime rate go up back in the days. EBV, we did it all, we been through it all. But now, I felt like a changed woman.

I was seated on the bench at the Stars and Stripes playground in Seton Park. I watched Eliza try to run around with the other children, but she was just too little to keep up. My baby was trying though. She was only one year old and could run her little behind off, falling every so often. I would help her move through the playground, picking her up and guiding her through the slide and monkey bars making sure she didn't hurt herself. We played on the swings and ran around awkwardly. I was laughing and she was laughing, having a great time. Afterward, I wanted to take her to McDonald's for a Happy Meal. It was becoming the perfect day.

There were other mothers in the park with their children, but I didn't know any of them and they didn't hurry over to befriend me. In fact, they were older and looked my way with some disdain in their eyes. I didn't know what they had against me, not knowing me at all, but I could tell they were stuck-up bitches who probably thought I was some young ghetto mother getting pregnant every year.

I ignored their foul looks and enjoyed being with my daughter. Only she mattered, no one else.

We spent over an hour playing in the park and I soon became exhausted and hungry. Eliza was also beat. I picked her up in my arms and carried her. Our next stop was to get something to eat. It was still somewhat warm and the sun was still in the sky shining down on me. I loved the sun. I loved the spring and summer and couldn't wait 'til we started having days like these continuously. Jack Frost and Frosty the Snowman could keep the winter; it was a desolate season.

I crossed Baychester Avenue with Eliza falling asleep in my arms. I didn't have a baby carriage to push her in, couldn't afford one. However, Tango promised to buy one for me since he knew how much of a burden it could be carrying my daughter everywhere. He wanted to do so much for Eliza and I couldn't wait.

I headed into the projects. My first mission: back to Tango's mother's place to change my daughter's diapers, freshen up a bit, and then head to nearest McDonald's. I was craving a Big Mac meal and some large fries. I just wanted to sit somewhere quiet and eat my meal in peace and not be bothered.

When I got to the building, there was Dandy exiting the lobby. She was only sixteen years old but had an ugly scar across her face that stood out. It was put there by Denise and her bitches last year; twenty-five stitches she received. They hated on my girl because she was too pretty, looking like Lauren London and down with us. Sammy and the crew retaliated heavily, and put Denise in the hospital. I was glad they did it and I wished I had gone along for the ride and added my slice of violence. But I had been too caught up in Rico at the time. Dandy was a sweetheart and she didn't deserve that kind of brutality toward her.

Despite the nasty scar that showed, she was always upbeat and positive. She was still in school and doing her thing. She wanted to become a fashion model, but she felt it was impossible because of her scar. But she was still very pretty and these niggas were still sweating her.

When she saw me, she didn't smile. Dandy always smiled when I came around, and she was always buoyant with conversation, but this time her expression was sullen. Her eyes showed great sadness and she gazed at me with this catastrophe showing on her face. Something was wrong.

Dandy walked my way like she had concrete shoes on, slow and heavy, and when we got face to face, she broke down in tears.

"Dandy, what's wrong?" I quickly asked. I couldn't console her because Eliza was in my arms and sleeping.

Dandy looked at me with her eyes flooded with tears. She was crying heavily. It was hard for her to speak at first. I thought some muthafucka put his hands on her, did something wrong to my friend. I was ready to fight for her, but she finally voiced to me what was wrong.

"Crystal is dead," she exclaimed.

"What?" I screamed out. I didn't want to believe it.

Dandy, still crying, said to me, "She was shot to death in the car with Dodo last night."

I felt myself about to break down with Eliza in my arms. Shock wasn't even the word on what I felt. I uttered out, "I just seen her the other day and she was good."

Dandy was in full-blown tears and heartbroken; so was I. It felt like I wanted to fall out. I had to leave. I had to get away. I just walked away clutching Eliza tightly and hurried into the building. The tears started to fall like raindrops and the pain overcame me like a thousand stab wounds penetrating my skin.

I couldn't get inside the apartment fast enough. No one was home and I was thankful for that. I figured the home aide took Ms. Davis for a stroll around the block since it was a nice day out. I went into the bedroom and placed Eliza on the bed and then I went into the bathroom, dropped to my knees, and sobbed like a baby. Another friend of mines was gone, murdered. We were dropping like flies. So many memories of Crystal were spiraling through my head. We had good times and bad times. Who was next? Who was left? It was me, Dandy, Winter, she doing a bullet in Riker's Island, Chyna, she skipped town for a while because she had warrants for her arrest, and Sammy.

Sammy. I thought about Sammy a great deal. Even though we were still at odds with each other, I missed her. She was my best friend, my sister, and I thought no one or nothing could ever separate us. I guessed we were wrong. With Crystal dead, time wasn't on our side anymore. It never was.

I sobbed in the bathroom for a long time. I had the door locked and the lights off. I wanted to be alone. I didn't want to be in Edenwald anymore. I didn't want to be around it anymore: the drama, the violence, the murders, and mayhem. I wanted a very different life now. I wanted to escape somewhere far. I wanted to rewind time and bring us all back together again, when we was solid, happy, and strong together like a brick wall.

Crystal's death hurt me a lot. It could have been me so many times, gunned down in the streets. Growing up,

Sammy and I, all of us, we always toyed with death. We always thought we were invincible. We risked our lives doing what we thought was fun for our gang and down for our crew. Now when you find yourself surrounded by death, the bulletproof vest comes off, and so does that giant S on your chest and you find yourself vulnerable to the world around you.

Tango came home to find me lying in bed with my sleeping daughter. It was early evening and the house was quiet and my pain was still throbbing through every inch of my body. He looked at me and already knew something was wrong. I didn't hesitate to let him know what it was.

"My friend Crystal is dead," I cried out.

He walked over and pulled me into his arms to console me. "What happened?" he asked.

"She was shot dead in the car with her man last night."

"That's crazy," he replied.

I cried in his arms and he didn't leave my side all night. He stayed with me. He was my rock. He was becoming the man I dreamed to be with. I loved him.

Chapter Twenty-one

Mouse

McCall's Bronxwood Funeral Home on Bronxwood Avenue was jam-packed with people coming to Crystal's home-going service. It seemed like every resident in Edenwald came out to say good-bye to Crystal. She was definitely loved and was going to be missed. It started to rain, so a lot of folks crammed themselves under the green awning trying not to get soaking wet from the rain. The street was lined with parked cars; passing traffic and the hustlers came out in droves to give their respect to Dodo's girlfriend. It was mostly YGC niggas in attendance. They were very saddened about Dodo's untimely and violent demise. They wore his gangster image on black T-shirts with RIP DODO, YGC 4LIFE embroidered on the front at Crystal's funeral. Dodo's home-going had been the previous day and a mob of people also came out to show their respect.

I came alone. Tango volunteered to watch Eliza for me while I attended the home going to say my good-byes. At first I was reluctant to attend, but if it was me, Crystal would have come to my funeral and I couldn't do my friend dirty like that.

Before I walked into the funeral home, I talked to everyone outside: Dandy, Erica, Nico, Sophia, Quinn, and a dozen other people from my old building. Everyone was saddened about what happened. We were talking. I found myself zoning out, thinking about old times. It was good to see old faces again, but it was hard to say good-bye.

I spent a half hour lingering outside feeling hesitant about going inside. I took a deep breath and entered the funeral home. The large foyer was flooded with people, family and friends. There was a mixture of folks clad in black and some in everyday attire, some faces I knew, and some I didn't. Some people were crying and other people were having a normal conversation about anything and everything. I moved toward the room where Crystal was lying in the casket. I could smell the flowers; they were all over. I signed the register book to show I attended the funeral. I then walked inside the main room. The rose room was able to accommodate 400 people. There wasn't an empty chair in the place. I slowly walked down the aisle with the white and gold casket at the end of it. I could see Crystal's body slightly protruding from the casket. The closer I came to it, the more tears I let go.

Her family was seated in the first two pews; they were weeping heavily, hugging and consoling each other. I saw her brothers and sister, but didn't acknowledge them. I couldn't. I was barely holding myself together. I was able to stand over the casket and gazed down at my departed friend. I was choking up, but maintaining. The mortician did an excellent job with her. She didn't look like plastic like so many others people I done seen. Of course her expression was deadpan and she was nicely wearing a beautiful white lace sleeveless gown. It looked expensive and it made her looked like an angel.

"Good-bye, Crystal," I whispered to her.

I leaned forward and kissed her on the forehead. I said my piece to her and pivoted on my heels and hurried away, feeling the anguish overcoming me. I hurried up the aisle, wiping away tears and wanted to leave the building. It was just too much to deal with.

I went back outside. It had stopped raining, but the sky was gray and the area too gloomy for my taste. People loitered around everywhere, looking casual. I needed a fuckin' cigarette. I asked a friend of mine for a Newport. I placed the smoke into my mouth and she lit it for me. I took a few needed pulls and exhaled. I closed my eyes for a moment and heaved a sigh and tried to free my mind from the awareness that one day, someday, we were all going to meet that same fate. I just hoped my day wasn't coming anytime soon. I wanted to see my daughter grow up. I wanted to live my life normally.

I took a few drags from the cancer stick and noticed the black-on-black Bentley parking across the street from the funeral home. Both doors opened and my eyes became transfixed on this burly, dark, and tall guy who anyone couldn't miss. And then I saw her exiting the Bentley: Sammy. She looked good. She was dressed to the nines and he looked dapper down in a black three-piece suit. They both crossed the street arm in arm and Sammy looked like she was the first lady of the United States.

I stood there and gawked at her, feeling some trepidation inside of me. I hadn't seen or spoken to Sammy in months, and there she unexpectedly was, coming my way with this mammoth of a man towering over her. But I figured she would come to show her respects at Crystal's funeral.

We both were friends with her, but no longer friends with each other.

Chapter Twenty-two

Sammy

I stepped out of Power's Bentley in my black lace sheath dress with the round neck and short sleeves and my legs showing like I was a supermodel. The dress was expensive, but money wasn't an issue to Power. He was spoiling me and I loved it.

I still couldn't believe Crystal and Power's cousin Dodo had been killed. Yesterday I accompanied Power to his cousin's funeral; now he was coming with me to my friend's funeral. It was only right. They both died savagely and it became a heinous crime in the hood. Who shoots a man five times in the back of the head at close range, and then my friend three times? It was a straight-up contract hit and overkill, and Power was ready to go to war with everyone. But word on the streets was that BMB was responsible for Dodo's death and it was an OG who killed him. I could smell it in the air: more carnage and mayhem to come. I wanted Power to play it safe and stay out of the streets for a while, but he was too hardheaded and too stubborn to believe he was also a marked man. He was determined to find the people who murdered Dodo and he wasn't gonna hide like some coward.

As we crossed the street, I saw her, standing there gazing at me like she had seen a ghost. She stood alone with a cigarette between her fingers. She looked good and was still shapely in the right areas. I saw that giving birth didn't make her fat or homely. Mouse was still Mouse. It was becoming an awkward moment, though, us running into each other like this after the way we left things. I didn't smile or frown, but stared at Mouse like she was a stranger to me for a moment.

I walked right by her and didn't say a word. I knew she was stunned, but I didn't know what to say or do. It was unexpected and I felt like a deer caught up in bright headlights on the fast freeway. I froze. Besides, I had to pay my respects to Crystal and her family and get my mind right. Mouse didn't say anything to me. She continued smoking her cigarette and looked the other way.

I walked into the funeral home and was greeted by a wave of people and they were giving me their condolences like I was family to her. I mean, we definitely were family, but we weren't blood related. Power was by my side and he was armed with a Glock 17 underneath his suit jacket. It was holstered and he was ready for anything that came his way. He scowled and stood like a giant in the room. People were shocked to see me with him. I just wanted to get everything over with.

I slowly walked into the next room where my friend's body was placed in this beautiful eighteen-gauge white and gold casket and it was inundated with flowers and pictures of Crystal from young to recent. There was mourning among the silence in the room. I approached slowly and took a deep breath. I stood over my friend's well-dressed body and said my good-byes. The tears fell from my eyes like a leaky pipe. I took another deep breath trying to control my outcry. I was stronger than that. I wasn't going to burst out into tears. I wiped them away, spun on my sandals, and addressed her family to my left. I hugged her mother and siblings and then walked away with puffy eyes.

Power was talking to some of his soldiers who came to the funeral. They were in some deep conversation nestled in the corner away from prying ears, discussing something privately. He was so engaged in talk with his cronies he didn't even notice me come out and exit the building.

I thought Mouse would have left already, but she was still lingering out front near the corner, alone. I stared her way. She noticed me watching her and didn't avert her eyes from me. Once ago, we were so inseparable and dangerous together; now I didn't know if I should stay or go—say fuck her and distance myself from that bitch, or go over and see how she was doing. We both said and did some terrible things to each other. We both got pregnant by Rico and we both went through hell.

Mouse gawked at me. I did the same. I wanted to fight it, turn around and leave, but I couldn't. It felt like something magnetic was making me stay and making me want to go over and talk to her. Why was it so hard for me to take the first step? She could take the first step too. I was letting my pride interfere with going over to her. I mean, I was the one who fucked Rico long after she was dating him. I did fuck her man behind her back and got pregnant by him. But she came at me on the corner, cursing and attacking me and she disrespected me. Was it becoming too hard to forgive and forget, especially after we had so many years of friendship and being sisters to one another?

Fuck it, just go over and speak to her, my inner voice screamed at me.

I swallowed the feeling called pride and decided to take the first step. I walked her way. We both were fixated on each other. There was still some tension between us. The last time we spoke it was on a sour accord. I took what felt like my umpteenth deep breath and coolly said to Mouse, "How you been?"

"Look, if you came over to gloat 'cause you got some nigga pushin' you in a Bentley, then don't," she snapped at me.

"First of all, I didn't come over for that. That's ya fuckin' problem, Mouse, you always jump to conclusions. I just fuckin' came over to say hi," I retorted.

We both scowled. It was already starting off rocky and fucked up. I was ready to walk away and say fuck this shit, but I didn't. My sandals stayed rooted to the ground in front of her. It felt like some invisible force was keeping me there. I said to myself, *let's try this again.* At first, it wasn't going too good. We both had a lot on our minds and frustration that we yearned to release.

"You know you a foul bitch, Sammy. I trusted you and you fuck my man behind my back?" she exclaimed.

I countered with, "I warned you 'bout that grimy nigga in the first fuckin' place, Mouse. You don't ever fuckin' listen!"

"So you ain't had to fuck him! You were my friend, my sister!"

"And I said I was sorry."

"*Eso fue asqueroso. Has estado una perra,*" Mouse hollered.

"Mouse, *no he venido a discutir,*" I shouted back, saying I didn't come to argue with her.

Our words were harsh at each other. We yelled and pointed fingers at each other. We started to draw attention to ourselves. We cursed each other out in English and in Spanish. It got to the point where we started drawing a larger crowd near us and then we both felt we were disrespecting Crystal's family and Crystal at her funeral. We took our conversation a block away to talk privately.

Alone and away from everybody, we both seemed to cool down. We had allowed our emotions to get the better of us.

"Mouse, I'm so sorry about everything that happened. If I could change time, you know I would and take away the hurt that I caused you. But I can't. I miss you. You were my best friend and the one person I could always talk to," I confessed. "And look at us; we fought over Rico. Are we serious? He's an asshole."

Mouse chuckled slightly. "Yeah, he is an asshole," she agreed with me with a minor smile.

With everything that was going on, my emotions started to get the best of me and my eyes started leaking like a faucet.

"I'm sorry too, Sammy. I just got caught up in everything and I wanted to have true love, but it was all a lie. I missed you too," Mouse proclaimed genially.

We had been away from each other for too long. It felt like we were falling apart without each other. I was the glue; she was the stitch. We hugged each other and reconciled right there at Crystal's funeral. It felt like her death was bringing our friendship back together again. We realized life was too short and we couldn't take the little things for granted. We needed each other to survive in this ugly and forever changing world.

Mouse needed my friendship again and I needed someone to deeply confide to.

It was still a little rocky between us, but we were patching things up and trying to make us solid again. I didn't want argue anymore and I didn't want to lose her again. Mouse and I had history; she was as much a part of me as I was of her.

When I left the funeral home I had all the contact information I needed to reach Mouse. She had moved back into Edenwald, but she was about to move soon and she wasn't staying too far from me. We promised to link up with each other the following day and catch up on lost time. With our reconciliation, it felt like a huge weight had been lifted off my shoulders.

I couldn't wait to talk to her. I had so many things to tell her about and I was sure she felt the same way.

Chapter Twenty-three

Tango

Tango played with Eliza in the living, pretending to be the boogie man, but with a large smile and goofy attitude. The one-year-old laughed and giggled loudly as Tango tickled her and swung her around the room like she was a bird. He was great with her. It was obvious Eliza was very comfortable around him. He didn't mind babysitting while Mouse went to her friend's funeral. He made snacks, they watched cartoons, and he was being a father to her. It was his family now, and he didn't care about Rico. Rico was incarcerated and missing out on a good thing: family.

It was getting late and Tango put Eliza to bed. He read her a bedtime story and tucked her in, and then he kissed her on her forehead and smiled. She was an angel in his eyes and he wanted to be in her life. Tango slowly shut the door and went into the living room. His mother was in her bedroom sleeping. He was alone for now. He went to the window and gazed outside. It was dark out and Mouse hadn't come home yet. He wasn't too worried about her. She was a big girl who could handle herself and he trusted her.

He didn't feel remorseful about murdering her friend, Crystal. It was just a job he had to perform. Crystal was simply at the wrong place at the wrong time. She had seen his face. He had to protect himself and his family.

But it did hurt him to see Mouse cry in his arms for hours. He consoled her. He felt he had no choice. He was responsible, but she would never find out because Tango planned on taking it to his grave. If the truth ever came out, there was no doubt in his mind that she would leave him for good. He could never lose her. Mouse thought he was working an honest job doing construction; she had no idea that he became a killer for hire.

Tango remained still by the living room window, watching the activity below his apartment. He lit a cigarette and observed the local hustlers hugging the block and the fiends continuously back and forth lurking for their next fix. With the weather becoming warmer it brought out everyone, from the hardworking residents to the despicable who swamped the neighborhood with their bad habits and transgressions.

Tango puffed and exhaled. Killing Dodo and Crystal didn't bother him as much as he thought it would. He was five grand richer and able to do for his family. That's the only thing that mattered to him: providing.

Mike wanted him to do another hit. This time it was brothers: double the pay, five grand for them both. That was $10,000 in his pocket and he could do a lot with ten grand. He knew Tango was able to handle it, pull it off smoothly and be ghost. Mike was content with the Dodo hit. Tango accepted the job; now it was a matter of timing.

From the window, Tango saw Mouse on her way home. She had walked from the funeral home to the projects. He smiled. He missed her. He doused his cigarette and planned to greet her as she stepped into the apartment.

Moments later, he heard her fidgeting with the lock and she entered. The minute Mouse walked into the apartment, Tango snatched his woman into his arms and hugged and kissed her passionately. It was an unexpected greeting for Mouse, but she was thrilled to have a man miss her the way he did.

"I missed you, baby," said Tango amicably.

"Where's Eliza?"

"She's 'sleep. I put her to bed an hour ago."

"How was she? She wasn't too much trouble?"

"She was fine. We had a good time. We played, watched cartoons, ate junk food, and she wore me out," said Tango.

Mouse smiled broadly.

Tango squeezed his woman gently in his arms and said, "Now it's your turn to wear me out."

"Is that so?"

"Yup."

The two kissed. Tango didn't ask her how the funeral was because he didn't care. Mouse seemed to be okay, being in a good mood. He just wanted some pussy. It seemed like they both were in a good mood. Mouse was happy to see Sammy again and having their much-needed talk. Tango wanted to love his woman down. He guided her toward the couch and pulled her down on top of him, where she straddled him. They kissed again and his hand was up her shirt, squeezing her tit. But before anything got started, Mouse said, "Let me go check on Eliza."

She removed herself from his lap and went into the bedroom. The door was ajar; she peered inside to see her daughter sleeping soundly. It was so angelic. Mouse smiled. She went into the bedroom and kissed her daughter on her soft, rosy cheeks.

"Things are definitely getting better, Eliza," Mouse whispered in the room. "Yes, they are. I have a good man in my life and he seems to be a keeper, and tomorrow, you gonna meet my best friend. We came a long way, baby girl, and Mommy is always gonna be around to protect you. I love you."

Once again, she kissed her daughter on the cheek and went back into the living to join Tango. He was seated on the couch buck-naked with his cock out, rock hard and ready for her to ride it.

"Tango!" Mouse shrieked lightly. "Oh my God."

"What? I told you that I missed you."

"I see you did." Mouse smiled provocatively.

Tango definitely knew how to make a bad day good.

The life he was now leading, it was natural to lie to his significant other. When Tango called Mouse to say he was going to be home late from work, Mouse asked why. "Some of my coworkers wanna take me out for a few drinks tonight, to celebrate my first month on the job," he lied. It came easily, one lie after another. But Tango felt he was protecting his woman from the truth. He was out stalking the Broughton brothers, Penn and Reason. They were also YGC and heavy in the streets and definitely no stranger to guns, drugs, and some murders.

Tango got an address for them, learned their habits, and knew about their location, their favorite places to be. He moved around them like their own shadow. He was ready to strike. He was ready to get paid.

The brothers stayed in a three-story tenement off of Jerome Avenue. Security was weak and the neighborhood was high with crime. Tango easily fit right in. He took the stairway to their third-floor apartment and effortlessly broke into their apartment using a pick and tension wrench. He already knew the Broughton brothers weren't home. They were at the local bar drinking. It's what they did: drink and have a reckless lifestyle with women. And he also knew they lived alone. Tango carefully went through the untidy apartment with dirty dishes in the sink, scattered clothes everywhere, remnants of drug use on the table, the trashcan overflowing with rubbish and a few guns being out in the open. It was the typical gangster pad. It was sloppy and Tango winced from the smell.

He took his position in the place. In one hand was a wooden baseball bat; in the next was a 9 mm. Now all he had to do was sit and wait and let his victims come to him.

Two hours later the front door opened and there was loud talking. The brothers had arrived home unaware that they had unwanted company. Penn was talking and cursing. Reason followed his older brother with the alcohol making him move sluggishly. They moved their way around the dark apartment and turned on the lights.

Reason plopped down on the couch and was ready to pass out. Penn removed the pistol from his waistband and placed it on the table along with his other collections of guns. He was ready to roll up some weed and relax with his brother. However, the minute Reason closed his eyes to rest and Penn settled in being unarmed and kicking off his shoes Tango emerged from his hiding place and attacked. He moved like lightning and struck like thunder. The baseball bat smashed against Reason's head, mashing his skull, and he toppled out of the chair and fell to the ground. He was fucked up. Penn went to reach for his gun but Tango was all over him, pistol whipping him with the butt of the gun and knocking him down to the floor.

Reason was knocked out cold from the blow, but Penn was conscious, bleeding from his head and scowling at Tango. He gazed up at the pistol aimed at him and cursed, "What the fuck, muthafucka!"

Tango had no reason to explain himself. He was there to execute a job. With no hesitation, he gripped the bat like Derek Jeter on the baseball field about to hit a homerun and swung at Reason; it almost took his head off. The Louisville Slugger smashed against his face spewing blood and immediately breaking his nose and then his jaw. Tango continually hit him with the bat so many times his body became unrecognizable. His face looked like ground meat. He broke every bone in the man's face and a pool of blood expanded underneath the body. To add insult to injury, Tango shot him multiple times.

Reason suffered the same fate. The baseball bat destroyed his slim body, almost breaking him into two pieces. Tango went ham on the little brother, knocking out teeth, crushing skull, breaking his nose, shattering his eye socket; and shot him multiple times in the face too. It was a nasty and appalling message, both bodies mangled with sick brutality.

Tango left the place coolly. It was back home to his woman. He needed to lie in her arms and take his mind away from work. When he arrived at his apartment, Mouse was sleeping with Eliza cuddled in her arms in his bed. Tango removed his clothing knowing it was contaminated with DNA evidence. The first thing tomorrow morning he planned on burning everything like he did before. He put everything in a trash bag, got comfortable in some basketball shorts and a wife beater, and joined Mouse and Eliza in bed. He nestled behind his woman and held her tight and whispered, "I love you," in her ear.

Chapter Twenty-four

Mouse

It was another beautiful day and I was going to enjoy every minute of it. I was happy. It finally felt like my life was going from shit to sugar. The landlord handed us the keys to our new apartment and we were about to move in, in a few days. I couldn't wait. It wasn't the house I shared with Rico last year, but it was something. It was ours, Tango's and mine. It was going to be our home. Tango put down a $3,000 down payment, which was a security deposit along with first and last months' rent. We were ready to go. We were ready to move out of Eden War.

After securing the apartment, he took me shopping. It wasn't Fifth Avenue in Manhattan or any upscale stores, but the department stores on Jerome Avenue. He bought me and Eliza a few things, even got Eliza her first stroller. I was content. I needed an upgrade. I had my Nikes, some Phat Farm, and some new earrings. Tango didn't buy anything for himself. When I urged him to, he said next time. The day was all about me. He always put me first and just for that, I was ready to suck his dick for an hour.

I exited the lobby pushing Eliza in her stroller. I was nervous and excited, ambivalent. I planned on meeting with Sammy today in the park. We were supposed to meet previously, but our plans got postponed because something came up on her end. It was sixty degrees outside. The moment I stepped out of the building, I took a deep breath and inhaled the warm weather into my lungs. Oh my God, I wished it could feel like this every day, just temperate and joyous. Everybody was coming outside to enjoy the day. It couldn't be wasted spent inside.

I walked to the playground on Crawford Avenue but Sammy wasn't there yet. She said by 2:00 p.m., but I was ten minutes early. I took a seat on the bench and let Eliza out of the stroller to play. The park wasn't crowded. It was a weekday, school was still in session and people were at work, so I had some solitude to myself to think and chill out. I couldn't wait to see Sammy's son. He was a few months younger than Eliza and belonged to Rico too. Thinking about that fact, it put a sour taste in my mouth, so I quickly had to think about something else before my mood changed for the worse.

Eliza didn't seem to be in the playful mood; in fact, she seemed cranky. I had to put her back in her stroller. I figured she was tired. I had a bottle ready for her and she drank half of it and went to sleep in the park. I lit a cigarette and waited for Sammy to show up, hoping she didn't stand me up.

A half hour went by and still no Sammy. I was starting to think she played me. I was getting upset. I felt stupid, naïve. I wanted to vent. I lit another cigarette and gave her another fifteen minutes to show; if not, then our friendship would be definitely over. I sat for another five when I saw Sammy entering the park pushing a stroller. I felt relieved; she wasn't playing me. She was hurrying my way looking nice in her designer jeans, white Nikes, and fall jacket, with her long, sensuous hair falling down to her back.

Sammy smiled at me.

We hugged each other and the first thing we did was take to each other's babies.

"Oh my God, is that her?" Sammy said, staring down at my sleeping Eliza with a smile. "She's so adorable. She looks just like you."

"Thank God for that," I said.

She laughed. "I know right."

I looked at Danny and he was too cute. Sammy had him in Sean John and he already had a head full of dark black hair.

"He's so handsome already," I said, but the sad news to me was he looked like Rico in all areas.

"I know. He's gonna be my little heartthrob when he gets older," said Sammy.

Danny was awake and moving around in his stroller, looking so energetic. I had to pick him up and hold him in my arms. He took to me already. I held him gently in my arms and grinned. He chuckled at me and made me wish I had a son too; but Eliza was still my baby who I loved to death.

"He's getting big already."

"Yup, pushed him out at six pounds and eleven ounces," she said.

"Eliza was seven pounds and eleven ounces."

"Whoa, she was a big girl."

"Tell me about it. She stretched my pussy out like a rubber band. She didn't know Mama still had use for her vagina," I joked.

Sammy laughed and commented with, "I know right."

We admired and complimented each other's babies and had causal talk. At first it did feel awkward being around her again, but as we talked, our old selves started to come back out. I sat down on the bench holding Danny. Sammy sat beside me. I couldn't let this snuggle of joy go from my arms. It felt like I could hold him forever. We talked about our kids, the baby formula we fed them or if we breastfed our babies. The ice was breaking between us and it felt good.

Danny was falling asleep in my arms. Sammy took him from me and placed him back into his stroller. Now both our kids were sleeping.

I sighed. Where did we start? "So how's life?" I asked.

"It's good. I met someone new," she answered.

"I see, saw him at the funeral. Big guy."

"Is he." She snickered.

"You crazy."

"He do me right, in all places," said Sammy.

"Good to hear."

"And you?"

"I met someone too. His name is Tango and he treats me like I'm his world," I boasted.

"You deserve it, Mouse."

I knew I did.

I started to tell her all the things Tango had done for me lately. I described my king to her and she seemed truly happy for me. She then talked about her man, Power, and explained how they met and kept it real with me, letting me know what he was about. He was YGC, a hardcore muthafucka in the game, and he was in love with Sammy. I was genuinely happy for her. After Rico, we found our kings.

Of course we talked shit about Rico. We both hated his guts. I didn't care for him. I didn't go see him at all. He was dead to me and my daughter. But Sammy let me know it was a different story with her.

"I still go see him, Mouse," she said to me.

I was confused. "Why?"

"It's a long story," she said.

"Talk to me, Sammy. I'm here," I told her, looking directly at her. I wanted to know what was going on.

We both were willing to let bygones be bygones and start over. It was a new year and we both were doing different and better things.

Sammy locked eyes with me and exhaled. I was listening. She went on to explain the situation with Rico. It started back last year with her date with Macky. I remembered. She didn't want to tell me what had happened. She told me about it now, how he tried to rape and beat her. She confessed that she felt so weak and vulnerable that she refused to let anyone know about it, but somehow she ended up telling Rico. Then Sammy hit me with the bombshell.

"I killed him, Mouse," she confessed with tears trickling down her eyes.

"Oh my God. What?"

"Rico set it all up. He had him kidnapped, brought me to the location, and I shot him in the trunk of a car."

I was taken aback. What the fuck was Sammy thinking?

"I hated that muthafucka. Now Rico is blackmailing me. It's the only reason why I go and visit him. He has this shit over my head."

I didn't know what to think.

She confessed about everything, about her and Rico's past, how they first fucked and how he steadily influenced her with lies and promises. It was the same way he did me. She was in tears and apologized for everything. I hugged and comforted her. She needed me. It was obvious she was holding everything in and it was tearing her apart. She went on to tell me about her dancing in Crazy Legs and how she would turn a trick every now and then to keep her lights on and feed her son. We both had similar stories.

Rico had manipulated us both.

After Sammy was done talking, I knew I had to tell her my story. She was listening and I began with telling how I was living in a shelter for a few months, struggling. I told her about Denise's cousin Dietra who was steady hating on me and always trying a bitch. I told her about that night I beat her almost to death and had to suddenly leave with my daughter in the cold before I got arrested. I mentioned moving in with Erica, and prostituting myself in Hunts Point.

"What?"

"Yeah, a bitch did what she had to do to eat," I said.

I let her know how Tango and I honestly met. I told it all. We both were in similar situations and look at us; we were still here, surviving and moving forward by any means necessary. I continued to apologize to her and she continued to apologize to me. We were definitely over Rico. But I felt bad for Sammy; he was trying to blackmail her into doing whatever he told her. I could see it was becoming a burden on her. I let her know that her secret was safe with me.

"I'm here for you, Sammy," I told her.

She nodded and wiped the tears away from her eyes. "I don't know how long I could put up wit' his shit, Mouse. You're lucky, he's out of your life completely, but me, he's gonna taunt me until he tries and break me," she proclaimed.

"We gonna do sumthin' about him," I said.

"I just want him to leave me alone."

"He will."

Right there on that bench, we both vowed to take our revenge on Rico. He did too much and he was continuing doing too much. Sammy was hurt and she was stressed. So we wanted to kill him, or have him killed. We were determined to destroy Rico somehow even though he was locked up in Attica. Where there's a will, there's a way. Sammy mentioned someone who had the muscle and clout to pull it off: Power. But it was risky, because she didn't want Power to know all her business, especially when it came to a grimy nigga like Rico.

We talked for hours and played with our kids. Sammy mentioned to me about our music being stolen and seeing one of our songs being performed on BET. I was dumbfounded. She then mentioned her run-in with Search at the club and how he disrespected her. I was also taken aback. Since when did she and Search have beef? But I did feel Search abandoned us. We were talented but our career wasn't going anywhere. Sammy asked me if I was still writing. I told her of course. I loved writing and I loved music. She admitted she fell off for a moment but started to get back on her pen game. We had some unfinished business to take care of. Fuck it, we weren't about to let Vixen Chaos die out. We worked so hard and came so far. Our setbacks wasn't going to be the final chapter in our books. There were a lot more chapters gonna be read and they were going to be some good ones.

From that day on, our friendship was mended again and I felt we were even closer. We shared our secrets, our darkness, and our pain with each other. I felt like a million bucks because I had Sammy in my life again. I had someone close to me I could talk to and I didn't want that to ever change.

I told Sammy I was moving, or we were moving away from Edenwald into our own apartment. She was happy for me. I was happy for her.

Chapter Twenty-five

Sammy

I sat near the bedroom window holding Danny in my arms, feeding him his bottle and gazing at the police lights that flooded the street below me. It looked like an army of cops were outside my window, over a dozen or two from corner to corner, and homicide detectives were walking around everywhere, canvassing the area and asking questions about the two dead men in the front seat of green Durango. They had been gunned down by a semiautomatic and from where I sat in my apartment I could almost see their bodies slumped over the steering wheel and the dashboard. It was a grizzly crime scene and more young black men were murdered.

I heard the gunshots an hour earlier; there were many of them, sounding like fireworks going off and they were so close in my bedroom, it felt like they were shooting at me. And it didn't take a genius to understand death followed. I was so close to the crime scene from my bedroom window that I could hear the detectives talking and almost could smell the nicotine on their breaths. It was the advantage of living on the second floor and near a hazardous street.

I was busy feeding my baby, but I admit, I was being nosey. I sat by the window like an old lady trying to figure who got killed. I overheard it was members from BMB. It was coming back on them. Someone in their gang were brutally killing YGC gang members the past few weeks and from overhearing Power talk whenever I was around him, he figured it was some OG, probably fresh home from prison. Power was in the streets twenty-four/seven, taking care of business and putting himself in the middle of this chaos. When the Broughton brothers were murdered savagely in their own apartment, it bothered him greatly and he didn't seem to sleep. He looked like a general at war. There were guns everywhere, from his place in the city to his cars and even on him. He stayed armed and stayed alert.

I worried about him greatly. He was determined to win and not get himself killed or locked up. Some days I pleaded with him to stay out of it personally, he had soldiers to crawl in the trenches and fight for him, but Power was a man of pride and he always said to me, "I ain't gonna never let my soldiers do what I won't do first. That's why these niggas respect me, 'cause they know a muthafucka like me is gonna be right out there in the trenches warring wit' muthafuckas too. I ain't some clown to hide behind his money and power. Bitch, I'm real like that."

He said it like he had something to prove.

I couldn't tell him anything. His mind was already made up. The only thing I could do for him was pray and hope he came out of this street war alive and with his freedom. Power stood out like a skyscraper in a small town. He was easy to spot and a lot easier to target and gun down. I fell in love with him and I didn't want my man dying on me. I didn't need another Rico. I needed a man who was going to be there for me all the time. But lately, Power's priorities had been to his gang and I was left on the backburner.

Yes, Power was giving me the world—money, clothes, jewelry and taking me out to some nice places—but I was still living in the projects, still around the violence, and still wondering about my future.

I thought about Mouse and her man Tango. Mouse looked so happy talking about Tango the other day that I did get somewhat jealous of her. Power had the money and the lifestyle, but it seemed like Tango had the passion and the undying commitment to his woman. I liked that. In fact, I loved that. Also, Rico wasn't in her life at all. She vowed to help me with the situation, but how? I felt so trapped that the minute I thought about it, I would start to tear up. I just wanted out, and I wanted to be happy. Why was it so fuckin' difficult to find it both, happiness and true love, without worrying about a bullet hitting you in the back?

I continued lingering by the bedroom window, observing the police do their jobs, and watching the neighbors loiter around the crime scene, behind the yellow caution police tape inhibiting anyone without a badge to come any closer to the bodies. The violent disturbance had awakened the entire block. But Danny was falling asleep in my arms. He seemed better now, fed and feeling safe against his mother's tits. He was aloof from this type of trouble, so far anyway. My son needed better than this. I didn't want to become that single black worrying mother with a troubled teenage son in the gangs or drugs and getting into all kinds of shit. I didn't want to get that knock on my door one late night or early morning, seeing police and giving you the news that your son is dead, shot down coldblooded like some animal. I didn't want that for Danny. I didn't want him to end up like his father. Danny had to be better than all of this. He had to. He was innocent now, smiling, playful, and always depending on Mommy, but in fourteen, fifteen, eighteen years, where would he be?

I cradled my child cozily in my arms as I gazed at the crime scene out my window. Those two dead souls out there; they were someone's child too, or were. But somewhere down the line they got caught up in the street life and look at them now. It was a fate that so many of my people have faced, men and women: death by some rival's hand.

I looked at my son as his pretty eyes succumbed to sleep finally and I vowed to keep him away from this. He was going to learn what life was like. When he got older, I would tell him about my past and tell him about his father—the man he was, or the man he wasn't. But right now, for my son to have some kind of chance when he got older, it started with me being the best mother I could to him. And that started with getting my life right and having things in order. I even thought about going back to school, getting my GED and maybe my degree down the line. I wanted to do something with my life. I wanted to better myself, for my son's sake. But how could that happen with Rico hanging this black cloud over my head?

I had seen enough. I closed my window and removed myself from the view outside. I placed Danny in his crib, made sure he was nice and comfortable, and then I went into the next room to smoke a joint and call Power.

I plopped down on the couch with a joint between my lips and my cell phone in hand. I called Power a few times but he wasn't answering. I sighed with frustration. Two things: I wanted to know if he was okay; and the second, I wanted some dick. Since this shit started in the streets, we hadn't been fuckin' like that. And I didn't want to cheat on my man, but I was horny. I smoked weed to calm down my nerves.

I called his phone again and it went straight to voicemail. I became frustrated and thought, could I put up with this shit, thinking that Power was Rico all over again, being in the streets and about to get his ass shot up or locked up? Fuck!

Mouse happily showed me around the small apartment like it was some palace she was moving into. It was in Harlem, not too far from 125th Street. It was a four-story walk up, no elevator, and kind of rundown, but Mouse was happy with it. The place wasn't furnished yet. It had two small bedrooms and a small bathroom that if you needed to change your mind, you needed to step outside. But it was her new home and I was proud of her.

"We were supposed to move to the Bronx, but that landlord started actin' fuckin' funny and Tango found us this place. At least I'm out of the projects, right?" she said with a smile.

"Yes, congrats on that," I said.

Our kids were with us. Danny was in his stroller and Eliza was hugged to Mouse's hip with a pacifier in her mouth. The tour of the place took a minute or less. Outside her bedroom window was an alley filled with trashcans and rats. There was a Chinese food restaurant underneath the apartment, along with an African hair braiding place, a public school two blocks down, and a few fast food restaurants and several bodegas crowding the area. It was your typical black neighborhood. But it was home and she had her man with her every night, supposedly.

"I can't wait 'til we get the place furnished. I'm thinking leather couches maybe, a flat screen over there, but Tango wants something simple," she said. "He wants to decorate the bedroom first and get busy in it." Mouse chuckled.

It was too cute, their relationship.

"I agree wit' him, Mouse. Just keep things simple. I mean, this place is only temporary right?"

"It is, but I'm ready to make my man a home, where after work he can come home and relax, kick off his shoes, drink his beer, watch his sports, and then, later, take care of me," Mouse said.

"That sounds nice."

"Yeah. I know it isn't much now, but I feel comfortable here. Don't nobody know me around here and I feel I can finally start over."

Starting over sounded so great, I thought. "Girl, I'm wit' you on that."

I could see Mouse decorating the small place lovely though. She always had an eye for decorating. When we were kids, we used to talk about living in huge mansions with like fifty rooms, and a big pool, and Mouse would go on and on how she would decorate each and every room. She would go into so much detail that you believed she done it before. She always did have a vivid imagination.

We stayed in the empty apartment for over two hours talking. We ordered some Chinese food from downstairs and relaxed on the floor at her place. I knew she couldn't wait until she got some furniture. We made the floor very comfortable though with a large quilt, some pillows, and a radio. Danny was crawling all over the place and Eliza was trying to get into everything when there wasn't nothing much to get into.

I was eating my egg roll and thinking about my own life while Mouse was tending to her daughter. My eyes saddened for a moment and when Mouse looked at me, she already knew something was wrong.

"Sammy, talk to me, what's goin' on wit' you?" she asked with concern.

I had to let her know. First, I told her that Rico called me collect the other day. Mouse sat up with me having her full attention and asked, "What the fuck did he want now?"

I knew she didn't mean to curse in front of the kids, but Rico could have that effect on a bitch.

"He knows about me and Power, and he wants me to not see him again, or he's gonna start talking about me to the authorities," I said.

"That clown-ass nigga," Mouse blurted out.

I went on to tell Mouse more about Rico, how he was pressuring me to sneak drugs into the prison for him, and how he had the audacity to pressure me into marrying him. Mouse couldn't believe her ears. She became so upset that I thought she would actually go to the prison and kill Rico her damn self.

"He's not gonna get away wit' this, Sammy," she vowed.

I didn't mean to turn her small housewarming to my problems, but as friends, we were always able to read each other, knowing when something was wrong without us telling.

"He just gotta go," said Mouse.

"I know. How we gonna do this?"

A sigh came from Mouse. She looked pensive toward the situation. While we had our kids we were talking about murdering someone. But how could we reach Rico inside the prison? That was the million dollar question.

The more time I spent with Mouse at her new place, the more we talked and the more I confessed about my private and personal life. We definitely had a lot of catching up to do. I told her about Power being in the streets too much and not spending any quality time with me. I was truly worried about him. Her advice to me was either leave him or love him the way he is.

"You know niggas like him don't change, Sammy," she mentioned.

She was afraid Power was going to hurt me like Rico did. She talked about Tango and his past, and boasted how he was now a hardworking man and trying to become a family man. I didn't need to hear all of that. But my dilemma: I leave Power and then what? I'm back stripping at Crazy Legs when I vowed never to return there again and living on ends meet, turning tricks in one of the backrooms to keep my lights on, fridge filled with food, and our rent paid. I couldn't do it. I couldn't keep on living like that. I admit I was scared.

We had such a long heart-to-heart that time went by and it was dark outside. The kids were sleepy and I knew it was time for me to head back to the Bronx. I was going to take a cab home. I hugged Mouse good-bye and went on my way. It was back to the Bronx and time to come up with a plan to get myself out of hot water.

Chapter Twenty-six

Tango

Tango stood over the body of Topple, a topnotch YGC member in the parking lot of his Bronx home. It was his third hit in one month. Topple was supposed to be a bad ass and untouchable muthafucka in the streets who everyone was afraid of. At first, there was a tussle, but quickly Tango got the better of Topple and he easily took him out like he was a bug underneath his shoe. The body was contorted in a vicious death, with multiple stab wounds to his neck and face, over sixty. The stainless steel combat knife thrust into Topple's neck like it was paper thin caused blood to gush out and left Topple fighting to breathe and survive. Tango kept attacking; he kept on stabbing. Once again, it was overkill. It was a sadistic message that had the heads of YGC taking notice and ready to take action.

YGC wasn't going to take the murders of their men lying down. They struck back with vengeance. Heavy BMB hitters like Young DJ and Puppet were gunned down in their green Durango, the shooters unknown. Another player named Jaguar was killed in front of his kids while playing in the park. And then another BMB gang member named Benny Hammonds was decapitated in his own home. Police were disturbed at what they saw, the man's head lying next to his own body and blood was everywhere.

Power had his peoples everywhere, to search and destroy, and to find out the man responsible for killing his cousin and a few of his soldiers. He promised anyone bold enough to find and kill the nigga fifty large, cash money in their hand. It was war. It was greed and every YGC member and those affiliated with the gang were on the hunt.

Tango stood over the body with his bloody latex gloves and the murder weapon still in his hand. He was more exposed with this kill. He was out in the open, standing in the dimly lit parking lot. He had put himself at risk of capture or being seen. Topple's body lay between two cars with his blood pooling on the ground. There could be a nosey neighbor watching from a window, or unseen eyes becoming a witness to the homicide he just committed. There were too many chances and he needed to depart quietly.

Tango secretly made his exit, removing the bloody gloves and planning to dispose of them in a distant trashcan. He didn't need any wise and skilled detective checking the local trashcans in the surrounding area for any incriminating evidence. He was smarter than that. The farther he was away from the body, the better his chances of not getting caught and getting rid of the knife and latex gloves. He tossed all evidence into a small plastic bag and carried it causally.

He walked a mile away from the body and finally tossed the bag into a trashcan on the corner. It was late and a chilly night. He finally made his way into Harlem via cab. He walked into his new apartment where Mouse was sleeping on an air mattress with her daughter. It was after midnight and he had a very long night. Before he decided to get into bed with his girl, he removed a wad of cash from his pocket and stashed it somewhere where he figured it would be safe. There was a loose floorboard in the closet of the second bedroom. It was deep enough to conceal anything. Tango had $10,000 bundled together with numerous rubber bands. It was his private stash. It was money he kept hidden from Mouse because he knew if she ever came across it he would have to explain it and he couldn't explain ten stacks in one month from working a normal construction job.

Tango showered briefly and joined Mouse in the bedroom. He felt refreshed and was ready for some sexual activity. But Mouse was sleeping with Eliza cuddled in her arms. So he did the next best thing: smoked a cigarette and jerked off in the bathroom. Tomorrow was going to be another long day for him; he had to go and see his parole officer. He already informed her of his new place in Harlem. She didn't have a problem with his relocation, it was within the guidelines of his parole, but she wanted to see proof of his employment. And thanks to a friend, he had some phony paystubs made up of the construction job he was allegedly working at. Not only was he trying to pull the blinds over Mouse's eyes, he had to outsmart his parole officer, too.

The last thing Tango wanted to do was lose his woman and go back to jail at the same time.

Chapter Twenty-seven

Mouse

Eliza was at the babysitter, giving Tango and me some quality time. And we definitely had some quality time together in our new apartment, fucking our brains out on the air mattress. He was banging my pussy out from the back, thrusting his hard dick into me roughly and smoothly like he was trying to put a baby inside of me. I moaned and cooed feeling his big dick work my center, with him grabbing my hips and the back of my neck throwing my petite, curvy frame into some sexual convulsion.

I loved him.

We sweated and grunted. I buried my head into the pillows and muffled my cries of ecstasy. The way his dick slid in and out of me it felt like the most purest sensation in my life. He pushed against me with a surge of pleasure rising inside of me like a tidal wave, touching every nerve.

"Fuck me, baby," I cried out.

He was a machine inside of me. Tango was in such a sexual trance, loving this good pussy that I didn't care how he fucked me or where he put his semen at, I just wanted to wrap myself in all of him and didn't think about getting pregnant even though I didn't want any more kids right away. Tango had me in bliss.

He pulled out of me and situated himself on his back, glistening in unadulterated sex. He wanted me to ride that big, delicious, dark dick. I popped up upright and moved my throbbing pussy over his dick. I took hold of his penis and straddled him, guiding him into me. He pushed against me; I slowly inserted himself into me. He started making gentle cooing noises in my ear.

"I know baby, this pussy is too good. You can't wait to get all the way up in it."

He groaned. "Um huh, ugh, ugh . . ."

I could feel his blood rushing and his nerves singing.

I started to milk that dick with my walls, pulling and tugging on him. He grabbed my waist and made the craziest sexual faces feeling my glorious insides work that large muscle. He was deeply enveloped, buried in my natural body heat and juices leaking, searing hot against him. He grunted and groaned, also squirming underneath me. He ran his hands over my chest and down my sides. He reached back to squeeze my ass, then down my thighs and all the way back up again. I enjoyed grinding on him. But I really loved when he held my hips and thrust up into me, hard and fast.

He was firmly thrusting up into me, not with speed so much, but with strength. It felt good. He felt too good. He ran his hands down my sides again, over my ass cheeks and reached farther around me to get his index finger wet. He then slipped the tip of his finger just inside my ass while continuing to thrust. In that instant, I doubled over, falling forward on top of Tango, moaning like crazy with my whole body gyrating. My legs clamped around him. I whispered in his ear, "I'm gonna cum if you keep doin' that."

He kept doing it.

I held his wrists and arched my back as we fucked. My mouth was open and my eyes half closed in bliss and lust. He watched me as I impaled myself on him. He was deep inside of me.

"Fuck me, don't stop," I cried out.

I moved quickly on top of him with my fingers gripping his wrists to the point where it was beginning to hurt. I began moaning more loudly with an animal noise echoing in the room. I trashed on top of him, my breathing rasping with him leaned back as waves of shockingly bright pleasure rocked his body with my every moment on top of him.

"You gonna make me cum!" I screamed out.

My nails dug into his skin and my movements increased even more. The air mattress began to rock and seemed to almost deflate. "Don't stop. Shit, don't stop!" I felt the pleasure coming. I threw my head back, yelping from the back of my throat and buried my face under his jaw. It was coming, for the both of us. I screamed against his neck as I felt my release pouring out of me. I clamped down on him and came like thunder. I bent back, away from him with my legs shuddering as I came again. I screamed again and threw myself forward onto Tango, baring my teeth.

He pounded me rough and with a final hard thrust he shot his load inside of me. I could feel it, every ounce of his semen swimming around inside of me. Oh my God, I couldn't move. I rested on top of him for a moment and felt his cum running out of me and on top of the bed.

We both were spent. I wasn't ready for another baby, but the way Tango shot his load inside of me, I was scared that at that moment, we conceived a baby in my tummy. I kept quiet though, relishing such good dick.

He got dressed and we talked for a while before he had to head to work. My pussy was still throbbing and sore the next day. But I loved it!

A special world for you and me
Un vinculo especial que no se puede ver

A special bond one cannot see
Nos envuelve en su capullo
It wraps us up in its cocoon
And holds us fiercely in its womb
The joy in my life
La alegria en mi vida
Please hold on to me and promise to stay with me
Y deja nunca solto
And let's never let go.

It was my love poem to him, the man I loved. The man I wanted to spend the rest of my life with. I was so in love with him that I wrote in two different languages. I sat in my new apartment thinking about how far I came. It wasn't much now, but I knew that in a year or two, we were going to be doing well. I planned on getting a job, part time, full time, it didn't matter and I wanted to go back to school. I needed to earn my degree and make something out of my life.

It was critical now I moved forward and not backward. It was time to chase that dream and knock down walls. While Eliza was sleeping, I was in the bathroom taking a home pregnancy test. My monthly was late by three weeks and I knew I was pregnant. The way Tango and I was fucking, and he never pulled out, it was inevitable. I had some morning sickness earlier and my chest felt sore.

I peed on the little stick and waited a few minutes for the results. I didn't want to be pregnant because now wasn't the time. We couldn't afford another baby and it was so dire that I was scared and thought about an abortion. But I knew if so, Tango would want this baby so bad. He talked about having kids. I listened. I wasn't sure. Eliza was only one. I was trying to get back on my feet.

The door was ajar and the apartment was still. I sat on the toilet waiting for the results to come through. I took a deep breath and picked up the stick. I was afraid to open my eyes and see the results. One line meant not pregnant, two lines meant oh fuck, my life was about to change again.

I took a deep breath and looked at the results, and there it was, what I already knew: I was fuckin' pregnant with Tango's baby. I felt ambivalent about the whole thing. Here I was about to go through the whole ordeal again: swollen belly, morning sickness, gaining weight, the emotions, and the uncertainty. I could only close my eyes and wondered if this one was going to be a boy this time. And how was I going to tell Tango, and Sammy?

I got up off the toilet and hid the pregnancy test. I had so many things going through my mind that for an hour I sat on the couch and didn't move. Eliza was sleeping like an angel and the apartment was still empty and unfurnished. I couldn't wait to get this place looking like a real home. It was the least I could do. I was about to become a mother again. Hooray, right.

Fuck me.

Chapter Twenty-eight

Sammy

I was glad Power finally had some time to spend with me, especially enough time to eat my pussy the way he did. I missed the way he went down on me. The streets was occupying too much of his time and I barely got to see my man. Shit, I felt that I had to be a rival with a gun in my hand for him to pay me any attention. A bitch was starting to get frustrated, sexually frustrated and not being paid any attention to. I didn't want to start having any doubts about this relationship. But tonight, he came to me, dick hard and his tongue ready to taste me. I didn't want him to talk about the streets or the bloodshed. I wanted to fill only good vibes from him tonight.

I was buck-naked with my legs spread, my pussy quivering; my clit was hard and I could feel it twitch and throb against his tongue. My juices were flowing to the point where Power could swallow them. He sucked and twirled on my pussy, licking my pussy from the bottom, to the slit, to the top. He opened my lips then he placed his mouth on my clit and started to apply suction to it. And it was followed by sticking his index finger into my ass and moving it around. I moaned and howled. I squirmed. I closed my eyes and went berserk.

"Power, I fuckin' missed you. Ooooh, don't stop, you gonna make me fuckin' cum!" I spilled out.

As I got closer to coming, I unconsciously rocked my hips, grinding into his face with my pussy squeezing and grasping at his tongue. My thighs shook and I felt it coming. I became really sensitive. He started swirling his tongue faster and I was about to come even faster. He used everything to please me: his lips, his tongue, his teeth, shit, even his gums. My thighs trembled, my clit tightened and then I flooded his mouth with my wetness, my moans filling his ears. I came pretty fast and hard. It was all over him. He didn't mind, the freak that Power was; he licked me clean and I loved it.

He made me cum several times like that before we fucked.

An hour into fucking and Power's cell phone rang. He was hitting this pussy from the back, damn near about to put my head through the headboard with his mighty thrusts inside of me. I cooed and I wiggled, backing my ass into him, but during mid-thrust, the fuckin' phone chimed. I begged for him not to answer it, this was our time and I wanted both of us to finish, but the muthafucka didn't listen to me. He pulled out, his big dick glistening with all my come and juices and he picked up the phone and answered like he wasn't busy with me.

"Yo, what up?" he said into the phone.

I rolled over and looked at him, *like seriously, you gonna do this now?* He ignored my disapproving stare and rejected the nasty attitude I threw at him.

"Where at?" I heard him ask. "A'ight. I'll be there in a minute."

Once again, he put the streets before me. And once again, I was feeling some kind of way. How he gonna leave this good pussy so easily, especially the way I sucked his dick and fucked him until we both released multiple orgasms, to be with his niggas and give them his time? I heaved a sigh of irritation. Power looked my way as he was getting dressed.

"Why the fuckin' attitude?"

"Because, we ain't fuckin' done yet," I exclaimed.

"You know I got shit out there to handle, Sammy, so stop actin' like that," he countered.

"You give everyone else ya fuckin' time, but your own damn woman. I'm gettin' sick and tired of this shit, Power," I barked.

"What the fuck you gonna do, leave?" he boldly shouted.

"Leave?" I was shocked he came out his mouth like that.

I thought about it. I wanted to, but where would I go now with no job and no real education to fall back on? Yes, I was a natural-born hustler, but when you have a son to take care of, you weigh your options. And besides, I was in love with him. I wasn't planning on going anywhere.

"No, but I might just fuck someone else," I boldly retorted.

He suddenly stopped dressing and glared at me. I didn't know why I came out my mouth and said what I said. It just slipped out. I was angry and I wanted to hurt him the way he was hurting me.

The way he looked at me, it felt like he was a bull seeing red. I became tense. I just stood there, naked and all, not knowing what he was about to do. He rapidly charged at me and wrapped his hand around my neck. I could feel his strength, his grip almost crushing my windpipe. Power lifted me into the air and slammed me against the bed. He shouted, "Don't you ever give away my good pussy, you fuckin' hear me? I fuckin' love you!"

I couldn't breathe at first. I couldn't answer him. The look in his eyes was almost satanic. The way he breathed down, it felt like a dragon breathing fire against me. He softened his grip around my neck and then exclaimed, "You want my fuckin' time, huh? That's what you want? You want me to finish fuckin' you."

I didn't answer. He roughly positioned me on my stomach, spreading my legs and succulent ass cheeks and I could feel him quickly fidgeting with the zipper to his pants. He held me against the bed forcefully with my face pushed into the mattress and his body weight pinning me to the bed and himself. Unexpectedly, I felt him slammed his dick into me. It was the other hole he penetrated: my ass. He was rough. I wrenched from the raw entry inside of me and he didn't care about my reaction. His dick was big, and without any proper lubrication, it felt like sandpaper down there. Power was Dr. Jekyll and Mr. Hyde: he quickly became this fuckin' lunatic, raping me anally, shoving my face into the mattress damn near suffocating me as he fucked me. I fought him, but he was too strong.

I could feel his dick rooted so far into my ass, I was scared he was going to tear something and fuck me up for life. He kept pounding and pounding into me. I wasn't a stranger to anal sex, but it had to be done properly, with finesse and time. Power didn't care at all.

"This is what you fuckin' want, this dick. Here, bitch, take this dick. Take this fuckin' dick and enjoy it," he shouted, mocking me.

I cried out. It was hurting. I felt his hand around the back of my neck; it cemented me into this position with my ass arched and his other hand pushed my back downward into the bed. He was in and out, stretching my anal and I was in tears. He was a huge man and there was no way I could fight him off of me. What had I gotten myself into? He was breathing heavily, enjoying me and I could feel him about to come again.

The minute he came, it seemed like he snapped out of some demonic trance. He quickly pulled his dick out of me and I felt weak and violated. Power pulled up his pants and instantly the look on his face was apologetic.

"Baby, I'm so sorry. I didn't know what came over me," he ruefully uttered my way.

I couldn't even speak. I had no words to say to him. I was utterly shocked at what he did to me. I was hurt. I loved this man, was in love with him, so why and how could he do me like this?

"Sammy, I'm so sorry," he repeated. He reached for me, but I recoiled from his touch. "Baby, I didn't mean to hurt you. I just got a lot on my mind right now and I snapped on you. I love you, baby. I love you."

It was hard to hear him say that he loved me when he physically raped me like I was some whore on the streets. I cried; he wanted to console me. Now, he wasn't in any rush to run out on me and see his crew. I had his undivided attention, but not the way I wanted it.

"Let me make this up to you," he told me in his most sincere tone. Power reached into his pocket and pulled out a wad of hundred dollar bills. I watched him peel away a few hundreds from his fat bulge and he placed the cash beside me.

"That's three grand right there, baby. Go out and buy whatever you want. I don't care. You deserve it," he said.

I looked down at the money. I didn't know what to think. Did he think he could pay me off after what he did to me? He continued to say, "I didn't mean to do this to you, Sammy. I just got a lot on my fuckin' mind. I just wanna find this muthafucka who's been killing my niggas and tear his fuckin' head off and piss down his gotdamn neck. I've been stressed, baby, really stressed. And if it weren't for you, I don't know where I would be."

I continued to be silent toward him. I dried my tears and felt some kind of way. A part of me wanted to just get up and go, leave Power behind. He was going through too much, putting me through too much, but there was a stronger part of me that forced me to stay and be with him. I needed him. He loved me and I loved him. And besides, I needed the cash. I needed his help. I felt to walk away from Power would have been suicidal. I started to collect myself. I started to ignore what he just did to me and write it off as if it was only rough sex. I would survive.

I picked up the money. Power smiled at me. "That's my girl."

I locked eyes with him and warned, "Don't you ever do that to me again."

He came near me and sat beside me. "Baby, best believe I never will. I'm sorry what I did to you and it won't happen again. I promise. You are my queen. And I promise you, once we find this muthafucka, whoever this OG is who's fuckin' wit' us and digging his own grave, everything's gonna be back to normal between you and me. We gonna take a trip somewhere. Vegas, Miami, how about the Caribbean? Yeah, the Caribbean sounds really nice, baby. We goin' there after we end this beef wit' these BMB muthafuckas."

I huffed.

Power looked at me momentarily, patted me on my knee, and then stood up. He continued getting dressed. I watched him get dressed and then observed him remove two pistols from the top drawer and conceal them on his person. He was a gangster of a certain magnitude, a hardcore killer. I could see it in his eyes that he loved the streets and he loved that lifestyle. I wanted to get away from it all, but how? How could I get away from it when I was in love with a man who idolized it?

Power kissed me on the lips good-bye. I savored the taste of him and felt brainwashed by him. He threw on his leather jacket, winked good-bye to me, and left his apartment. When the door shut, I got up myself, placed the money in my pants pocket, and got dressed. What could mend today's wrong was going out tonight and enjoying myself with friends at the club, and then, tomorrow, go shopping and buy whatever I desired. Fuck it, I deserved it. I lived poor for too long now and now it was my time to shine.

As long as Ms. Wilson got paid her money, she didn't mind watching Danny all night. And I was paying her handsomely, one hundred dollars a night to babysit for me; the bitch didn't complain not once. Fuck it, I could afford it now. I was dating and fucking one of the biggest hustlers in New York City. Power's reputation preceded him. Nobody fucked with him, and through stories I'd heard, those who did would later regret it with their life or their families' lives. And when it was soon known throughout the tri-state area that I was his girl, I was getting so much respect from everyone that it felt like I was the first lady of the United States.

My reputation was growing, but as it did, Rico was becoming more threatening. When I stopped answering his collect calls, the letters came in the mail. He was fucking with me, taunting me with this black cloud of guilt and extortion over my head and mentioning Macky in his letters, bringing up the past, making noise when I wanted silence and trying to rock the boat. In one of his letters, he even stupidly wrote:

I'm hearing you think you a queen again, got your king now, so Rico's forgotten now. Yeah, right, bitch. I'm gonna always be around and always in your life. You have my son, so don't get cute and think some other nigga is gonna be a daddy to my seed. You don't want him to end up like Macky now. We know you are the hand of death, Sammy. What skeletons do you keep in your closet? You know I got the key, right, so don't fuck with me. I haven't heard from you and I'm still waiting on your answer, and you know a nigga ain't trying to hear no. Get at me soon, and for your sake, please don't keep me waiting long. I love you.

I quickly got rid of the letter and was so upset, I wanted to scream. Rico obviously wasn't going to go away. I needed to get my mind off things, so I decided to hit the club scene. I didn't want to party alone, so I invited Kawanda, a girl named Lisa, and Mouse. I told them that drinks tonight were on me.

Kawanda and Lisa were willing, but Mouse was still unsure. She told me that she needed to find a babysitter. I urged her to come out, maybe have Tango watch Eliza, because it'd been too long since we went and hung out, and actually had a good time. I needed to unwind. I needed my best friend with me.

Club Eight Ball in the South Bronx was always a lively and entertaining place to be on a Thursday night. It was where all the hustlers, shot callers, and players went to have a good time, via flaunting, flirting with the ladies, popping bottles, and doing business. It was a huge club with several VIP rooms and a long wraparound bar that carried every drink available to man.

There were always plenty of bitches in the place for the men to flock to. The men came with their A game and the ladies came dressed like they were about to walk down Hollywood Boulevard, showing off what their mamas gave them.

I was no different. I walked into the place clad in a very low-cut, red minidress with clinched ties on the sides and my six-inch stilettos that stretched my defined legs to the heavens. I felt like I could touch the ceiling in my shoes. I was with Kawanda and Lisa, and the minute I stepped into the club all eyes were on me, gawking and hypnotized by my beauty and outfit.

Of course we got our own VIP and ordered Moët and Cristal, all on Power's dime. We danced with each other and got our drink on. The DJ was blending some of the sweetest mixes and we all got hyped. The Moët had me feeling so right. And the atmosphere was what a bitch needed. But every so often I would look around to see if Mouse had shown up.

Two hours into partying and drinking I was starting to give up hope that Mouse was going to show. Maybe she couldn't find a babysitter. It wasn't a big issue, but the minute I thought that, there she was, entering the club; and she didn't come alone. I assumed she was with her man, Tango. I didn't mind him coming along; as long as he was making my friend happy, then I was happy.

Mouse started to look around for me. I stood up and waved her way to get her attention. I could see her searching. I tried to shout for her, but the music was just too loud. The man she was with, he was attractive and tall and older. I admit, Mouse picked a winner in my eyes. She was wearing tight blue jeans, heels, and a tight Guess shirt underneath a leather jacket that highlighted her tits. Tango, he looked pensive and looked like he didn't want to be there. He was dressed in a leather jacket also, and his demeanor to me read thug from head to toe.

Mouse finally spotted me waving frantically her way. She smiled and she and her man came over. I hugged her, introduced her to Kawanda and Lisa, and the formal introduction was made to Tango. While Mouse and I talked and got our drink on, Tango was the quiet type. He didn't speak much and he didn't drink much either. It felt like he was cautious about something, like he didn't want to be around us, or didn't want to be in the club at all. I asked him a few questions, to get to know him better, but his answers were terse. So I stopped talking to him completely. But Mouse and I were having a great time, reconnecting and partying. We even spat a rhyme for everyone. It was one of our old-school joints that we used to perform when we were young teens. It felt like old times again and I didn't want this night to ever end.

An hour and a half after their arrival, Tango looked like he was ready to go. He was constantly looking around, and would sit with his back against the wall, not willing to get up dance with his woman and have a good time. That type of behavior made me think he was doing some grimy shit out there in the streets, because only a nigga who acts like that, always looking around, quiet, too cautious, he's definitely doing dirt. Mouse said he was working a legit job. I assumed he was lying to her. But it wasn't my business to get into. I just dealt with Mouse and learned my lesson long ago not to make the same mistakes twice.

Around 2:00 a.m., I got a surprise visit from Power. He decided to show up to the club. I didn't know how he found out what club I was partying in, but there he was, entering with his harrowing-looking entourage and looking menacing himself. As he and his group of thugs moved through the crowded dance floor, I couldn't help but notice how much respect he got from everyone and each person parted like the Red Sea allowing Power and his men to move easily without any problems. Power looked like a Don in his turtleneck and bling-bling gleaming on him like the sun. He towered over almost everyone in the place and his bald head glistened with his thick goatee neatly trimmed and his ink-black eyes probably searching for me.

When he saw me seated in VIP, he slightly smiled and came over. His goons made our comfortable area abruptly cramped with their presence. They didn't hesitate to take over our fun. They snatched up our bottles and helped themselves and started harassing my girlfriends. Power gave me a kiss and said, "I see you decided to have some fun with my money."

I shrugged. "I needed to get my mind off of things."

"Hey, I ain't complaining. I like seeing my woman having a great time."

He made me take a seat on his lap and wrapped his arms around me. I didn't mind. We started to show off. He fondled me gently, whispered something naughty in my ear, I chuckled at the comment and then he grabbed the chilly Moët out of the ice bucket. It was his mindset to take over and run things wherever he was at. He smoothly took things over at my small party.

Mouse was nestled against her man. They both were quiet. I noticed Tango became extra uncomfortable. He had his fingers locked and was faintly crouched forward with Mouse's arms wrapped around him. It looked like he was ready to leap. He looked at my man like it was going to be a problem between them. Power turned and noticed the man's eyes on him. He took a swig of Moët, locked eyes with Tango, and asked, "Nigga, you know me?"

"Nah, I don't," Tango replied coolly.

"Then why you clockin' me so fuckin' hard?" Power chided.

Oh shit, I thought. The last thing I needed was problems. I tried to defuse the situation before it escalated into some serious. "Power, this is Mouse's man, Tango. He's wit' her."

"I don't care who he wit', he needs to correct his fuckin' eyes," Power exclaimed.

Power's entourage was all scowling a great deal at Tango. They all looked like they were ready to tear him apart. The funny thing, though, Tango didn't look nervous at all. He didn't even flinch. He kept his cool. He didn't fuss back.

"We were just leaving," Mouse chimed.

Good idea.

She stood up, grabbing her man, knowing it was about to get ugly. Tango didn't fight with his woman. He stood next to her with this smirk on his face. The smirk angered Power. He pushed me off of his lap and stood up also, ready to confront Tango. And his wolves were ready to attack. I became nervous.

"What's ya name, nigga?" Power demanded to know.

"Tango," he replied gruffly. "It ain't no beef wit' you though. I just came home not too long ago."

All eyes were on him and Mouse. Power stood at his full height, looking like a black grizzly bear in the room with his claws showing and teeth exposed, ready to gnaw at the man.

"We're leaving," Mouse chimed once again. "Sammy, it was so good seeing you again. We had fun."

I didn't say anything. Mouse pulled Tango out of the fire quickly and I felt relieved. Power shouted out, "Fuck outta here, nigga, YGC in the fuckin' building." He then glared at me and exclaimed, "What the fuck you got this clown-ass nigga around you?"

"He came wit' my homegirl," I explained.

"I don't give a fuck who he came wit'. I don't trust this nigga yo, sumthin' funny 'bout him, my niggas."

His crew nodded and agreed. "I feel you, my nigga." They looked fiercely at Tango until he and his woman were finally out of the building.

"Tango," Power uttered. "Yo, I want ya niggas to find out about that nigga, see who he run wit' and what he about."

"We on it, Power," Mitch replied. Mitch was a pit bull who always had his teeth showing; he was the young and vicious killer in the mix. When Power gave him orders, he didn't ask questions. He just did what he was told.

I just prayed this drama, it ended here, in the club, and didn't escalate into anything critical. I had Mouse back in my life and I didn't need anything or anyone else fuckin' it up for me.

Chapter Twenty-nine

Mouse

The first piece of our furniture set arrived today and I was happy. Seeing the three-piece living room set being delivered made me forget about the small drama in the club last night. I wondered what that was about; most likely boys being boys, trying to boast who got the bigger dick. I didn't think anything of it. Tango did have his past and maybe it was nothing. While Tango was at work, I was busy decorating our apartment, turning the cramped, ghetto-looking place into our home. We could finally afford a few nice things. We had gone down to Aaron's and decided to rent our furniture by the month. It saved us a pretty penny and the set I picked out, it was a metal and wood sectional sofa set in dark truffle, perfect to enhance my home décor. The whole thing went for $1,500. We picked up a fifty-five-inch flat-screen TV, too.

Gradually, my place was coming to life. We had a used bedroom set in the master bedroom, and in the second bedroom I painted the walls sky blue, placed some Disney drapes over the windows, and set it up for my daughter's room. It was also going to be the baby's room. I didn't tell Tango about the pregnancy yet. I wanted to find the right time to tell him.

All morning, I was decorating and cleaning, and started cooking, while tending to Eliza when she was awake. Changing diapers, making bottles, and becoming a housewife, yeah, this was the new me. But I didn't mind it at all, it beat sucking dick in Hunts Point and living with a bitch who used me and took me for granted. I never wanted to go back to that.

While Eliza was sleeping in my bedroom, I continued working in the second bedroom. I wanted to do the floors over. They were dull and creaky. I wanted to make this bedroom feel like magic. Tango had called me and said he had a surprise for me after work and suggested that I try to find a babysitter for tonight. He was taking me out to dinner. I couldn't wait. I loved being with him from sunup to sundown. We were a couple and the next step I assumed would be marriage. Yeah, I was ready to get married. I wanted something different and Tango, he definitely felt different. He felt so real to me. It was a sure thing that this was legit and we both weren't going anywhere.

Yes, I was happy.

I started in the bedroom closet. It was filled with mostly jackets and some of Eliza's clothing. I turned on the lights and looked around. I noticed there was a squeaky and lose floorboard. The minute I stepped on it, it popped up like a seesaw. I looked at it and something caught my attention. I kneeled down curiously and removed the floorboard and to my surprise there was money underneath it. It was a wad of bills, mostly hundreds and fifties wrapped tightly around a few rubber bands. I picked it up and couldn't believe my eyes. There had to be close ten or fifteen thousand dollars in my hand. Where did this money come from? Did it belong to Tango or was it left there by the previous owners? So much money, I didn't know what to think. If it belonged to Tango, then it was obvious that he was doing something illegal out there. I went from being angry to disappointed, but I couldn't jump to conclusions. I had to give Tango a chance to explain himself.

***

The Blue Hill restaurant was classy, and it was expensive. It was uptown, near Washington Square Park. It was a place where presidents and kings and queens would dine. Where fat bankers would take their wives and pink-shirted bros would bring their high-heeled girlfriends. The décor was breathtaking with its high ceiling chapel of twirling meat, and butterscotch banquettes projecting a beauty more natural than that of the nip-tucked Upper East Side ladies who dined there. There was plenty of civil conversation and people I was very unfamiliar with.

But here we were, Tango and I, two urban natives from the projects still trying to find ourselves in the world. I tried to dress for the occasion, wearing a long skirt and blouse, my long hair styled in a French bun and having just the right makeup on and the jewelry Tango bought me. I had to look good for my man, classy. It was the first time I saw Tango in a blazer; it was blue and he wore a collared shirt underneath looking like the Renaissance man himself. I was proud of him, but in the back of the mind, I couldn't stop thinking about the money I found hidden in the closet.

We had causal talk, sipping on water while waiting for the waiter to bring our meals. I ordered a pepper-crusted rib-eye for forty-five dollars and a scattering of under-crisped vegetable sides. It was expensive, but Tango told me to order whatever I wanted; price wasn't an issue tonight, which made me more suspicious. He had the main course in American cuisine, a surf and turf and steaming mashed potatoes. It looked good.

"You look so good, baby, like royalty. No bitch in this place can't compare to my woman," Tango complimented me.

I smiled. "You look good too, like a million bucks."

"You know ya man tries."

"I know, baby."

"We comin' along, ain't we? I love the way you furnished the place. It looks good."

"Thank you."

Eliza was staying with a friend for the night. Tango wanted to have some fun. God knows what else he had planned for us. But I gave it to him, he was spontaneous and outgoing. The club scene didn't work for him, but he would put all his effort into trying to please me and make me happy.

When the meal came, I knew I wasn't going to be able to finish it all. It was just too much. They sure gave you your money's worth here. But I was going to try. I remembered plenty of days when I went hungry, not knowing when I was going to have my next meal and believe me, everything nourishing to my body, I didn't take for granted; nothing was about to go to waste. Tango started digging into his dish. He ate like a hungry man and didn't care who was watching him. He still had somewhat of that prison mentality inside of him at the dinner table. I had to school him most times, remind him that he wasn't locked up anymore and he could take his time consuming his meal.

While we dined, I asked him, "So how's work?"

"Work is good, baby. I'm catching on and the bosses' are happy with my job performance. I really like my job," he proclaimed.

"Really." I raised my eyebrow almost shouting out, "Nigga, please." I had a feeling that he was lying to my face. I started to think and analyzed the situation. He did bring home paystubs, but he never brought home any work tools. And I noticed his hands; especially his fingernails were too clean for him to be doing construction. And then how was he able to afford so much so quickly? So many questions and not any answers. I couldn't deal with dating another man in the game, and now that I was pregnant with his child, it was even more critical between him and me.

"Tango, have you been honest with me?" I asked.

"Yeah, baby. Why the third degree so suddenly, babe?" he replied calmly.

"How can we afford to eat here, Tango? My dish alone is almost fifty dollars, and then the wine and the rent-a-car ya driving. The furniture. What is all this?"

"I've been workin' hard, baby, trying to provide for my family. And the car, my peoples hooked me up."

His peoples. His peoples were always hooking him up with something, from money, pussy, to driving a nice-looking Intrepid. What else were they hooking him up with?

I looked at him. I didn't know what to respond with. My heart felt heavy because my womanly instincts told me that he was somehow back in the streets and doing something crazy out there. I wanted to believe Tango, but it was hard to, especially with the money I found in the closet.

Tango sat there so cool that he looked like a snowman. It was the right time to tell him the news.

"You need to provide all right, and do it the right way," I replied, sitting up and looking at him intently. "I'm pregnant."

The look on his face showed he was shocked. "What? You pregnant?"

I nodded.

"Oh shit, baby. You about to have my baby, seriously?" he exclaimed excitedly.

I thought the entire restaurant heard him. He was ecstatic and smiling largely.

"Yes, Tango, I'm about to have your baby, so you need to start being honest wit' me about everything," I stated seriously.

"Baby, I am being honest wit' you."

"Then explain the fifteen thousand I found in the bedroom closet."

"The what?"

"Tango don't play fuckin' stupid wit' me," I cursed abruptly.

"Why you in my shit?"

"It's my place too," I spat out.

I found our special dinner turning into a nightmare.

"I worked hard for that."

"Doin' what?"

He didn't answer me. He scowled. He sat back in his seat and looked like the cat caught his tongue. It was clear he was hiding something. A guilty man he was. I saw the future of him, or us, falling apart if he didn't quit whatever illicit act he was doing.

"You need to stop it," I sternly said to him. "If we gonna be a family, Tango, then whatever shit you doin' out there, stop it. I'm pregnant wit' ya child and my heart can't take if you get locked up or killed out here. I love you."

All he could do was look at me. My eyes were hard and my heart was on pins and needles.

"I'm not gonna get locked up, baby, or killed," he replied.

"How you know? Do you see the future? You Superman out there on these streets, huh? You're on parole, baby, and any violation, they gonna send ya ass back to jail. I already have one baby father incarcerated, I don't need another. 'Cause I swear to you, I will abort this child out my damn womb because I refused to raise two babies by myself," I proclaimed through my clenched teeth. I wasn't having it. I meant every word of it. I would be a fool to keep this child inside of me when the man I loved was risking his own fuckin' life or freedom.

Things were becoming heated in the restaurant. It looked like I was getting through to Tango. But he replied, "It's hard out there, Mouse, and I'm only tryin' to make it right for us."

"You think I wanna put up wit' this, Tango? I'm tired, baby. I don't need that type of drama in my life. I went through it wit' one man. I'm not gonna go through the same shit wit' the next one. I will walk, Tango. I swear to you, I will fuckin' walk and not look back."

I didn't want to walk away from him and the new life we started to build together. I was scared. I couldn't go back to staying with Erica and working the track. Just the thought of it was making me sick to my stomach. It felt great to have my own place. And if I had to work three fuckin' jobs to maintain and feed my daughter, then so be it. But I refused to go backward. I refused to go back to the shelter. I was tired of everything, from the streets to the evil I felt surrounding me.

The tears ran down my face and my eyes were saddened by the uncertainty of my future or our future. I wanted Tango to be the one, but he lied to me. And I was scared to ask how he was making that much money. Was it dealing drugs or something much more sinister?

"You don't need to walk away, baby. I'm done wit' it. I promise you. I can't lose you," he said.

"Don't tell me shit you think I want to hear, tell me the truth."

"It's the truth, baby. What I made, we can make good on. It's enough to keep our heads above the water," he said.

"And is the construction job for real?" I asked.

"It's not."

"So you lied to me."

"I know and I'm sorry."

I took a deep breath. I hated when someone lied to me. I hated when the man I loved lied to me. My look toward him was disappointment and uncertainty. But he made a promise to me and I felt he would uphold his promise. I really didn't want to walk away. I didn't want to do this by myself. Tango was a good man to my daughter and he was a great man to me. He rarely talked about his past. From what I knew, he used to be a bad-ass muthafucka back in the days and had the hood on lockdown. But now he was supposed to be a changed man. I would think doing ten years' hard time would change any man. And he wasn't getting any younger. He had this good pussy to come home to and a good woman attached to it. Why would any nigga want to fuck it up?

"I won't lie to you again, baby," he assured me.

I could only look at him and hope he was for real. I didn't want our relationship to go sour. I took a chance allowing him into my life and my daughter's life and the thing I feared the most was it coming back on me, thinking that whoever he harmed out there wouldn't hesitate to come harm his family in retaliation.

"Just love me and be honest wit' me, Tango, that's all I ask."

"And I will."

We continued our talk and our dinner. It would have been a shame to ruin such a lovely evening. We had dessert and our quality time was good. We spent over two hours in the restaurant. When the bill finally came, it was almost $200. Tango pulled out his wad of cash while all the other patrons in the place were paying via credit or debit card. We looked so ghetto fabulous when Tango peeled off several twenties and a fifty to pay with.

We had to do better.

After dinner, Tango and I drove to Times Square and took a walk around there. We held hands, conversed, and enjoyed the peaceful and warm evening. Spring was almost here. It felt good not being bundled up in a winter coat and gloves, but to show off my outfit and walk freely among the crowd of people in the square and take in some decent entertainment. In the city, I felt like someone else. I wasn't Hector's daughter. I wasn't that bad-ass gangster bitch representing EBV or Edenwald. I wasn't that prostitute sucking dick in the front seat of a car or fucking tricks for money. I was just me, Mouse, a beautiful woman out with her man and enjoying the evening. No one looked at me funny and no one was judging me.

After Times Square, Tango and I went for a walk in Riverside Park, where the Hudson River and the New Jersey shoreline across the bay provided the most beautiful view during the night. Tango held me in his arms and once again proclaimed his love for me.

I was all smiles.

I didn't want this feeling and this moment to ever end.

Chapter Thirty

Tango

Tango navigated the rented Intrepid through the busy Manhattan streets with Mouse nestled comfortably underneath his arms. He had one hand on the steering wheel and the other arm around her. She was half asleep. He was all smiles. Despite the minor mishap over dinner at the Blue Hill restaurant about his occupation and the money she found in the closet, it was a marvelous evening. He couldn't believe that he was about to become a father again. Mouse was going to be his seventh baby mama with his next youngest child. He hasn't seen or spoken to any of his kids in years. But he felt that this one was going to be different. Boy or girl, he was going to be in his child's life no matter what.

He made a promise to Mouse, to stop his dangerous activity on the streets. That meant no more killing. He had lots of blood on his hands, already committing several murders and he had gotten word on the streets that he was on Young Gangster Crew's most targeted list. Tango found out through a friend that there was a pricey bounty on his head. A snitch reported to YGC that they noticed Tango lingering around a few victims before their demise. They put two and two together, noticing how the bloodshed started up right after Tango's release. But now he kept a low profile and killed with subtly, so he thought.

Tango squeezed his woman tight. He couldn't wait to get back home and spend some more quality time with his woman. He was ready for some intimacy. Mouse always had him aroused, and the fact that she was pregnant and having his baby, he couldn't wait to get some of that pregnant pussy. He was excited. The only thing that worried Tango was income. With him giving up killing, how would he make his money? He didn't have any legal work experience or carry any trade. The only thing he knew was the streets. He had been conniving his parole officer. The bitch was too stupid to tell fake paystubs from real ones or his peoples was just that good in forging fake documents. But he knew a good thing never lasted for too long. He had to find new means of employment somehow.

He was cruising on the Bruckner Expressway, in the Bronx and going to check on Eliza. Then after that, head back home and be in good hands for the remainder of the night.

Tango drove through the Bronx streets. It was late. He listened to Hot 97 and made a left on Third Avenue. Once on Third Avenue, Tango glanced into his rearview mirror and had the assumption that he was being followed. It felt like the same headlights had been trailing him since he crossed over the Willis Avenue Bridge.

Mouse was sleeping, so he didn't want to disturb her, or even worse, scare her. His pistol was underneath the driver's seat and plus he had a .38 in the glove compartment. He drove carefully and continuously looked through his rearview mirror to see if his belief was right. He knew he was right; there was a car following them. Tango kept his cool and his speed limit moderate. He continued driving north on Third Avenue. It was almost a ghost town at 3:00 a.m. The shops and bodegas were closed, traffic sparse, and not a resident in sight. It was a part of the Bronx that slept and remained quiet during the afterhours.

Tango came to a stop at a red light, and with the car idling at the intersection he slowly reached underneath his seat to remove his pistol without trying to wake up Mouse. He kept cool and breathed easily. His attention was fixated in the rearview mirror, watching the following car approach closer and closer. In his mind he felt danger coming his way. It angered him that muthafuckas had the audacity to try him while he was with his woman. But maybe he was jumping to conclusions. It could be nothing, he wanted to believe. But if it wasn't, then how did they find him? And how did they know it was him?

The car approached slowly and stopped parallel to his ride at the red light. Inside the blue Charger were two black males, very young and looking like thugs. Their rap music blared and they bobbed their heads to the explicit lyrics. Tango gripped his pistol slyly. It was fully loaded and cocked back, ready to start blasting if needed. He glanced into the car and remained deadpan. The two black males glanced his way then averted their eyes from him.

Once again, it could be nothing, or something; Tango wasn't about to take that chance. Mouse was with him and he would do anything to protect her. He raised his pistol slightly while his right arm was still wrapped around Mouse. His foot was on the brake and he was ready to react.

The two males glanced his way again and then smirked. It seemed like the red light was taking forever to change back to green. He was out in the open, feeling vulnerable. Things were becoming too on edge.

The light finally changed green and the Charger drove off, not being a threat. But the real threat came out of nowhere. All of a sudden multiple shots were fired at his car. It came from two black male pedestrians emerging from out of nowhere. They rushed his way with their guns blazing. His car was under fire. Mouse woke up to the frightful sound and screamed with the passenger glass shattering around her. Tango slammed Mouse down into the seat, returned fire, and then pressed down on the accelerator. The car sped away at a high speed with the passenger windows shattering as bullets ripped through the car. He could still hear the shots ringing out. Tango drove several blocks away from the gunmen, thankfully escaping the threat. Mouse couldn't stop screaming and panicking though. One minute she was sleeping and comfortable with her man; next thing she knew, she woke up frightfully startled in a war zone.

"What the fuck, Tango! What is goin' on?" she screamed.

Tango didn't answer her. His attention was on the streets. He drove fast and constantly kept looking in his mirrors to see if anyone was following him. They had set him up. He was furious. He thanked God that he survived the hit, because it was amateur hour. But Mouse could have been killed, and if that had happened, then Tango would have rained down some biblical shit on everyone in the Bronx.

Mouse couldn't stop shaking. She continued shouting. She wanted to know what had happened. Why were they shooting at them? "Answer me, Tango!" she heatedly screamed. She even physically tried to attack Tango while he was driving almost causing him to sideswipe a parked car.

Tango was highly angry. He frowned. His blood was boiling. Muthafuckas had the audacity to try to kill him and his bitch on this perfect evening. The only thing on his mind was revenge, death.

"You better tell me sumthin', Tango. What the fuck!" Mouse shouted. She continued to punch and smack Tango as he was behind the wheel.

Tango had to pull to the side and park the car. Mouse was going to make them crash. He climbed out of the car to think and to get away from Mouse. But Mouse wasn't having it, though. She jumped out too and ran around the car and continued hitting on Tango, punching him in his chest, shoving him, and wanting to know who tried to kill them.

"I fucked up, all right!" Tango screamed back.

"What are you talkin' about, you fucked up! What did you do?" Mouse was crying. She was still shaky and couldn't believe what had happened. The rent-a-car was shot up; bullet holes were in the doors and the windows shot out completely. The front seat had shards of glass in it and they didn't know where the gunmen were at.

"What did you do?" Mouse asked intensely.

Tango gazed at his woman. He raised his arms and locked his fingers behind his head. He exhaled noisily, trying to keep his cool. It didn't feel safe. He wanted to console her and let her know everything was going to be okay. He was going to take care of everything, and do it his way. But the way Mouse looked at him, it seemed like she didn't want any more dealings with him. She seemed fed up. He became nervous; he felt his worst nightmare was about to come true, that she would walk away from him and leave him for good.

"Baby, I can fix this."

"Fix what? They tried to kill us, Tango. They shot at us!" Mouse screamed so loudly, her voiced echoed for blocks.

"We need to get back in the car and go," he suggested.

Mouse walked around hysterically. She didn't sign up for this shit. Tango had his fist clenched and holding the pistol in the other hand. It was still outside. The section they stopped at felt like a standstill. As Mouse ranted, Tango repeatedly looked around the area, keeping his guard up and making sure they didn't come back to finish the job. YGC and Power had to be the ones behind the attempt on his life. He knew it.

"I'll tell you everything, baby, but we just need to go, get out of sight," he said.

Mouse looked reluctant. She gazed at Tango with so much discontent that she wanted to walk away and not get back inside the car with him. It had been such a lovely evening, and then it all went to waste. She had so many high hopes and dreams for them; now his past or his stupidity was coming back to haunt them, or most likely, destroy them both.

"Mouse, just get inside the damn car so we can go," he hollered.

"Don't curse at me, nigga!"

Tango sighed with frustration. The more they lingered in the street the more likely trouble would come their way, either from the gunmen searching for them or the cops coming to investigate the disturbance in the area.

Mouse unwillingly got back in the car with him. Tango drove away, distancing himself from the area but the damage had already been done. Mouse sat with her arms folded across her chest and frowning a great deal. Her tears fell like water from melting ice. She wanted to hit him again, punch Tango in his face so hard he would have the taste of her knuckles in his mouth for a month. But she didn't; she rode silently, pondering and nervous like hell. Who was this man, really? She loved him but there was still that awkward mystery about him. People don't try and kill you for no reason. Once again she thought, was it his past finally catching up to him or did he fuck with the wrong people?

When they arrived home, Mouse was all over him. She was ready to pack her bags, or pack his bags and throw him out. She was loud and so angry, the way she felt she could knock down mountains. Again, she wanted to punch him in the face. He had put her life in danger, and what if Eliza was with them, then what? She would never be able to forgive him or herself if anything happened to her daughter because of her incompetence. Tango had to explain himself. He couldn't lie his way out of this one and no one wasn't going anywhere until she got a reasonable explanation from him. So he went on to say that he owed a drug debt to someone large in the streets and they had some harsh words. Tango said it got physical between him and the drug dealer. Mouse didn't believe him. She threatened to leave him.

"Baby, I can fix this, believe me," he sternly shouted.

"Fuckin' how?" Mouse retorted.

"I know I fucked up, but give me a second chance. I'm tellin' you the truth," he exclaimed.

Tango knew he couldn't tell her the truth that he was a psychotic killer, murdering rival gang members in cold blood and being paid $5,000 a head. It would surely drive her away for good. He would do whatever to hide the truth from her, even lie when earlier in the restaurant he made a promise to never lie to her again. But he felt this was different; he was about to lose the best thing that ever happened to him. And he was ready to fight tooth and nail to keep his woman.

They argued heatedly. Their spat went from room to room. Mouse couldn't hold back her emotions and her hands; she repeatedly hit Tango from his chest to his face.

"You so fuckin' stupid! You so stupid, Tango. Oh my God!" she yelled.She wanted to hate him, but it was hard.

Tango didn't retaliate; he knew she was upset. He played defense and tried to block all of her outraged swings thrown at him. She was heavy-handed and had quick hands. Tango was surprised. She needed to vent, and if she used her hands in doing so, he didn't care. He knew he was wrong. The shooting kept replaying over and over in Mouse's head. She came so close to death. And the frightful feeling of her daughter almost becoming an orphan tonight it made her fume even more.

"I want you to get the fuck out, Tango." Mouse was crying.

Tango didn't budge. He didn't plan on going anywhere. He was ready to fight for his relationship and fight in the streets. They weren't going to get away with this. Tango gazed desperately at Mouse, his eyes pleading for another chance. He approached lightly; Mouse was ready to swing on him again.

"I said get the fuck out!" she screamed madly.

"Mouse, baby, I ain't goin' nowhere. I love you too much to let you go, baby. I do," he proclaimed coolly. "You know I do."

He continued approaching her carefully like she was a rabid dog and he was the trainer trying to tame her. Mouse cried. Her fists stayed clenched. Every bone in her body said to let him go, but the way Tango stared at her, there was something in his eyes that hurt them both so much.

Tango reached out to her; she recoiled from his touch. She didn't want to be held or consoled. She wanted peace of mind.

"Baby, I promise you, that life ain't me anymore. I know I made a mistake. I know I fucked up. I got out, felt the pressure and went back to my old ways, and dabbled in that life again. But since you came into my world, I'm ready to give it all up, like I promised you in the restaurant. My life don't mean shit if you and Eliza ain't in it," he strongly proclaimed.

Unrelenting pressure stirred inside of Mouse. She heard him, but could she believe him? Her contemptuous gaze stay aimed at Tango. When he stepped closer, she took two steps back.

"Why are you ruining this wonderful night for me?" she questioned sadly.

"Baby, I didn't ruin it; they did," he chided.

"I don't know if can do this wit' you, Tango."

"Baby, don't say that, please don't. Yes, you can. We a family, baby. You and me, we one, Mouse. I love you. You hear me? I fuckin' love you," Tango expressed with conviction.

Mouse cried. It was hard to look at him. Tango dropped down on his knees and gazed up at her. He clasped his fingers together. He was pleading and begging. Without her, he felt useless.

"Mouse, I love you. Marry me," he loudly proclaimed.

"What?"

"I said marry me. Let's just start over and be different. Let's take that money and leave this city, all three of us. I'll find a trade and do anything to keep you in my life. But I can't lose you."

Was he serious? "And you think the people who tried to kill you are suddenly going to forget about you because you left town?"

"I'm tryin' here, baby. I'm gonna be that good man for you. I'm ready. I'm fuckin' ready," Tango said with some tears in his eyes.

He was still on his knees with Mouse standing over him. She took a deep breath. What to do, what to think? $15,000 wasn't much, but it could be a good start somewhere else. But she wondered if he would live that long or stay free even longer. With his seed inside of her, Mouse was dubious about him, but he made it feel so real and legit when he talked. He had so much passion inside of him when it came to loving her that it almost felt unprecedented in her life.

Her mind told her to leave, but her heart was screaming to stay. The tears flow and the core of her soul didn't know how to react. Tango was on his knees begging to marry her. All she could say was, "Yes."

She said yes, because she truly felt that things would get better with them. She said yes because she was definitely in love with him, and it may have sounded crazy, but she was ready to become his ride or die bitch, because he was definitely riding for her when she had nothing. She said yes, because she was already sucked in, her mind, body, and soul entangled like a knot around Tango.

She said yes, because deep in her heart, she didn't want to lose him and be alone again. It was a scary world out there and even scarier when you had to be in all by yourself.

Chapter Thirty-one

Sammy

I had to calm my man down somehow. He was angry and troubled. And I did it the best way I knew how to: being on my knees with his big black hard dick thrusting in and out of my mouth. I wanted to take his mind off the streets. Power had been really stressed lately and I could see everything that was happening, it was getting to him. The other day, another one of his promising lieutenants was killed in the South Bronx, gunned down by rivals. And now the streets were on fire, burning with law enforcement and joint task forces kicking in doors and making arrests, seizing his product and a few hundred thousand dollars of his money. The bloodshed, the violence, and the cops, it was impacting his business. He was losing money and losing men. The pressure had been set on high. And I was starting to see Power less and less because his priorities were toward his business and fierce retaliation on his enemies rather than being with me, when I needed him.

I was going through my own trials and tribulations, but loving him and not being selfish, I put him first. Like any real bitch would do.

My head bobbed back and forth against him. His dick inside my mouth, pulsating with me having a strong desire to please him. He was naked and moaning from my lips tasting him. He gripped the back of my head, my long hair entangled between his fingers and he pushed my head forward. I was thinking about so many ways to make him cum. I was kissing on it, licking his tummy, sucking his dick, cupping and massaging his balls, hearing his moans, feeling his groin pulsating as I sucked him deep while rubbing his belly with one hand and his legs and balls with the other.

The thought of tasting his cum made me hungry enough to swallow it. I wanted Power to come with a bang. I did him nice and slow, liking to take my time. I loved spending some extra attention to his mushroom tip, kissing it and licking on it, jerking him off all together. He pumped his dick into my mouth while on my knees staring up at him, deep throating his large cock and playing with his balls.

"Ugh. Ooooh, ugh, ugh, shit. Suck my dick like that, baby, it feels so good. Ummm, shit."

I played with his head with my tongue and I felt his dick spasm inside my mouth. He was about to come soon and I was ready for him. My thick, full lips slid on his dick like they were on ice. I could feel it. He was about to release that stream of white liquid. He needed to bust that good nut. After a few more sucks and licks, he freed himself inside my mouth and I didn't hesitate to swallow his semen and having some of it dribble out. I could feel his hot cum sliding down between my breasts and swimming inside my mouth. He shuddered from the intense orgasm he experienced and his cum had a very strong flavor and it was definitely an acquired taste.

"Ooooh, I definitely needed that, baby," he said to me like I just gave him a deep tissue massage.

I stood up and wiped my mouth. I was happy that he was pleased. Now I needed my own release, and I wasn't talking about sex. The minute he came, got what he needed, like on timing, there was someone at the door, knocking with a sense of urgency. He was always busy;

his phone was constantly ringing or someone was coming by the place to talk to Power. He got up from my good sex to see who was at the door, while I removed a cigarette from my pack and walked to the window. The city was lit up in the night. It was a temperate evening and I just leaned against the glass like I was despondent. I inhaled the nicotine. I heard a man in the other room and while they were discussing something important, I was thinking about my own problems. I'd got another threatening letter from Rico the other day and he was calling me collect on a regular. The man was a fucking nuisance in my life. He just refused to see anybody happy if it wasn't him or if I wasn't with him. I also got another visit from Detectives English and McGowan. They wanted to ask me some more questions about Macky's death. I continued lying to them, keeping cool, but it was obvious that with Rico still alive this secret wasn't going to go away. So I had to do something about him.

I pulled on the Newport and gazed out the window like I was in a daze. I continued to hear Power and one of his goons talking in the next room. I overhead the man say, "Yo, we on that nigga. It's definitely Tango, that bitch nigga. C-Lo saw the nigga lingering around the club the other night before, in the dark, looking suspect, before one our niggas was killed."

"That nigga from the club the other night, he ain't got yet?" Power said.

"He gonna get got, boss."

Why were they talking about Tango? I knew something was going on.

I suspiciously eased out the bedroom to listen to more of what he had to say. Power was behind his bar making himself and his friend a drink.

His soldier went on to say, "It's definitely him. He the OG fresh outta prison and we got his friend, Sheldon, to give the nigga up, you know, wit' a little persuasion on my end, boss. We almost killed that nigga tryin' to get him to talk."

"We got what we want, so I want him dead," said Power.

"Got you; but one problem?" said the thug.

"What fuckin' problem, Mike?"

"He ain't been around lately. He like, went underground."

"What you mean he ain't been around! The nigga ain't invisible, right?"

"Yeah."

"So find the muthafucka and take care of him," Power shouted.

"Ayyite."

I couldn't believe what I was hearing. I stayed hidden from his view. Why did he want Mouse's man killed?

What did Tango get himself into? And why did my man have a hard on for his murder? I didn't know Tango at all but he was making my friend very happy and it was so good to see her happy. It was so good that we both had someone in our lives we cared for and who loved us. Now, Power wanted to snatch that away from my friend.

What the fuck? I thought.

When Mike made his exit from the apartment, I hurried back into the bedroom. I went by the window and looked out of it, pretending I was standing there all along. Power walked into the room with a charged attitude. He lit a cigar and said to me, "Yo, I gotta make a run and take care of some business."

"Now?" I replied with some attitude.

"Sammy, let's not start this shit again. You know I'm a busy man," he returned.

"You get yours and then right out the door, huh."

He put on his pants and shirt, ignoring my statement. The nigga was hard to deal with sometimes, for real.

When he was completely dressed, he looked my way and asked, “What’s up wit’ ya friend, Mouse? Have you spoken to her lately?”

“Why you worrying about her for?” I asked.

“I was just asking; don’t take it any other way.”

He looked at me and I looked right back. I knew why he was asking, but I played naïve. Something severe was brewing.

“We’ll talk when I get back,” he said, throwing on his jacket.

When he left, I felt the shit was about to hit the fan, and I never been so nervous in my life. I didn’t know if I should warn Mouse that her man was in danger. Was it my business to get into? I thought about calling her to get some information from her. And when I did, her phone was going straight to voicemail. I hung up, feeling frustrated. Someone was about to have a very bad day, and with my relationship with Mouse getting better, Tango was in the mix of something with my man and I knew that when push came to shove, I would have to choose: either have my friendship with Mouse or my loving relationship with Power.

Part of me said, *Why couldn’t Tango stay locked up?*

I had to go to him for help. Even though I knew he was plotting to kill Mouse’s man, Tango, I needed Power to help me deal with Rico. He was the only one who had the connections to have a man killed inside prison. For that to happen, I had to be honest with him and tell him everything. I came to him in my best lingerie: a bright red short lace baby doll with the open crotch thong. It had the fingerless, lace-edged gloves with ribbon restraints.

He was in his living room, smoking his cigar and counting money.

"Baby, can I talk to you for a minute?" I asked in my sweetest voice.

He stopped counting money and looked my way. When he saw what I had on, his eyes widened with delight. "Damn," he uttered first. Then added, "Of course, baby, what you need?" He patted his lap indicating that he wanted me to take a seat on it. I did.

Power placed his arms around me and held me affectionately. "You look so good baby, I might fuck around and get you pregnant tonight," he joked, or at least I thought he was joking.

He noticed the troubled look on my face and read that I had a problem. He stopped being facetious and began serious. "You got a problem wit' someone?"

"A matter of fact, I do," I said.

"Who, and I'll take care of it."

I was glad to hear that. I took a deep breath and said, "It's Rico."

"Ya baby father?"

I nodded.

"Ain't he locked up?"

"He is, but he's blackmailing me," I told him.

"Blackmailing you? How?"

Now the last thing I wanted to do was tell him about the murder I committed, and then it was an extra person who knew my secret; the less who knew, the better. But how could I exactly explain it to him without implicating myself? Power would want to know everything. He wasn't just going to accept the half truth of my story.

He was waiting for me to explain myself. This was going to be hard. But I had to do something. With every passing day, Rico was becoming more of a threat to me. I haven't gone to visit him in weeks and I never wrote him back and denied his collect calls. I was pushing the envelope the more I ignored him. He wasn't going to tolerate it for too long. Expressing myself to Power, it was going to be daring, or just stupid, but I had to take some risk. If he loved me the way he always proclaimed, then my confession to him would not hinder me and he wouldn't forsake me.

"I killed a man last year," I confessed.

I could tell the way he looked at me; the news came as a shock to him or he thought I was lying. He replied with, "You bodied a nigga, fo' real?"

"With Rico's help," I said.

I had his undivided attention. I went on to tell him everything, about Macky trying to rape and beat me last year. I told him how Rico and I linked up, talked about Mouse briefly, and how I used to hustle for Rico. I kept talking and talking like I was in an interrogation room and coming clean to the detectives. But I didn't tell Power about the detectives who came to visit me. I was too afraid to let him know about any of that. The last thing I wanted him to think was that I was a snitch. I needed him to trust me fully. I went on to explain how Rico was blackmailing me and why. If I wanted Power's help, then I had to be exactly honest with him.

I went on to say that he was the only man who could help me because he had the effectiveness to arrange a hit out on Rico. Power had muthafuckas everywhere ready to do his dirty work, and for the right price, anyone could get got, no matter where. And I strongly needed Rico permanently out of my life. I planted in his mind that Rico wasn't just a threat to me but everyone else.

"I never liked that nigga anyway," replied Power.

I felt my heart pounding like drum beats. He knew it all now, so how was it going to play out? Would this turn against me or would it benefit me? He was quiet for a moment, contemplating something.

"He gotta go, then," said Power.

I smiled.

But there was more.

"I'll help you, on one condition," he continued. "You need to help me with a certain problem too."

I was listening. I was definitely willing to help my man out by any means necessary. Whatever he needed done, I was there for him.

Power rubbed my leg and held me closely. "You help take care of my situation and I promise you, Rico will be a dead man by week's end." He sounded so certain of that. It was pleasing to hear.

"What you need help wit' baby?" I asked, being so fuckin' naïve.

"I need help killing that nigga Tango. Word is out on the streets is he the muthafucka out there bodying my niggas and now he went underground? He ain't been around lately and I need that nigga found ASAP," he said.

What? I couldn't believe what I was hearing. But there was more.

"I need you to get in contact wit' ya friend Mouse, and help me set up her man. You do this for me, I do that for you," he said.

I was flabbergasted. Power was using me to help kill my best friend's man. He knew how close Mouse and I was, and he saw the advantage in it. But how could I do this to my friend, snatch away her happiness? We recently reconciled our beef and were close again. If I didn't do this, Rico would bury me for sure really soon. But if I did, it would destroy Mouse. We were talking again and I knew Mouse found true love with Tango. Doing this would surely tear us apart again and make us bitter enemies. But my freedom was at stake.

I felt like a pawn on a fuckin' chessboard. I had Power moving me here and Rico moving me over there. I didn't know what to do. I felt I didn't have a choice. I had to think about my son and my own fuckin' future.

I locked eyes with Rico and found myself saying, "I'll do it."

He smiled. "That's my girl. That's why I fuckin' love you, 'cause you ride wit' ya nigga."

I did. And when Tango was dead, Rico would see his demise and maybe, finally, I would be free.

To be continued . . .

PAR

ORDER FORM

URBAN BOOKS, LLC
97 N18th Street
Wyandanch, NY 11798

Name (please print): ____________________

Address: ____________________

City/State: ____________________

Zip: ____________________

QTY	TITLES	PRICE

Shipping and handling: add $3.50 for 1st book, then $1.75 for each additional book.

Please send a check payable to:

Urban Books, LLC

Please allow 4-6 weeks for delivery